The Calico Tapestry

a supernatural mystery

by

Evelyn Roberts Brooks

ISBN: 978-0-9843781-6-6

for my sisters
Diana, Martha and Susan
with love
and gratitude…
thank you for
showing me the way
to love books and reading
from an early age

Books by Evelyn Roberts Brooks

Nonfiction

FORGET YOUR TROUBLES: Enjoy Your Life Today
GET HAPPY TODAY: Your Path to Lifelong Happiness

Fiction

The Gypsy Talisman
The Weeping Cameo
The Calico Tapestry

The Calico Tapestry

ONE

Madeline Clark opened the door to her room upstairs and turned on the light to dispel the dark shadows. She sighed and sat on the edge of the old canopy bed, the mattress sagging beneath her, wondering what she would do now that Mrs. Lawrence had refused her request.

There was a musty smell in the room. She wrinkled her nose in distaste, wishing she didn't have to spend the night with her young son in this sprawling house filled with strangers. At least, they were strangers to her, and more of Mrs. Lawrence's family were on the way to spend the rest of the holidays with the older woman. They would stay a few days and finish up with an at-home New Year's Eve party before everyone went their separate ways again.

Madeline had gotten the impression that Mrs. Lawrence expected something important to happen while her family members were gathered.

It had been a gamble, Madeline reflected, driving all the way here to petition Mrs. Lawrence for aid. And she had lost.

Under other circumstances, it would be a delight to visit here and turn it into a lively adventure for her little boy. The spooky old mansion was situated in the craggy hills just beyond the outskirts of Malibu, California, near the county line.

Acres of uncultivated land surrounded the house, leaving it isolated, lonely and yet starkly beautiful with its impressive ocean view. They'd driven up a winding, rutted canyon road, with only a few scattered houses in the distance. There were no neighbors nearby.

Frowning, thinking of her diminished options, Madeline decided to rest for ten minutes and see what new plan she could come up with. She idly turned to plump the pillows.

With a gasp, she leapt from the bed.

There on the pillow lay the severed head and tail of a small gray field mouse. She gave a shudder of revulsion. Trying to be practical, she reached for the wastebasket, but couldn't bring herself to handle the dismembered mouse.

No doubt, she thought wryly, it had been a special gift from that calico cat she'd seen wandering downstairs earlier.

Feeling this was a sign to leave, she decided to let her hostess know she wouldn't be staying after all, then quickly pack and get herself and her son out of here. No one could convince her to sleep in that bed now, nor even in that damp, drafty room. It seemed a certainty that to do so would bring on unpleasant nightmares.

Memory of her dead car battery struck her at once. Even though she couldn't drive off, that still didn't mean she had to sleep in this room.

She grabbed her purse and opened the door, anxious to get away. When she stepped into the hallway, a warm furry animal slithered past her, going into the room, rubbing against her bare legs. Madeline gasped, then laughed at herself for overreacting.

It was just the cat, thirteen-year old "Calli." It regarded Madeline and blinked twice. The calico cat was a beautiful female with large patches of black, white and ginger-orange markings.

"Out," she told the cat, pointing to the hall.

Its whiskers moved and its tail fanned the air. Calli had seen the mouse on the bed. Before Madeline could stop it, the lithe cat jumped onto the bed and began toying with the mouse's head as if it were a rubber ball.

Disgusted, she left. In the hall, she took several deep breaths to compose herself and then went into the bedroom adjacent to hers. Without turning on the light, she advanced toward the side door which connected this room with the one she had just left. She fumbled with the key, turned it, tested the knob to be sure the door was locked, and then pocketed the key automatically.

She wanted to be sure her small son, whom she had tucked into bed in this room shortly before finding the dead mouse, did not wander in to find her if he awoke during the night. She was grateful that Tommy was asleep and had been spared the sight of the hapless mouse.

That blasted cat! Now that her initial shock had worn off, Madeline was annoyed that Calli was allowed to roam freely and deposit its hunting trophies wherever it pleased. Why hadn't someone warned her? Apparently her guest bedroom was a favorite of the cat's or it would not have returned so readily to play with the mouse.

She longed to be safe in her cozy apartment in Hermosa Beach, but that was more than fifty miles south on the Pacific Coast Highway, and she had no way to get there. She'd sleep in here tonight with her little boy, then get auto service in the morning and be on her way home.

Madeline had moved to that small apartment from San Francisco only six weeks previously. Craig, her ex-husband, had threatened more than once to take four-year-old Tommy away from her.

During the divorce last year there had been a bitter custody battle, but Madeline had won full custody once the court had evaluated reports about the domestic violence she was escaping. Still, she knew from stories other parents in her support group told in anguished detail, that it was not uncommon for a thwarted parent to kidnap their own child and thus grab illegal custody.

Through a real estate friend now living in the Los Angeles area, Madeline located the Hermosa Beach apartment which she was now subletting, furnished. She got a new cell number, and made her friends promise not to give Craig the phone number or her address.

In spite of these precautions, Madeline was nervous that her ex-husband would carry out his threats to steal Tommy and transport him to another state where she could never find him.

After Madeline filed for divorce, she and Tommy had moved to a studio apartment in the San Francisco area so she could keep her job at a jewelry boutique where she designed and created unique pendants and other jewelry.

One day she'd gone after work to pick her son up at the day care center and had been informed by the new staff assistant that the boy's father had already done so. In a panic, she phoned the police. The next day, Tommy was returned to her, unharmed but confused.

In that heart-stopping fear she'd never see her son again, Madeline became determined to save enough money to escape with Tommy to another city. To support them, she'd start a business of her own. First, she economized in every possible way to fatten her bank account, and then moved south to Los Angeles.

Madeline quickly discovered that she could not make enough money selling a few pieces of handcrafted jewelry now and then, even when she set up a web site and advertised her wares.

After much deliberation, she decided to continue making the jewelry but also give lessons in jewelry-making and tapestry work. Since needlework was a long-standing hobby of hers, she felt confident that the new combination would be successful.

She'd been wrong.

Her advertising – online, in local papers and via colorful flyers she put on car windshields in parking lots and on bulletin boards in laundromats – had generated a trickle of customers and two students. Being in business for herself was not the profitable venture she had envisioned in her daydreams while working in the jewelry store for a paycheck.

Madeline was well aware that she needed more money. Her savings were dwindling fast, and there was little income to reverse the tide. After careful calculations, at night after Tommy was safe and asleep in his bed, Madeline saw that no matter how much she scrimped, she only had enough funds remaining to carry her for two months more.

It was hard to believe they were at the end of another year, but it was almost New Year's Eve.

Determined to be at home for Tommy until he started school, she sought every means possible to stretch her funds. She had even forced herself to call Craig from a public phone on Christmas, to ask for the child support he was court-ordered to pay but was six months behind in remitting.

"I'm not going to give it to your friend Gina so she can mail it to you," he'd said. When Madeline protested that the law was on her side, he laughed and said cagily, "You can have the money, dear. I'm not withholding it. It's set aside in a special bank account."

She didn't know if that was true or not, but there was no point accusing him of a lie because the conversation would get derailed. "Then just give Gina a check–"

"I'll transfer it to you. Give me your account information and the bank branch address."

Madeline was afraid to agree to that condition. She knew Craig was clever, and could probably find a way to track her if she gave her bank account information to him.

He wasn't going to ask her outright for her home address, because he knew she'd refuse. But if he could trick her into giving him a location to pinpoint her on the map, then he'd be able to track her. And through her, reach Tommy.

She was silent on the phone. Her throat tightened at the very thought of losing her precious son. After three miscarriages, Tommy's birth had been a true miracle. He meant more to her than mere words could describe and the prospect of life without his sweet presence was appalling.

Craig chuckled softly in the silence, no doubt guessing her thoughts.

"No bank info," he said, "no money. It would be irresponsible of me to give your child support money to someone else, on the vague assumption that she'll deliver it to you. What if Gina keeps it? Then I'd look bad in court, and you would suffer. Sorry, babe. No can do. Just give me your bank name and account number. I'll go online and transfer six months' worth right now. I bet you need the money pretty bad, don't you?"

"I'm fine. We're fine." She'd hung up the phone, and let out a huge sigh. She'd have to come up with the money she and Tommy needed on her own, without any help from Craig.

Someday she'd fight him for the money and use it to set up a college savings fund for Tommy, but for now, she had to put their safety in the top priority slot, and avoid letting her ex-husband know how to find her.

Then, while reading the paper one morning at the laundromat, Madeline came across an article that sparked an idea: she'd have an exhibit to draw attention to her work! The article told of an upcoming museum exhibit on "The History of Cats in Art."

She read that the museum had tried in vain to borrow a century-old tapestry from a wealthy widow named Mrs. Agatha Lawrence who lived near Malibu. The needlework was called "The Calico Tapestry" and it was said to be the portrait of a patchwork-colored cat named, aptly, Calico.

Madeline learned that Mrs. Lawrence repeatedly refused to loan the tapestry for exhibits, even charitable events, but no reason for this was disclosed in the newspaper.

Excitedly, Madeline reasoned that if she could induce the widow to endorse her own exhibit by loaning the famous tapestry, the resulting publicity would surely give her new business the boost it so desperately needed.

She wrote a persuasive letter asking for an interview with Mrs. Lawrence, and to her surprise, her request was granted.

That morning, with her son Tommy strapped into his car seat, Madeline drove up to the rambling Victorian mansion with its many gables and ornate trim. The faded, weather-worn wood was gray and uninviting. The first impression was that the house must be deserted, because it looked so neglected and overgrown with weeds. But from all she'd been able to learn about Mrs. Lawrence, the woman was significantly wealthy, and apparently an eccentric.

She forced herself to smooth her hair and take Tommy by the hand, then approach the front door and ring the bell.

An Hispanic housekeeper, Rosa, opened the door but informed Madeline that Mrs. Lawrence was not available since she was napping.

Madeline had no choice but to wait. As the hours passed, she fed her son all the snacks she'd brought in the car for him, and tried to keep him entertained.

Finally, Mrs. Lawrence agreed to see her.

Madeline went into the living room where Mrs. Lawrence waited, unsmiling.

A tall Christmas tree stood in the bay window, decorated with old-fashioned glass balls and bows. The white lights sparkled among the branches. A few wrapped gifts remained on the velvet tree skirt.

"Is one of the presents for me?" Tommy asked.

"No, honey. Shhh." Madeline gripped Tommy's hand tighter, sensing he was about to bolt to check the gifts. She quelled her sudden nervousness in front of Mrs. Lawrence. She'd prepared an entire speech that was designed to be persuasive, and all she had to do was open her mouth and say it. She began, "Mrs.—"

"No," Mrs. Lawrence said.

"Pardon me?" Madeline looked at her in confusion.

"You want to take The Calico Tapestry and my answer is 'no.'"

"Then why did you invite me here?" Madeline stopped, seeing from the expression on the older woman's face that being annoyed with her would not help matters. "Well, thank you for your time." She turned away, muttering under her breath, "I guess…"

She took Tommy out of the room.

Outside, when Madeline got in her car to leave in defeat, she found the car would not start. Dead battery. Confused, she saw that the headlights had been switched on, draining the battery during the hours she'd waited to see Mrs. Lawrence.

Madeline knew she had not put the lights on, but why would anyone else do so? Someone playing a prank?

"Tommy?" she asked, "did you put the car lights on, honey?"

"No, Mommy."

Tommy knew better than to play with any knobs, levers, switches or dials on the car, but perhaps he had done it and was afraid to admit it in case he got scolded for it.

Madeline noticed that Mrs. Lawrence was watching them impassively from a downstairs window.

For a moment, Madeline simply looked back at her, then put aside the sudden suspicion that the old woman had turned on the headlights for some strange reason of her own.

However, as she returned to the house with Tommy, she noticed there wasn't even a wheelchair ramp anywhere in sight. How would Mrs. Lawrence have come outside?

Back inside, Madeline said to Rosa, "I'm afraid I have a dead battery. And my cell phone doesn't get a signal here. May I use your phone to call for the auto club?"

Rosa shook her head.

Madeline looked at her, wondering what was going on. "I'll pay for the call, if that's what you're worried about."

Mrs. Lawrence joined them, her power wheelchair making a sibilant noise. "No phone. I had it turned off yesterday."

"Yesterday?" The timing seemed very strange to Madeline. Was the woman telling the truth, or just being obstinate about helping?

"The only people who ever called me were asking for money," Mrs. Lawrence said. "But you and your little boy can spend the night. I know you must be disappointed about the tapestry, but you see, I had a dream last night that I should not give it to you."

Madeline looked at the woman, but did not trust herself to speak. *A dream?* She could hardly believe what she had heard.

"In the morning," Mrs. Lawrence continued, "when my nephew Luke comes by with the groceries, he can help you."

"I don't suppose there's anyone who could drive me down to a gas station?" Madeline didn't want to stay here. The place gave her the creeps.

Mrs. Lawrence cocked her silvery head, and added, "He's a handsome young bachelor. You might want to stay and meet him even if your automobile was in working order! He'll inherit a lot of money when I'm gone." The old woman laughed, then abruptly turned her wheelchair around. "Rosa will show you where to sleep. She'll give you food, too. Good night."

"Um, yeah, good night," Madeline said. "Thanks."

"Mommy?" Tommy tugged at her skirt. "I'm hungry."

Rosa smiled at them. "Come in the kitchen."

So Madeline left her car and brought into the house her needlework bag, their jackets and the backpack of toys she kept in the car to amuse Tommy. Her hostess, via the housekeeper, supplied nightclothes and fresh linens, plus a simple supper of soup and sandwiches.

While eating, Madeline tried to get information from the housekeeper. Rosa was friendly enough, but somewhat closemouthed, and Madeline had to admire that loyalty.

Madeline did manage to learn that Mrs. Lawrence, who had lost the use of her legs when she suffered a stroke two years earlier, had a male attendant living on the ground floor, in a room adjoining the study that had been converted into a bedroom for the invalid.

The attendant's name was Jason Malone, and the black-haired, bearded man had given her a friendly enough smile when he poked his head in the kitchen doorway to say good night to Rosa.

"And, hey, we've got company," he said, noticing Madeline and Tommy. "I hope you stay a few days. We could use a pretty face around here." The calico cat approached the kitchen, then caught sight of Jason and instantly hissed at him. The cat's fur stood up and she bared her fangs. He laughed uneasily. "Guess the kitty doesn't like my after-shave."

Now, remembering the borrowed nightgown she'd left in the bedroom next door, Madeline moved toward the hall, bracing herself to see that dead mouse again.

She stopped by her son's bed, dimly outlined by the narrow shaft of light coming from the open door to the hall. She leaned over to kiss her son and make sure he had not kicked off the covers.

The bed was empty.

"Tommy?" she whispered, thinking he might be hiding, waiting to pounce on her and then shriek in delighted laughter.

She ran her hand over the wall by the door and located the switch, but when she turned on the overhead light, she saw immediately that the small room was empty of anyone but herself.

Maybe he'd gone down the hall to the bathroom. With quickening steps, she went in search of her son. He was not in the bathroom. She ran up and down the hall, flinging open doors on both sides, snapping on lights and taking a cursory glance to be sure he was not hiding anywhere.

"Tommy?" she called out, panic constricting her voice.

There was no reply, except the creaking of floor boards as she ran the length of the large house. Outside, it began to rain. Tree branches rubbed against bare windowpanes, squeaking eerily.

What if he had awoken and then, confused by the strange surroundings, gone wandering in search of his mother? Madeline drew in a sharp breath, imagining her son alone and lost. He must be terrified!

She saw a flight of stairs going to a third floor, and hurried up them. The stairs were dark, and the overhead light did not work. She trailed one hand on the wall to guide herself by touch.

At the top of the narrow stairs was a closed door. It opened easily. A cold moist draft of air blasted Madeline's face and blew her hair into her eyes.

"Tommy?" she called out.

Madeline knew that old houses like this had dozens of rooms, possibly even secret hiding places. How would she ever find a four-year-old child? What if he had fallen, and was unable to answer when she called his name?

Myriad possibilities bombarded Madeline's thoughts and she feared Tommy was in danger.

In the third floor hallway, Madeline found a light switch that worked. A yellowish glow illuminated the hall, casting menacing shadows as she hurried from one empty room to another, calling her son's name, her voice echoing strangely.

At the last door, third from the stairs, she rattled the knob and pushed hard but it would not open. She realized it was not stuck, but locked. She looked for the key but did not find one.

Pressing her face against the door, she cupped her hands around her mouth and shouted Tommy's name. Although there was no response and no sound from inside, Madeline was suddenly certain that her child was locked in that room.

TWO

A deep voice behind Madeline barked, "Get away from that door."

Startled, Madeline turned and saw Jason Malone. She thought Rosa had said Jason slept downstairs, but maybe she'd misunderstood. "Is this your room? I'm looking for my little boy."

"Go downstairs."

"You've seen him?"

"He's probably in the kitchen, getting cookies. Mrs. Doyle is always baking."

She hesitated. Her maternal instinct said Tommy was behind this locked door, and needed her. She saw the coldness in Jason's brown eyes, but then he smiled and she felt she had imagined it.

"This old house is getting you upset." He gave her a little push in the direction of the stairs. "You have some milk and cookies, too, when you find your kid in the kitchen. You'll both sleep easier through this storm."

She suddenly remembered the mouse, forgotten in her concern over Tommy. After she finished telling Jason about the head and tail she had found on her bed, he laughed.

"No wonder you jumped to the conclusion that something happened to your son. Calli is a good mouser, but she shouldn't be a house cat."

So the cat's name was Calli. And she was a good hunter. "This has happened before?"

He shrugged.

She sensed his impatience. He was waiting for her to go and she realized he wanted to enter the locked room without letting her see inside. Was it possible this odd, dark man was actually hiding Tommy in there?

Madeline became determined to find out, but she knew she could not physically overcome Jason, who was built like a tank.

13

"Oh, hey," she said, aiming for a casual tone, "I'd love to peek in this room and satisfy myself he's not playing hide and seek. You got the key?"

"No."

They looked at each other for a long moment.

Mustering a cheerful smile, Madeline said, "Well, then, I'm off to the kitchen! Thanks so much for your help!"

She walked briskly to the stairs and descended, feeling his cold glare on her back as if it were tangible, but forcing herself to avoid turning to look at him. At the bottom of the stairs, she slipped into a nearby room and waited a few seconds, listening hard.

Her caution was rewarded when she heard Jason come partway down the stairs, pause as if looking for any sign of her, and then return to the third floor.

Madeline slipped out of the room and stealthily followed Jason upstairs. The hall was black now. He had turned out the light.

She tiptoed toward the locked room where light spilled out from the crack beneath the door.

Clenching her hands to stop the trembling, she moved quietly forward and put an ear to the door, hoping to hear Tommy's voice or some other telltale sound.

Too late, she remembered the chunky tourmaline earrings she wore. The gemstone grated against the door. In the absolute stillness, the noise was deafening.

She held her breath, wondering if Jason had heard it. No footsteps approached from the other side of the door and so she breathed more easily, deciding she was being far too jumpy. Then she recalled the way Jason had silent come up behind her earlier. She had not heard him until he stood directly behind her and barked out that command to get away from the door.

The back of Madeline's neck prickled. Quietly, she backed away from the door. She'd have to find another way to learn if Tommy was in that room.

Jason was a formidable foe. It would be more sensible to get the housekeeper to help.

Grateful for her soft-soled boots, Madeline glided down the hall away from the locked door and its dim glow. She had moved only a few feet away, however, when the hall was in total darkness and someone grabbed her shoulders and spun her around.

"Why are you spying on me?" Jason's meaty hands dug into her slender arms. He shone a powerful flashlight directly in her eyes.

She blinked and averted her head. "Let go! What have you done with my son?"

"I told you I don't know anything about him." He pushed her aside roughly. He turned off the flashlight.

"Why are you doing this?" she asked, terror for her child making her brave. "What have I ever done to you? We only met today."

The hall was silent except for the sounds of the wind and rain outside. It took a few seconds for Madeline to become aware that she was alone. Jason Malone had vanished as silently as he'd appeared.

She started toward the locked room, but stopped. Turning, she went downstairs instead, believing it was only futile to battle Jason alone. She hurried down the two flights, glad the other floors were well-lit. She shook off the gloom of the third floor, praying all the while that she would find her son with Rosa in the kitchen, chattering away in his high-pitched voice about the paper goldfish mobile they had made yesterday to decorate his bedroom.

As Madeline ran past the dining room, she tripped on a bump in the long Persian rug and nearly fell. Catching herself, she kept going to the kitchen, feeling as if she couldn't get there fast enough. She needed to see with her own eyes that he was safe, secure and happy.

He would probably be surprised to see her, and to find out that she was worried. Madeline resolved to explain to her son carefully that what he had done was naughty and he should not wander off on his own again. Especially not while they were staying in this strange old house.

She pushed against the swinging doors that led into the huge old-fashioned kitchen. The darkness that greeted her was a shock. Her son was not sitting happily at a counter munching cookies with Rosa. No one was there.

"Tommy," she screamed. "Tommy!"

But there was no answering cry from her child.

"What on earth is the commotion about?" asked Mrs. Lawrence, wheeling toward Madeline. "This is no time of night for a game of hide-and-seek."

She watched the older woman approach, silently borne by the well-oiled motorized wheelchair. Mrs. Lawrence was dressed for bed in a lilac-flowered, ruffled negligee that seemed too large for her wasted body. Lying open on her lap was a thick book on astrology.

"I'm sorry to disturb you," Madeline said, "but my son is not in bed and I can't find him. I'm afraid he has been kidnapped."

"Are you always this dramatic when your child is out of your sight for a few minutes?" The old woman took off her glasses, rubbed her eyes tiredly, polished the glasses with an edge of her robe and put them back on.

Madeline quickly explained about finding the mouse's head and tail on her bed, and then discovering her son was not where she had just left him, sound asleep.

"Should I assume you have looked in all the likely places for him, like the bathroom?"

"Of course," Madeline said. Why did she have to keep explaining this, when they should all be looking for Tommy? It was so frustrating. "I hoped he would be down here with Mrs. Doyle, having a bedtime snack, but no one is in the kitchen."

The older woman stared at her. "I see you did a lot of research about me, in your quest to snatch my tapestry from the wall, but Mrs. Doyle hasn't worked for me in years. Four or five, at least."

"I don't understand."

"Why do you jump to the conclusion that your boy has been kidnapped? Who would come all the way out here in a rainstorm? And why?" Mrs. Lawrence looked askance at Madeline. "You told me earlier that you are short on funds and that is why the loan of my tapestry is important to you. Only those who can afford a ransom have their children kidnapped."

"My ex-husband doesn't care about ransom. He wants Tommy, and I suspect that he's taken him. He did it before, but the police caught him before he could leave the state."

"Then why would you tell your husband – pardon me," she amended, seeing Madeline's quick frown, "I mean, your ex-husband – why would you tell him you were coming here?"

"I didn't. But I did tell a neighbor in my building, because she saw me loading Tommy in the car with extra toys, and I explained the mission I was on, to get the tapestry. If Craig managed to find out where I live now, then she obviously told him where to find me, probably thinking she was being helpful. He's very good at convincing women that he's harmless."

"One of those, eh?" Mrs. Lawrence looked wryly sympathetic. "But no one knew you would be sleeping here tonight. Wouldn't it be far more likely that your ex would wait at your apartment for your return? If he has indeed located your address, which from your tone I gather you wished he had not."

Madeline rubbed her forehead. "All I know is that my little boy is not in bed. I need to find him. Do you have a flashlight I could borrow? I'm going to look outside. Maybe he wanted another toy and thought it was still in the car."

"A flashlight? Let me think…"

"Wait. Jason has one. He's the one who suggested Tommy would be downstairs." Suddenly feeling reticent about confiding in this stranger and complaining about the woman's own employee, she said, "There's a locked room on the third floor. Perhaps Tommy is in there and can't get out. Do you have the key?"

"I thought you wanted to look outdoors," the older woman mumbled, stifling a yawn. "Before you do all this running around and Nancy Drew-ing, why not check the boy's room? He probably came down for a drink of water and went back to bed while you were roaming around on the third floor."

More to humor her hostess than because she believed her, Madeline hurried upstairs and opened the door to Tommy's room. She turned on the ceiling light. The boy was asleep in bed. He mumbled softly, as if disturbed by the light, and kicked off his covers.

Relief flooded Madeline. She pulled the blankets up around his shoulders and kissed his warm brow.

17

She darkened the room and tiptoed out, closing the door softly behind her. On impulse, steeling herself for a shock, she went next door, flipped on the light and turned toward the bed.

There was no sign of Calli, and there was nothing unusual on the bed. All signs of the dead mouse were gone. The bedspread had been neatly turned down. Robe and slippers were invitingly laid out for her use.

THREE

Madeline awoke abruptly, sensing a presence in the room. Her eyes flew open and for a moment she was confused by the unfamiliar surroundings. Thin moonlight seeped through gaps in the filmy curtains. The storm had stopped.

Earlier, after telling Mrs. Lawrence that Tommy was indeed as safe as the older woman had predicted, Madeline returned to the second floor and shared her son's bed, knowing she would sleep more soundly with him safely by her side.

Now, hearing the soft breathing of her son, Madeline wondered if that slight noise had woken her so thoroughly. It seemed unlikely. She closed her eyes and turned on her side, but sleep eluded her. She could not seem to shake off the unpleasant sensation that she was being watched – studied – by someone, or … something.

She wondered if that cat had managed to sneak in the room. She sat up and tried to see in the darkness, hoping Calli wasn't bringing another trophy.

Suddenly her thoughts of the cat ceased.

With a sharp intake, she recoiled against the headboard. "What – what do you want?" she asked the man staring at her from across the room. She clutched the bedcovers and pulled them higher, hiding Tommy safely. Now he looked like a lump in the bed, or an extra pillow.

Her hands were cold. Her jaw ached from the tension of waiting. She prayed that Tommy would not wake up, prayed even harder that the man was unaware there were two people in the bed, not just one. She was grateful for the darkness and hoped the intruder would not shine a light on her.

"Is that you, Jason?" she asked, annoyed.

The man shook his head, frowning. He came closer, and the hazy light around his face cleared so that she saw his features. He definitely wasn't Jason. This man was clean-shaven, and much better looking than Jason Malone.

A small smile appeared on his lips, as if he knew what she was thinking. She flushed in confusion.

He continued to look at her with an unfathomable expression in his soulful eyes. He was tall. Taller than any man she'd ever met, easily over seven feet in height.

As he neared, moving so slowly that Madeline would not be sure he was actually moving if his features were not growing larger and clearer, the man's mouth moved but no sound came out.

Slowly, she inched the blankets higher, to hide her movement as she leaned sideways and groped on the floor for her boots, thinking she could startle him by throwing one. She grabbed a boot, and slowly straightened, waiting for the right time to throw it.

He came closer, his mouth still moving.

"I can't hear you!" she said in a whisper, half-choking on her words, afraid of waking Tommy.

Her eyes grew wide as she saw a shimmering veil surround the man with a diffuse white-gray light as if he had lit a cloth-covered lamp.

Then Madeline saw his feet, and understood why the man appeared so unusually tall: his feet were not touching the floor. He was floating mid-air.

An intense chill shook her under the warm blanket. She wanted to scream for help, but who would come? Who would hear? She and Tommy were alone on the second floor of this big drafty house. They were alone, and at the mercy of this… creature. She shivered, realizing he was not human.

Blue rays emanated from the stranger's bare feet. He moved closer.

Her whirling thoughts filled with questions of what he could want, why he was there, and whether he intended to harm her and Tommy. She saw the man's mouth move again soundlessly and wondered if she had actually spoken out loud and he was trying to reply.

The being shook his head, as if he had read her thoughts. All at once she had an overpowering sensation that he meant them no harm. He made a gesture toward the lump in the bed. Madeline was instantly wary. He had seen Tommy!

"Don't you dare hurt my son," she cried out, unthinking. Then, realizing she had confirmed what the being might only have guessed, she bit her lip, and shook her head. "He's not here. I'm alone."

Again she felt a wave of compassion from the being and hesitantly said to him, "You … you are not going to do anything bad to us, are you?" Emboldened by the apparent friendliness of the being, she went on, her voice sounding braver than she felt inside, "Why did you wake me up?"

She thought she was going to get an answer this time. It seemed as if the man or being was trying desperately to tell her something, but once again either he was unable to speak or she was unable to hear his words. There was a look on his face that she could only interpret as concern, and kindness.

Just as her fear began to dissipate, a heavy mist formed around the man's lower half and she saw for the first time a slender silvery cord attached to his head and floating behind him across the room. The cord tightened and jerked the man backwards.

A look of surprise creased his handsome face. At an ever-accelerating speed he moved back the length of the room, pulled by an unseen force faster and faster toward the window. And then, as Madeline watched in astonishment, he went out backwards through the closed window and vanished.

She sat perfectly still in bed, staring at the dark window. The boot dropped from her fingers and thudded on the floor.

She was certain she'd been awake the past few moments. But if she wasn't dreaming, then what or who was that being? A ghost?

Adjusting the covers over Tommy, she smoothed his hair. He was still asleep, thankfully.

Hesitantly, questioning the wisdom of doing so but unable to stop herself, Madeline got up. She moved her arms and legs slowly, trying to relax her stiff muscles, aware how rigidly she had sat throughout the uncanny experience.

She walked to the window, reached out a hand, stopped, then touched the glass. Yes, the window was closed, as she had thought. It was a chilly winter night and she would've felt a draft if someone opened it. Earlier, she had locked the window, needing that extra measure of security after the scare she had been through when Tommy was missing.

Testing it, she discovered the window was still locked.

Moving the curtains aside, she looked out. The moon was high. The sky was studded with rain clouds. The wide expanse of rocky slopes around the house was empty except for the scrubby vegetation, cactus and sagebrush that grew there naturally.

The stranger was nowhere in sight. The silvery rope that had yanked him backwards was gone. There was no sign, no clue, no evidence at all that he had been there.

FOUR

The tantalizing smell of fresh-baked bread greeted Madeline when she went downstairs Thursday morning. It was still early, and Tommy was not up yet. Unusual, since he was normally awake and full of energy long before his mother wanted to be.

She was tempted to postpone her errand until after breakfast, but she turned her back on the kitchen and slipped out the front door, hoping no one had observed her. She wanted to take care of this before Tommy was up and running around.

Vividly recalling the strange visitation in her room during the night, she wanted to check the ground beneath her window in case there were footprints, the marks of a stepladder, or some other tangible evidence that the intruder had been a living, breathing human.

Although it had rained the previous evening while she was searching for Tommy, when Madeline had looked outside after her glowing visitor went out the window, the sky had been mostly clear and the moon bright. She felt fairly confident that it had not rained again after the man's visit.

The ground was wet but not soggy. The air was misty. Seagulls flew overhead, making their raucous cries. A dull rhythmic pounding spoke of the surf nearby, on the other side of the Pacific Coast Highway. The waves sounded closer, more threatening, than she had noticed yesterday.

Pulling her corduroy jacket more tightly around her, wishing for something warmer, she crossed the unkempt lawn and turned a corner, studying the many windows until she found the one she wanted. Congratulating herself for her foresight, the young woman stopped beneath the window where Tommy's teddy bear perched on the sill inside.

Carefully, she scrutinized the earth, bending to be sure she did not miss anything important. After several fruitless moments, she straightened and admitted defeat. She still did not believe it was a ghost. Whoever he was, he had some reason for trying to scare her.

The memory of the man's worried face and the sensation she'd had that he wanted to help now seemed farfetched.

Madeline looked up at the spacious house. The peeling gingerbread trim needed paint. The window frames were cracked and roof tiles were missing or broken. She slowly walked toward the back of the house, gazing up at the ornate balconies at some windows. Sun-blistered wooden steps led up to the wide rambling veranda and from there into the kitchen and other rooms she had not yet seen.

Voices came from the kitchen as she approached, and the smell of breakfast reminded her how hungry she was. She'd get Tommy ready to go, then they'd eat and wait for Mrs. Lawrence's nephew Luke to come with groceries. He'd be able to help her with the dead battery, and then she'd be on her way, no worse for the trip other than a few attacks of nerves.

She started to go in the kitchen door, but realized she'd have to explain herself, so she hurriedly went around the house to the front. As she approached the door, she glanced up and thought she saw someone watching from a window. There was a slight movement of curtains, then all was still.

Probably just a breeze, she told herself sternly, not liking the uneasiness this house and the people in it made her feel.

It was getting warmer and the sun felt good on her back, yet she could not shake off the sense that she was being watched. She scanned all the windows but could see nothing unusual. Then high above, on a wrought iron belvedere, a noise... and a small movement. With a snap of her head, she focused all her attention on that spot, backing up a few steps in an effort to see better.

She bumped into something. Turning sharply, she gasped and shrank back.

"It's you!" She pointed a trembling finger at the young man she collided with.

He stared at her, baffled.

With a scoffing noise, she decided everyone here was crazy and she'd better leave as soon as possible. She sped into the house, slamming the door behind her and trying with fumbling fingers to secure the chain lock.

FIVE

Madeline came downstairs with her son in time to see the housekeeper unchain the front door and admit the young man Madeline had bumped into outside.

Quickly, before she could be noticed, Madeline pulled Tommy into the dining room. The table was set for breakfast. Mrs. Lawrence was already eating.

She plopped her child into a chair and poured him a glass of orange juice from the pewter pitcher on the buffet. "Good morning, Mrs. Lawrence."

The older woman was buttering a piece of rye toast. The scraping was the only sound in the room. She glanced up and smiled cordially.

"Excuse me," Madeline said, "but your housekeeper just let a strange man in and you mustn't let him get me. He tried to last night but then he went down a rope and out my window. That is, Tommy's window, since I bunked in with him last night." Hearing footsteps approach, she said in a rush, "Mrs. Lawrence! Please. You've got to help me."

The old woman chewed her toast. She looked up as the good-looking young man in jeans and a red sweater came in. "There you are, Luke," she said, tilting her head for the kiss he planted on her wrinkled cheek. "You're just in time for breakfast. Take a seat and I'll ring for Rosa to bring another placemat and napkin." She picked up a porcelain bell by her coffee cup and rang it loudly.

"He's, uh, your nephew?" Madeline turned to stare at the man.

"Didn't I tell you he's a handsome fella?" Mrs. Lawrence said. "Luke, this girl you're gaping at is Madeline Clark, and that nice-mannered young man is her son Thomas. They're guests of mine, so treat them well."

Luke smiled. Rosa came in and bustled around him, happily serving him a plate and making sure he had everything he needed. He slid his placemat around the table to sit next to Madeline.

"He's the one you said would help with my car?" Madeline asked Mrs. Lawrence, feeling disoriented. She was positive that Luke was the man she'd seen last night in Tommy's room. He looked different now. More... solid, but it was him. What she'd seen during the night had been a shadow or weaker version of the vibrant man beside her now.

"You keep staring at me," Luke said to Madeline. "Have we met before?"

"No. That is... sort of."

"Sounds intriguing."

Madeline noticed that Jason was watching them from the hallway, seeming interested in the conversation. Calli loped towards the dining room, but stopped when she saw Jason. The cat hissed at him, and raised a paw as if to strike at him. Jason backed off.

When he caught Madeline staring, Jason gave a lopsided grin, held up his toolbox and continued on down the hall, apparently on an errand to fix something.

The cat wandered into the dining room, no doubt drawn in by the breakfast smells.

With a glance after Jason, puzzled by something, Madeline turned her attention back to the breakfast table.

Tommy piped up. "Can I have another muffin, Mommy?" After she refilled his plate with fruit and half a muffin, Tommy said to Luke, "Are you going to be our new Daddy? We need one."

Madeline winced. "Why don't you run upstairs and get your backpack of toys? And then you can play with your trucks over there," she added, pointing to a corner of the room. After Tommy scooted away, she said, "Ever since I got divorced last year, he's been asking when 'we' are getting married again."

Taking pity on her embarrassment, Luke asked, "Have you known my Aunt Agatha long?"

Shaking her head, Madeline explained the reason for her visit, and why she and Tommy had to spend the night. While talking, she darted looks at Luke, wishing he would at least admit that he'd been in Tommy's room last night, instead of continuing this pretense that he didn't know her and had never seen her before this morning.

As if reading her thoughts, Luke said, "When we met outside, you said something that didn't make sense–"

"It is apparently a habit of hers," Mrs. Lawrence said, stroking Calli. She fed the cat a bite of egg from her fork, and then continued eating from it herself. "Just before Rosa let you in, Madeline barreled in here demanding protection from you! And last night, she claimed her son was kidnapped, when all the time he was safely asleep in his bed."

"But–" Madeline began.

"Seemed like such a sweet girl, too," Mrs. Lawrence said, "and she writes polite letters."

"I'm not as crazy as it sounds," Madeline said, feeling the need to defend herself.

Tommy looked up from the corner where he was playing with toy cars. Noticing his interest, Madeline took a moment to take him into the kitchen to stay with Rosa, so he would not be frightened by her story.

When she was back at the dining table, Madeline suddenly felt foolish. This once-elegant dining room, with its magnificent cut-glass chandelier and the fine old oak table and velvet-cushioned chairs seemed so sane, so safe, so normal. To speak of strange glowing apparitions that floated above the floor and mouthed silent words seemed ludicrous.

At Luke's urging, she told them what she had witnessed, explained that it was Luke's face she had seen, and then braced herself for their scornful laughter.

She did not expect the reaction she received.

Mrs. Lawrence turned to her nephew and sighed. "Luke. Shame on you."

"Then, you believe me?" Madeline asked.

Jason slowly walked past the open doorway.

"Of course I believe you," Mrs. Lawrence said. "My nephew is a talented psychic. He frequently has out-of-body experiences."

Madeline looked at the two skeptically.

"So that explains my headache this morning," Luke said. To Madeline he added, "I usually remember my trips – also called astral

27

projection in case you've heard of that term. No? I see you find all this overwhelming. If it is any consolation, I apologize for disturbing your sleep."

Mrs. Lawrence chuckled softly. "I bet she didn't mind."

Madeline reddened. "I was terrified. I've never seen a … a ghost before."

"I'm not a ghost." Luke grinned at her.

"Are you sure you didn't climb in my window and put on that act to spook me?"

"You may as well believe us, child," Mrs. Lawrence said, steering her wheelchair away from the table. It whined faintly as she maneuvered toward the door. "Come along, and I'll show you my book collection."

While they followed Mrs. Lawrence down a hall to the library, Luke whispered to Madeline, "Don't be frightened. You're like a cave man encountering space travel for the first time."

"I hate flying."

He smiled. "By the way, it's okay if you don't believe in ESP, but it might be a good idea to humor my aunt."

"Why?"

"You're staying for the seance tonight, aren't you?"

They walked into the book-lined library where Mrs. Lawrence was busy pulling books from a low shelf onto a coffee table.

"Seance?" Madeline repeated. "No thanks. I'm leaving as soon as you jump start my car battery."

He gave another impish smile. "What if I refuse to help until after the seance?"

SIX

While Luke hooked jumper cables between Madeline's dead battery and his car, he said, "Aren't you lucky I came prepared?"

"Next you'll tell me that you sensed I had car trouble," she said. "But is that why you came here today? To put on a seance for your aunt? She said you were bringing groceries."

"Multi-tasking. That's my middle name." He started his car engine and indicated that she should turn her key.

She did, but the car wouldn't start.

He revved his motor. "Try again!"

She kept trying, but it was useless. Shaking her head, she got out of her car. "Thanks anyway, but I guess it needs more than a quick jump."

Checking under her hood again, he held up a broken fan belt. "Looks like your car wants you to stay."

"Could you drive me down to a mechanic shop or something? Really, I need to get going."

"Spooked about the seance?"

"Don't be ridiculous," she said.

"For the record, she's not my aunt. She's my great-aunt. My mother's father's sister, if you follow me."

"If you really have psychic powers, I wish you would put a spell on her—"

"What for?"

"Make her change her mind about letting me borrow The Calico Tapestry. It would help me a lot if I could be the one to exhibit it, and get the publicity for my new business."

"Sorry my powers aren't that variety." As he closed her hood and put his jumper cables away, he said, "I used to wish my psychic abilities would go away. It can be a burden, though I don't suppose you understand what I mean."

"I think I do," she said. "It must be strange to wake up with a headache and not know where you were during the night. And I guess people are always asking you to predict a winner at the racetrack or the stock exchange."

"Lottery numbers. That's the big request."

She looked at the house, thoughtfully.

"Listen," he said. "I'm sorry I scared you. I hope you'll forget the whole incident and put it out of your mind."

"You kept trying to tell me something."

"I did?"

"When I first saw you in the room, I couldn't see your face clearly, and I asked if you were Jason. You shook your head and started trying to warn me…"

"Warn you? Are you sure about that?"

"No… but you kept frowning. And there was something else. It's like you could read my thoughts." She rubbed her arms. "I was afraid you were going to do something to my son."

"Let me make it up to you, okay?

She looked at him curiously. "Drive me to a gas station?"

"I'll do that later, I promise. But if you stay for the seance, I'll do my best to talk my aunt into letting you borrow that tapestry. I know she can be a tough old bird, but she likes me for some odd reason, and she owes me a favor or two."

"That'd be great. Wow, thanks so much." Madeline shot him a wide smile, and he looked at her as if seeing her in a new light.

"Aunt Agatha?" Luke said, when they returned to the house and found Tommy and Mrs. Lawrence in the library with Calli the cat. "I'm afraid my powers as a mechanic are not the greatest. Madeline and Tommy need to stay a while longer. Okay with you, isn't it?"

"Naturally," the woman said.

"Thank you so much for understanding," Madeline said. "Would you like to stay here a while longer, Tommy, and play with the cat?"

"Yeah. Is he mine?"

"He is a she, and only to play with while we visit here. Wait a sec, I'll get a picture of you together." She dug out her cell phone. Even though she didn't have service to make a call, she still had battery power to use the camera feature. She took several photos, and then the cat streaked off as if glad to escape the child's too-tight hugs.

Tommy dashed off after the cat.

"I guess I'd better get him," Madeline said.

"He'll be fine. It's nice to have young people in the house," Mrs. Lawrence said. "Purely selfish motives, my dear. A brood of money-hungry relatives will descend on me this afternoon. They say they're coming to keep me company in my lonely old house." She snorted. "I know better! There's not one of them that doesn't wish I'd hurry up and die, so they could get hold of my money."

"I'm sure they don't wish that," Madeline said.

The old woman peered up at her. "Do you Ouija?"

"Excuse me? Do I … weegie?"

Luke smiled. "She wants to know if you like to use the Ouija board?" He pointed toward a table where a Ouija board and tripod pointer were set up.

"I've never tried anything like that." Madeline knew her tone added the words, *And I never will* but she didn't want to be rude by telling them she had no intention of delving into the occult.

"Never mind, dear," Mrs. Lawrence said. "I'll teach you how to use the tarot cards later. Then when the locusts descend I can keep my blood pressure down by sitting with you in a quiet corner and see what the cards say. You see? You'll be doing me a favor by staying."

Madeline gave a guilty start, thinking of her real reason: The Calico Tapestry which Luke promised to help her get. Or at least try. She caught his glance. He winked.

During this, Tommy came back without the cat. He regarded the old woman in the wheelchair. "I like to play cards, too. Do you know how to play Go Fish?" He looked puzzled when the adults laughed.

"I'm going to rest for a while," Mrs. Lawrence said, pointing her wheelchair toward the door.

After she left, Madeline said to Luke, "I really appreciate how nice you and your aunt are being to Tommy and me. And Rosa, too, she's been great about keeping Tommy in the kitchen with her when I need a helper."

He gave her a sharp glance. "I feel you're deliberately leaving someone out of that compliment. May I guess Jason Malone?"

"I forgot about your 'powers' – I'll have to watch my step around you."

"Just an ordinary guess. Anything you want to tell me?"

She hesitated, wanting to tell Luke about the scary experience the prior night when Jason kept her out of the locked room on the third floor, but her son was in earshot. Tommy was susceptible to nightmares and she didn't want to frighten him.

"Probably my imagination," she said lightly.

Although she knew the weather forecast was for more rain, when water suddenly pelted the library windows, Madeline gave a small cry of surprise.

"Are you always this jumpy?" Luke looked at her, then smile reassuringly. "It's the house. Kinda creepy sometimes."

"I don't expect you to entertain me. I'm sure you have other things to do for your aunt. If you'd just watch Tommy for a moment, I'm going to dash out to the car for a few things before it starts raining any harder."

"Want me to go for you?"

"I know what I want, and I can grab it fast, but thanks anyway."

When she came back into the house a few minutes later with her latest needlepoint project, a pillow she was making for a client, Jason Malone slipped out of another room and followed close on her heel, without saying anything to her.

Uneasy, she quickened her step, heading for the library, almost running in her effort to escape Jason. She thought of calling out to Luke for help, but decided that was melodramatic. The mood of the house was affecting her. She was usually more practical than this. But even though she chided herself, she hurried to get away from Jason.

Behind her, he made soft clucking noises, implying she was being chicken.

Her cheeks flaming, she reached for the library doorknob.

As he passed, Jason leaned in so his lips were next to her ear. He kept his face forward and did not look at her. His lips barely moved as he whispered, "Get out while you can. Take your kid and beat it. Don't believe anything Luke tells you!"

She turned sharply, wanting to ask him to explain.

But he sped upstairs, out of sight.

SEVEN

"And this is my daughter Nancy's husband – Frank Miller," said Mrs. Lawrence, finishing the introductions to Madeline by flapping a hand toward the short balding man.

"Pleased to meet you," Madeline said, feeling the curious stares from her hostess's family.

Luke watched in amusement.

They were all gathered in the living room for pre-dinner appetizers and drinks. In addition to the old woman's two middle-aged children from her first marriage, a son-in-law, and a grand-daughter, there was also a young woman who wasn't a relative but hoped to be. It quickly became clear to Madeline that Daphne Pfeffer was determined to marry Luke.

They spent some time exchanging Christmas gifts. "I'm sorry I did not know you would be here," Mrs. Lawrence said to Madeline.

"Oh, please, no apologies needed," Madeline said.

Madeline was relieved to notice that Jason Malone was not around, either uninvited or perhaps it was his evening off. She had looked into the kitchen earlier to see if Rosa needed help, but had been shooed away cheerfully. In passing the dining room, she noticed there were places set for only eight people. That meant Jason was not expected to join them later on, and she was relieved.

Her son Tommy was in the kitchen having an early supper under the watchful gaze of the housekeeper, with whom he had become fast friends ever since Rosa allowed him to help knead dough for the soft rolls she prepared for dinner. Madeline considered herself fortunate that Tommy had a safe place to eat and play. She didn't feel it was appropriate for him to be part of the scheduled seance.

In fact, she'd decided that this gathering of locusts, as Mrs. Lawrence had termed them, was not only no place for a child, it was no place for herself. She felt distinctly out of her element, and under-dressed for the occasion. Since she hadn't planned on an overnight stay, she was still wearing her boots, corduroy jeans and a sweater.

The others were in holiday finery, particularly Daphne, whom she learned was a model and actress.

Mrs. Lawrence's oldest child from her first marriage, Brad Calhoun, offered Madeline a glass of wine. She accepted it with a smile.

"I hear you're one of us," he said, smoothing his hair with a practiced hand. Bradford Junior was fifty, or nearing it, and desperately trying to hide his age. The skin around his blue eyes was too tight, too smooth and wrinkle-free to be natural. His teeth were arctic white and unnaturally even. He wore a chocolate velour pullover with tight jeans and held his trim physique erect, never seeming to relax. Luke had told her the man was an actor, and she felt that explained a lot.

She took in his manufactured appearance and smiled to herself, wondering how many hours he spent each day to keep up the facade of youth.

"One of you?" she repeated, puzzled.

He held up his left hand and pointed to the bare ring finger. "Divorced. I've been married three times. Struck out. From now on, my motto is casual hookups only. No more trips down the aisle. You?"

Trying not to be shocked by his blase attitude, she said lightly, "Just once. I'm leaving my options open." She sipped her wine and glanced around the room as if fascinated by the decor, wishing he would leave her alone, but too polite to dismiss him outright.

The living room was decorated elegantly for the holidays, with gold and silver ornaments in huge crystal bowls, and ribbon swags on the mantel. The satin furniture was upholstered in varying hues of sea green and aquamarine blue, but red and green tasseled throws here and there added a holiday feel to the room. A collection of Santa Claus figurines in porcelain, pottery and glass filled a massive display cabinet in one corner.

Madeline couldn't help noticing how luxurious all the decorations were, and thought in contrast of the spindly three-foot-high tree that she and Tommy had decorated with homemade paper ornaments.

But looking at the people gathered here, she knew that her tree had been trimmed with love, and in contrast, there was a sense of the holidays being impersonal with this family. Maybe that impression was only because she was an outsider, she reminded herself, wanting to be fair.

Outside in the hall, a large grandfather clock struck the hour.

Looking around, Madeline tried to remember all the names she'd heard. Nancy Miller was seated on a striped couch with her fifteen-year-old daughter Frances. The two were clearly having an argument but were keeping their voices down and no one but Madeline seemed to notice them.

Fragments of their heated sentences reached her ears and she was startled to hear the blatant scorn pouring out of the mother and daughter, with their look-alike short, dark curly hair. It was clear to Madeline that the mother was drinking too much, and she wondered if that was part of the problem.

Luke was bent over the large stone fireplace, striking match after match in an effort to get the kindling to catch. She started to join him, then noticed Daphne sidle up and offer her assistance with her gold cigarette lighter.

Jealous, and annoyed with herself for the reaction, Madeline immediately turned her attention to the tapestry hanging over the mantelpiece.

"I see you are admiring our old Calico," Brad said, gesturing with his glass.

Madeline gave a small start, having forgotten Brad was at her side. "Yes," she said feebly, "I suppose I was." She looked at the faded old tapestry, carefully avoiding the sight of Luke laughing with Daphne. "It looks very much like Calli, doesn't it?"

The memory of the dead mouse came back to her, and with it, her appetite vanished. She put down her plate of cheese and crackers on a side table and sat in a wing-back chair. The fire was now lit and blazing cheerily.

"It's a family tradition," Brad said, pulling up a chair and sitting next to her. "My grandmother made the tapestry. Her cat was the model. Striking, isn't it? Bigger than life, of course, but the colors are good. Seems to me they used to be stronger, more vivid, but maybe that's my imagination."

"Probably not. If you examined the tapestry, on the reverse side the yarn will be more intense in color. Even though this room doesn't seem to get direct sunlight, the colors fade, especially after a hundred years. And of course, being hung above a working fireplace is not the best place for it."

"Sounds like you know your stuff."

She flushed at his tone of sardonic amusement. "Needlework is a hobby of mine. Actually, a business. I mean, I wish it were a business." She grimaced, hating the way his presence made her feel tongue-tied. She didn't know why she was letting Mrs. Lawrence's relatives affect her so much, but there was an atmosphere in the room of uneasiness and rancor.

He eyed her closely. "What exactly are you doing here?"

"Your mother invited me. I had hoped she would loan me the tapestry for an exhibit to promote my business, but she turned me down. Car trouble left me stranded."

"Until I saw my sister brought along Daphne, I assumed from the way you look at Luke all the time that you're his date tonight."

"No, I'm not," she said, looking around casually but being careful not to glance in Luke's direction.

Brad laughed, not unkindly. "He's a good guy. A bit strange with all that hocus-pocus stuff, but otherwise harmless. You'd be better for him than Daphne, but you've probably already decided that, haven't you?"

She didn't like the insinuation, but didn't know what to say.

"Okay," he said with a gesture of surrender. "Act high and mighty if you want. I won't give away your game. If I was your age and trying to support myself and a little boy, I'd do the same thing."

"Which is?"

He didn't seem to notice her coldness. In a conspiratorial whisper, he said, "I'd maneuver my way into a rich family. That ploy of trying to borrow mom's tapestry is a good one, I'll admit, but pretty transparent. And then the trick of a dead battery. That's great. What did you do? Leave your headlights and radio on to drain it? Disconnect some wires so you'd be invited to stay here until it could be fixed?"

Her temper simmered just below the boiling point. If he had not been Mrs. Lawrence's son, she'd have let loose with a rejoinder that would set him back a few gray hairs. With effort, she merely said, "I better go check on my son." She walked away quickly.

In the kitchen, Madeline calmed down by playing with Tommy for a few minutes.

"I like it here, Mommy." He finished a grilled cheese sandwich.

"Rosa is a good cook, isn't she?" Madeline smiled at Rosa.

"Eat as much as you want, Tommy," Rosa said. To Madeline, Rosa added, with a meaningful nod toward the living room, "You need a break from the party?"

Madeline flushed guiltily. "Mrs. Lawrence is very nice, but–"

"Luke is too. Those others…" Rosa shrugged. "I hear they want Mrs. Lawrence to have her youngest son declared dead so they can get more money when she dies."

"That's terrible. I didn't know there was another son."

"It would not surprise me if one of them tried to make things go faster." Rosa looked at her meaningfully.

Murder? Madeline darted a look at Tommy, who was happily watching cartoons on TV. "But Mrs. Lawrence is so old," she whispered to Rosa. "Can't they just wait?"

Rosa nodded in agreement, then drained the potatoes and began mashing them with a stainless steel ricer.

"Anything I can do to help?" Madeline asked.

Rosa shook her head, smiling. "Go back to the party. Tommy is fine here. I enjoy having a little boy with me."

Madeline was too curious about something to leave just yet. "You mentioned another son. Where is he? And how can they simply have him declared dead?"

After putting the potatoes in a serving dish and then onto a warming tray, Rosa said, "He went off to that war in Iraq and never came back. Seven years ago, Mrs. Lawrence got a letter from the army that he was 'Missing in Action.' She never heard nothing more about him."

"That's so sad. I remember seeing in a movie that seven years is the length of time you have to wait before you can have someone declared dead. Why doesn't Mrs. Lawrence go along with the rest of the family? Does she believe her son is still alive somewhere?"

"She don't talk about him. I never met him. He was gone three years already, maybe four, when I started working for Mrs. Lawrence. But I saw his picture."

"What's he look like?"

"Blond. Blue eyes. Skinny. But something in his face I didn't like."

"What do you mean?" Madeline waited for Rosa's reply but the housekeeper seemed unsure how to explain.

"Not a nice person, I think. I am glad he did not come back."

"Doesn't sound like anyone I'd like to meet."

Rosa filled more serving dishes. "Dinner is almost ready. You want to leave Tommy with me?"

"Thank you, Rosa, but I don't want to impose and it's already past his bedtime. I'll get him settled upstairs and then I'll check on him throughout the evening. I really appreciate the help you've given me."

Upstairs, she got Tommy settled in with picture books from his backpack so that he could pretend to read in bed the way he'd seen her do. She knew from experience that he would be asleep within a few minutes of opening the first book.

"Good night, Tommy tom-tom," she said affectionately, hugging him tight.

"Night, Mommy mom-mom," he said with a sleepy giggle.

"I'm going to dash down the hall to the bathroom and then I'll check on you again before I go downstairs for dinner. You gonna be okay up here, my big man?"

He nodded.

Smiling, she left the room, and when she poked her head in a few minutes later to check on him, he was already asleep. The book had fallen from his hands. She picked it up and smoothed the covers over his shoulders.

She felt uneasy about leaving him alone without an intercom, but reasoned that with everyone downstairs, Tommy would be safe in the bedroom by himself. She had seen Jason drive off earlier in a battered pickup, so apparently it was his night off. She hoped he'd be gone for a long time.

Nonetheless, she made sure the windows were locked and checked the connecting door to that bedroom she had occupied briefly. She started to lock the hall door as well, but decided that could be a hazard rather than a safeguard.

She stopped her thoughts from spinning about emergencies, but could not shake off the feeling that Tommy should not be left unguarded. She debated the idea of staying with him, but she was really hungry and it couldn't hurt to go down to dinner.

As she turned off the light and left the room, she checked the time, and decided to come back in a half hour.

Thinking of the seance to come, she wondered if Luke would hold true to his promise to help her borrow the valuable old tapestry. If so, then all this would be worth it.

EIGHT

"You sure are a nervous little mother, aren't you?" Daphne said when Madeline slipped into the living room where everyone was having dessert and coffee. Daphne's makeup was still flawless, and she smiled cautiously, as if the movement would cause instant wrinkles she wanted to avoid. "That makes a dozen trips upstairs in the past hour."

"Shut up, Daphne," young Frances said, blowing a bubble with her gum and popping it noisily. "Just because you'd make a rotten mother–"

"Enough," Frances' mother said, drinking brandy. "I won't stand for any more rudeness from you. One more outburst and you can go home."

"Chill." Frances flopped into a corner chair and draped her gangly legs over the side. "It's raining too hard. I don't have my driver's license. If I left you here, you'd get pissed. And you always tell me not to hitchhike." She put another piece of gum in her mouth and chewed vigorously.

Mrs. Lawrence sighed as she surveyed her only grandchild.

Madeline quietly moved to the table by the window where she served herself a bowlful of warm cherry cobbler and poured cream over it from a silver pitcher. She looked through the silverware for a large spoon to eat with.

"Need something, Maddie?" Luke walked up to her. With a backward glance toward the Millers, who were still arguing about teenage Frances' lack of manners, he added, "Fun crowd, isn't it?"

"I refuse to answer," she said with a smile. "I want to stay on your good side." She found a spoon and took a bite of the cobbler.

Indicating two vacant chairs, he said, "Can I bring you a hot chocolate to go with that?"

"How did you know I didn't want coffee? Oh. Of course. There I go again, forgetting you're–"

"Different? Really, though, it was a lucky guess. I don't go around reading everybody's mind. It'd drive me crazy. There'd be no room in my head for my own thoughts."

They sat while she ate.

"How do you deal with it?" she asked.

"I learned years ago how to filter out stuff. Usually I'm only aware of someone's thoughts if it's urgent or important."

"Like… murder, for instance?"

He put down his cup of tea. "What makes you say that?"

She looked at him. "I'm new here, and I'm leaving soon."

"But there's a reason you said it."

"Look. You don't have to be psychic to pick up the bad vibes in this house." She studied his lean face and saw the worry in his clear blue eyes. "You've already had the same thought. Your aunt is in danger, isn't she? That's why you stop by with groceries and probably other excuses to check on her, and let him know you've got an eye on things."

"Him?" Luke asked.

Madeline noticed Brad Calhoun hovering a few feet away, near the dessert table.

Mrs. Lawrence called out to Brad, "Where's my coffee? Make sure you pour decaf or I'll be up all night!"

"Yes, Mother." Brad filled a cup and hurried to the old woman's side.

Once he was out of earshot, Madeline said to Luke, "Rosa thinks that some of the others are planning, or at least wishing for, your aunt to die soon."

"Money is a magnet for many people. They don't care what they do to their souls in the pursuit of riches."

"But it's not a magnet for you?"

"I like what money can do for me. But I wouldn't pay that kind of price for it. I'm more interested in evolving my soul than sending it backwards." He smiled. "Besides, I happen to love my aunt and I hope she'll stick around a long time. Don't look for trouble here, Maddie. Let's not blow kitchen gossip out of proportion."

She felt chided. She stood up. "I better check on Tommy."

"Again?"

"Just because your girlfriend thinks I'm a nervous mom doesn't mean I don't have good cause for it. In this house." She walked away quickly.

On her way out of the room, though, Mrs. Lawrence stopped her.

"Not going to bed already are you, Madeline?"

"No, ma'am. I was going to be sure my son didn't kick off the covers."

"Still worried he's going to be kidnapped?"

Madeline winced. The old woman's voice was loud, and everyone stopped talking to stare at them.

"Why would someone take your kid?" Brad asked.

Madeline shook her head, not wanting to get into this now, here with these people.

"Oh, I get it," Brad said. "Another ploy to get money. Stage a kidnaping, hit my mom up for the money as a 'loan' to pay the kidnappers, then hightail it out of state."

"What?" Madeline stared at him. "That's crazy."

"Yeah, crazy like a fox," Brad said.

Mrs. Lawrence sighed. "Bradford. Go eat another piece of pie. And be sure the dining room is cleared for the seance."

Madeline breathed more easily, seeing the old woman wasn't impressed by Brad's tall tales. After everyone went back to their private conversations, she said to Mrs. Lawrence, "Thank you. I'd like to do something to repay your hospitality."

"I enjoy having you and Tommy here. I'd much prefer you for relatives than the ones I've been saddled with. Except Luke, of course. He's a gem. But you've already noticed that, haven't you?"

"Am I that obvious?" she replied, half to herself. "You're the second to comment."

"Who was first? Rosa? Or am I being a nosy old woman? I haven't forgotten how sensitive young girls can be about their romances."

"It's not a romance! And I'm not all that young anymore, either." Madeline smiled. "Anyway, it was your son Brad. He thought I was Luke's date until Daphne showed up with the Millers."

"Brad? Hmm. I'll bet that's not the only comment he made. I can tell from your tone he didn't make a favorable impression on you. He rarely does, more's the pity. I'm sure Brad could be a charming man if he wasn't so afraid."

"Afraid of what?"

Mrs. Lawrence looked startled. "Musing out loud, dear girl. I suppose it's never easy for a mother to stand by and watch her offspring ruin their lives. But what can I do? I did the best I could, gave them every advantage, tried not to spoil them, and gave them wings to take off on their own flight pattern."

"I'm sure you've been a wonderful mother, and grandmother too."

"Flattery! Don't stop, I love it. I get few compliments." She shrugged, but the anxious look on her lined face did not go away. "He's a grown man. It's up to him to choose his own direction. But I see I'm depressing you. I forgot you are a mother, too, with hopes for your own son. You are so young, so innocent! I wish I could do it all again, with what I've learned since."

Mrs. Lawrence shook her head sadly and seemed to grow older and more hunched in her wheelchair.

"Agatha?" It was Frank Miller. "Can I break in? I need to talk to my mother-in-law in private before we get busy with the readings."

"Frank!" Mrs. Lawrence wagged a gnarled finger at him. "I see where young Frances gets her atrocious manners."

"That's all right," Madeline said, feeling like an outsider. "I do want to check on Tommy."

As she moved off, Daphne quickly joined her. "I'd love to see this paragon of yours. Mind if I tag along?" Daphne looked stunning in black jeans and a pale silk shirt whose neckline was filled with a dozen slender gold chains. Her blonde hair was shiny and sleek, and everything about her seemed to be direct from the latest fashion magazine.

Madeline felt at a disadvantage in the same casual outfit she'd worn the previous day. Unable to think of a polite way to refuse, she shrugged and led the way.

Going upstairs, Daphne said, "You don't much like me, do you? I don't mind. Not many girls do. My mother says it's because they envy me."

With her hand on Tommy's doorknob, Madeline said, "I guess you're waiting for me to agree with your mother, but to be honest, I don't. I think the reason is you're not very likable. You've got a chip on your shoulder, and you push people away with that attitude. But why don't we call a truce, since we'll be in each other's company the rest of the evening?" She held out a hand to shake.

Daphne looked at Madeline's hand, then examined her own perfect manicure as if searching for any flaws. Then, without a word, she turned on her heel and went downstairs.

Madeline let her hand fall to her side, frustrated. She was angry with herself for bothering to make the effort. She should have just smoothed things over and kept her mouth shut instead of feeling the need to be honest. She knew she had just made an enemy, and it was a mistake she'd regret. Squaring her shoulders, she turned the knob and went in.

NINE

"I can't wait 'til I get my license," Frances said, flopping down next to Madeline on an uncomfortable couch. "Then I won't have to stick around for these stupid seances. Relatives. Ugh." She jammed her hands into her torn jeans and stretched her legs out straight on the floor.

Her mother immediately sang out, "Posture, Frances!"

"Sit properly dear," Frances mimicked. She wriggled upright, then grinned sheepishly at Madeline. "I bet you think I'm incorrigible. That's what my dad calls me." She sighed. "I am, too."

"You're a normal teenager from what I can see. It's hard being in-between things in life, isn't it?"

Frances nodded, pleased to have someone offer understanding. "They're sending me to a girls' academy next year. To give me class. Or something. It'll be a waste of money. They might as well bury me alive and get it over with." She chewed a new piece of bubble gum, loudly cracking and popping.

Madeline couldn't help giving a start when a bubble popped near her ear. "Maybe you'll make new friends there and like it."

"Hey, there's Calico – Come here, Calli!" The cat obligingly leapt into the girl's lap. "Don't you like cats?"

Madeline hadn't realized she had moved away from the cat. "Not that one."

"Why not? Did she bring you one of her famous trophies? A lizard? A bird?"

"Mouse."

"Cool."

"But don't tell me you're psychic, too. Does it run in the family?"

"Maybe." Frances idly scratched the cat's ears. "My psychiatrist says I'm a disturbed adolescent. Luke says I have telekinetic powers." Seeing Madeline's puzzled frown, she explained, "I can move things without touching them."

"Do you… do this often?"

"Luke says I need to develop my ability before I outgrow it. He says I need to learn how to control it and make it work for me in a positive way."

Madeline laughed. "That does sound like something he'd say." Involuntarily, she glanced across the room where Luke chatted with Daphne. The blonde beauty caught the glance and gave a cool one in return.

"So you've clashed with Daphne already," Frances said. "Don't worry. Everybody does eventually. But she never gives up. She's always hanging around Luke, hoping to get that ring."

"A wedding ring?"

"Not just any ring. The big honking diamond my grandma's got tucked away. She can't wear it anymore on account of her arthritis, but I've seen it. I figure I haven't got a chance of being the one to get it. Kinda gaudy anyway. I think it's like four carats or something."

"I hope she has it in a bank vault or a safe." Madeline couldn't help thinking of Jason Malone and all his skulking around the house, possibly in search of valuables just like that diamond ring.

"Maybe if I can get control of my TK powers, I could call the ring to me." Frances laughed. "As if it works that way."

"Does your power come and go, on its own?"

The teen shrugged. "One guy that investigated me said it was poltergeists. You know, mischievous ghosts that throw things around the room. Another guy said it's me doing it. Happens because I'm a disturbed adolescent."

"So that's where the label came from?" Madeline teased. "Doesn't it scare you when it happens?"

"No. Should it?"

"It would me," Madeline admitted. "I don't like for things to happen without my control."

"That's because you're not gifted. And you're not used to being around people with ESP and stuff like that. You get used to it. Luke's the best though. Did you know he even helps the police?"

"I've seen TV shows about that. What does he do?"

"He goes in a trance and tells them where to find missing kids or dead bodies. Stuff like that. Didn't he tell you?"

"No," Madeline said. She glanced over at Luke, who appeared to be deep in conversation with Daphne.

"Luke says we all are born with psychic powers, but we forget how to use them."

"Well, I'm sure I don't have any."

"Or maybe they're latent and they'll come out at the right time." The teenager studied her. "That Daphne's a real bitch. You and Luke make a cute couple. Are you in love with him, or is it just lust?"

"Good grief, Frances. We just met yesterday!"

"Call me Frankie if you want." Frances put the cat on the floor. "Haven't you ever heard of love at first sight? I think it's romantic. Maybe you're soul mates. Tell him to go sit under the Christmas tree so you can unwrap him." She giggled.

Uncomfortable, Madeline started to get up. "I'm going to see if Tommy needs a drink of water or anything."

Grabbing her arm, Frankie pulled her back down. "I won't talk about Luke anymore, okay? I get it. You're embarrassed and I'm being too confrontive. My therapist says I need to tone it down. So tell me about the mouse Calli brought you. Was it dead or still wiggling?"

"Quite dead. Just the head and tail."

"Gruesome."

"Yeah. Found them on my pillow just as I was about to lie down on that very spot."

"What else?"

"I opened the door and turned on the light–" Madeline stopped, remembering something significant. She finished thoughtfully, "and I found the, well, the objects, on my bed."

"The head and the tail."

"That's right." Madeline was remembering the way it happened, trying to be positive she opened the door, that it had not been ajar. No, she was certain. The knob was stiff and old fashioned, and she recalled having to make an effort to turn the knob and swing the door inward.

But if she had to open the door, that meant someone else had shut it, because she had left it open.

This meant someone, a human, not the cat, had deliberately gone into the bedroom she was going to sleep in, and placed those macabre objects on her pillow. Then they'd gone out, probably closing the door automatically without thinking of the significance it would have for her.

But why would anyone want to do such a thing? And who could have done it? Mrs. Lawrence didn't go upstairs because her wheelchair did not have a ramp, lift or elevator to allow her access.

Maybe the cat is at fault though, she mused. Perhaps the wind blew the door shut or it swung closed by itself after the cat dropped off its gifts on the bed. Or maybe somebody happened to walk by and shut the door after Calli had been in there.

The bed was not in full view of the doorway, so the mouse parts would not have been noticed by a casual passerby. Since all the other rooms had their doors shut, someone like Rosa might have automatically shut the one she'd left open.

That would explain the mystery, Madeline thought with relief, feeling foolish for her paranoia.

"The reason I asked what else," Frankie said, breaking in on Madeline's thoughts, "is that there should've been more than the head and tail."

Madeline came to attention. "More parts, you mean?"

"I've got a cat at home, and I've been around Calli forever. I did a report on cats for school one time and I had to do a bunch of research."

"What did you learn? That could be related to what happened to me."

"There should've been the pancreas, too. Gross, huh? But true. Cats leave all three things. Better take another look on your pillow and see what you missed."

"Good to know." Madeline grew thoughtful. She knew without looking upstairs that she would not find any mouse organs. Disgusting thought, but at least Frankie's report told her one thing: it had not been Calli who left the mouse head and tail on the bed.

Someone deliberately placed them there, to scare her. As a prank? Or for more sinister reasons?

Yesterday there had only been four other people in the house besides herself and Tommy. Mrs. Lawrence, Rosa, Luke… and Jason Malone.

Frankie said, "You okay? Sorry I got so graphic about the dead mouse. I'm too blunt. Another of my many flaws. Can I get you a drink of water or something?"

"What? Oh, no thanks, Frances. Don't worry about it."

"I hate that name. You're supposed to call me Frankie, remember? All my girlfriends do," she added shyly. But then her brash facade was back in place. "If you want. Doesn't matter to me." She got up. "I'm getting another cup of hot chocolate. Want one? My dermatologist said chocolate's bad for my skin but what difference will zits make when I go to a school full of girls?"

After Frankie left, Madeline did not move. She sat, wondering about Jason and what his motive could be for acting so strange.

Gradually she became aware of an argument being conducted in whispered tones a few feet away. She started to get up, but realized the three people involved didn't know she could hear them.

To avoid attracting attention and causing embarrassment, she stayed and listened helplessly. And what she heard made her understand why Mrs. Lawrence should be afraid of her relatives.

TEN

"Now Agatha," Frank Miller said to Mrs. Lawrence in a voice as smooth as chocolate mousse, "be reasonable. This old house is falling apart. It's much too big for you. You rattle around in here! And you can't even use two-thirds of the space because of stair access. Plus, in your condition, don't you think you'd be better off in a nice apartment complex with plenty of neighbors on hand in case of emergency?"

"Pretty speech," Mrs. Lawrence said. "How long did you rehearse it?"

"You don't even have a phone anymore," her daughter Nancy, Frank's wife, put in. "We'll all help you move, Mother. You won't have to lift a finger."

Madeline watched the old woman's growing annoyance. She felt bad for Mrs. Lawrence, but as an outsider she didn't feel her comments would be welcome.

"There's a new assisted living community I heard about," Nancy said. "Wait. I think I might have the brochure in my purse."

"Might?" As everyone turned to stare, Madeline realized she'd spoken out loud.

Brad frowned at her. "I hardly think this is any of your business." To his mother he said, taking the brochure from Nancy, "Look at all the features. No upkeep worries. Not that you seem to worry about upkeep around here, actually."

Madeline wondered why Mrs. Lawrence let them talk to her like this. It must be painful, to have your own children treat you with such disdain. She wasn't fooled by their pretense at concern for Mrs. Lawrence's welfare. This land was valuable. Even if the house itself might end up being a tear-down, the property would sell for seven figures.

"Your concern for me is touching, children," Mrs. Lawrence said.

Madeline winked at the old woman, who gave a small nod in acknowledgment of the support.

"You know how much we love and adore you, Mother," Nancy said, and the others around her murmured assent. "We only want what is best and right for you." She took the assisted living brochure from her brother and laid it in Agatha Lawrence's lap.

"Is that so?" Mrs. Lawrence asked sweetly, and waited for their nods and yeses and of courses before barking, "Then leave me alone! I love this old house as you call it with sneers on your lips. My grandfather – your great-grandfather, Brad and Nancy – built this house in 1897 for his bride. It was based on the floor plan and design of the house that his father built for his bride in Boston in 1865. Do you hear those dates?" She pounded the arms of her wheelchair for emphasis. "This house is full of history! Tradition!"

Madeline was proud of Mrs. Lawrence, but she could not help agreeing in part with the others. It was a rundown and shambling old house, no question about it.

They were cut off from neighbors by miles of winding canyon roads, sagebrush and rock-strewn hills. No telephone. No internet connection. Mrs. Lawrence was dependent on rural mail delivery, radio and television to keep in touch with the outside world. She could not drive a car, not since her stroke, and could not walk.

Wondering how it felt to be dependent on others to help her move about if she wanted to go outside or shopping, Madeline thought once more about Jason Malone. She supposed that living out here limited the choice of attendants who were willing to isolate themselves. That's probably why Mrs. Lawrence had hired Jason in the first place. Certainly it couldn't be because of his charming ways.

"Tradition has its place, Mother," Brad said. "But so does good old-fashioned common sense. It's not safe for you to stay way out here anymore."

"I see," Mrs. Lawrence said. "It would be safer for me to be in the city, with all the muggers and robbers and vandals and gang members and–"

"Now, Agatha," Frank chided. "You're exaggerating. But let's not get sidetracked. Won't you at least look at the brochure? I've seen the apartments. And they're really nice. They even have a ramp for your wheelchair, built in."

"In other words," Mrs. Lawrence said, "it's the ideal haven for the old and infirm. Tell me. Is this paradise actually a nursing home?" She brushed the brochure from her lap to the floor. "Oops."

Madeline held back a snort of laughter.

"No, Mother," Nancy said, picking up the brochure. "We wouldn't try to put you in a home. Not unless you wanted it, of course?"

"You three must think I'm a silly old woman. Let me set the record straight. I didn't attract and marry two of the smartest and savviest businessmen Los Angeles has ever known by being a dumb blonde!"

Madeline couldn't help glancing in Daphne's direction, but the blonde model was busy yawning, her mouth wide and gaping. Luke saw the yawn and caught Madeline's eye for a quick smile at Daphne's expense.

"God gave me brains," Mrs. Lawrence said, "and I know how to use them. Don't underestimate me."

"We know all about your Phi Beta Kappa key, Mother," Brad said, "so don't bore us with the story again now. We have guests."

"Brad!" Nancy said. "Cool it!"

"Bore you, Brad?" Mrs. Lawrence asked her oldest child. "I wouldn't dream of it. Only children like you are allowed to bore their parents and get away with it, not vice versa. By the way, you might want to rephrase your comment."

"Uh, which one?"

"You don't have guests tonight. I do."

Frank cleared his throat. "If you don't like the idea of assisted living, Agatha, then how about a smaller house? Something with no stairs. We could find one in our neighborhood for you, I bet."

"So you could keep an eye on me?"

"That's right," Nancy said. Frank impaled her with a look. "I mean, no. Not the way you mean it, Mother. You don't need watching. I didn't mean that."

"Be quiet, Nance," Frank said. "You never know when to keep your mouth shut."

There was a moment of stunned silence.

Mrs. Lawrence looked at all of them, one by one. When her gaze reached Madeline, she said, "How do you like my family so far?"

Madeline didn't know what to say, so she just smiled helplessly.

Mrs. Lawrence turned back to Brad, Nancy and Frank. "So you'd like me to sell this old rat-trap and get modern."

"You wouldn't have to live with chrome and glass, Mother, if that's what you're afraid of," Brad said. "I'm sure we could find something more traditional for you. And you could even take some of your furniture so it would feel like home."

"How generous of you," Mrs. Lawrence said.

"Then it's all settled!" Frank clapped his hands together, relieved. "Let's have a drink on it, and then I guess it's time for that seance of yours, Agatha, unless Luke is going to flake out on us."

"I'm still here," Luke said. He added another log to the fireplace where the embers glowed. "Ready anytime. You know me. I can go into a trance just like that." He snapped his fingers, instantly closed his eyes and let his head loll, pretending to be out.

Madeline smiled, liking his ability to lighten the mood. She'd felt so uncomfortable being caught in the middle of a family argument but didn't want to draw attention to herself by leaving abruptly.

"Frank," Mrs. Lawrence said, "if it wasn't the holiday season, I'd tell you what you could do with that drink of yours." Her voice quavered, and she seemed surprised by her emotion. "Nothing is settled," she said more firmly. "Not the way you think."

"But, Mother!" Nancy wailed.

"I know why you are doing this. Just as I know why you want me to have Patrick declared dead."

"You mean Uncle Patrick?" Frankie asked.

"Enough, Frances Jane." Her parents spoke in unison.

The teenager wandered over to the fireplace and jabbed at the burning logs with a brass poker.

Calli the cat explored the floor beneath the dessert table, then approached Madeline and stared at her. Relenting, Madeline patted her lap in invitation and the cat settled there as if they were old friends. Smiling to herself, Madeline stroked the animal's soft fur.

"Money." Mrs. Lawrence said it so softly that at first no one reacted. "That's what it all boils down to. Plain old hard cash."

"What are you saying?" Nancy commented, all innocence.

"You seem to think the stroke impaired my brain in ways besides these useless old legs."

"Didn't it?" Brad asked. "I thought you said the doctor–"

"Those young doctors don't know half as much as they'd like us to think. I know what I told you. But he was wrong! My mind works fine. I can still count."

"What is that supposed to mean?" Nancy asked, confused. "I know you can count, Mother. What's that got to do with downsizing?"

"Everything!"

"Shut up, Nance."

"You shut up, Frank. She's my mother! I have a right to find out what she means."

"I'll spell it out for you, dear daughter of mine. Dear, greedy daughter of mine–"

"Mother!" Nancy protested.

"I thought I told you to shut up," Frank said, his jaw tight.

Mrs. Lawrence said to them, "You three want me to sell this old house. You want me to sell it to that nice Abby Whozit–"

"Her name is Amy Horowitz," Brad said.

"Whatever. And she's going to pay me a decent price. And then the developer she sells it to will have the house razed and build condos here. I can see the ads already. Ocean view. Secluded. Quiet. Exclusive gated community near Malibu." Mrs. Lawrence looked at them steadily, her two children and her son-in-law. "What's your cut going to be?"

"Her offer is fair," Brad said. "Be realistic. No one would want to live in this house. It's a wreck. It shouldn't matter who wants to build what here. Sell while you can instead of holding out for more. The money in the bank will bring you peace of mind."

"Who says I don't have peace of mind, right here, right now?"

"Don't risk losing the sale," Frank said.

"You'd like it if I could get an indecently high price, wouldn't you? That would mean you'd inherit all the more when I die."

"We don't want you to die, Mother," Nancy said. "Don't talk that way."

"Grow up, Nancy! I didn't raise you to be such a whining brat. Let me finish," Mrs. Lawrence said. "I'm 'bored' by the petty interruptions. Do your squabbling at home, on your own time and your own turf."

Madeline silently cheered the old woman.

"I know what you're going to say, Ma," Brad said. "And you're wrong. We only want to see you in a healthier and safer environment. Closer to town, closer to your doctors. It would make us all feel better."

"I won't honor that statement with a reply," Mrs. Lawrence said. "I know what you want. I'll sell this house and spend a fraction of the profit on a new place, banking the rest. Then I'll have your brother Patrick declared legally dead and rewrite my will. Very clever move, from your standpoint. If he does reappear or if we find he has a wife or child, then Patrick or his heirs would have no legal recourse. No way to get his fair share."

Brad snorted. "And then after you sign the new will, I suppose one of us is going to bump you off?"

Nancy darted a look at him, as if picking up her cue. "This isn't an old Hitchcock movie, Mother. I don't know why you insist we are after your money. We just want you to be happy." She sniffed. "Keep your nasty money for all I care!"

"Good," Mrs. Lawrence said. "I'll do just that." She tapped her chin, as if considering a new idea. "Perhaps you are right and I should make a new will." She glanced over at Madeline, who was still stroking the calico cat. "I'll leave all my money to…"

"To that girl?" Brad asked, outraged. He glared at Madeline.

Mrs. Lawrence chuckled softly, watching their faces closely as she made her announcement. "No… To Calli."

The cat chose that moment to purr loudly.

Mrs. Lawrence laughed loud and long.

ELEVEN

Mrs. Lawrence followed Madeline out of the living room, maneuvering her power wheelchair skillfully but limited by its capabilities. "Please wait, dear!"

Madeline stopped and turned.

"I'd like to speak with you a moment. Would you humor an old lady and come into my bedroom where we can have privacy? I won't keep you long," she added, seeing Madeline's glance upstairs toward Tommy. "You can check on your little boy when we're through. Unless you are worried about him and it will be a distraction?"

Feeling foolish for checking on Tommy so often, realizing it was an insult to her hostess to think something bad would happen to the boy here, Madeline said, "I'd love the chance to chat."

Reminding herself that this was just a house and there was no need to be so easily spooked, she fell in step with the older woman's wheelchair.

They went down the hall and into a large airy bedroom that was furnished elegantly. The walls were crowded with framed photographs and paintings. Madeline couldn't help noticing what an active and interesting life Agatha Lawrence had led, with many photos showing outdoor sports like sailing and tennis, as well as trips to Europe and China.

She realized how hard it must be for an active woman to be bound to the wheelchair.

"Please have a seat, dear."

Madeline looked where the woman was pointing, and sat down on a turquoise embroidered silk settee.

Mrs. Lawrence stopped her wheelchair in front of a gleaming walnut table covered with photographs in silver and porcelain frames. She selected a large photo of a blond young man, gazed at it a moment in silence, then turned it to show Madeline. "My son Patrick."

"Rosa told me that he's been missing a long time, after going to war in Iraq. Have you heard anything new recently?"

The older woman shook her head sadly. She held up a smaller picture where a younger Patrick was holding a dummy puppet and a blue ribbon. "He won first place at a talent show for ventriloquism. Of course this was years before he joined the army and went away. Seven years ago this month is when I got that letter. I already had his Christmas gifts wrapped and ready for him under the tree, in case he got a leave of absence to come home for the holidays. Otherwise, I would've mailed a package. Instead... the letter came."

"It must have been a horrible shock."

"You'd think that seven years would dull the pain, wouldn't you? To be honest, Patrick was a difficult child and a rebellious young man. He was my change-of-life baby, an unexpected addition to the family. Still, he is my son. I love him." Mrs. Lawrence put the photos back. "You understand motherly love. I've seen how you look at your boy. I don't have to explain how love pours out from a mother's heart even when it is not returned or appreciated by the child."

Madeline didn't know how to offer comfort. She could not imagine how it would feel to have Tommy not love her, or to reject her. How it would hurt! Mrs. Lawrence must be a very giving person, she decided, in order to keep on loving Patrick when he didn't reciprocate.

Finally, she said, realizing only a few seconds had passed, "But you love him, and you don't think he's dead. You feel you'd know in your heart if he was really gone."

"That's right." Mrs. Lawrence smiled. "I don't think he's dead. But the others do. Or at least they pretend to, because it eases their guilt over what they want me to do. Whether they believe it or not isn't important, I suppose. Nor is it even important what I believe."

"Why do you say that?"

Calli came in through the half-open door and rubbed against Mrs. Lawrence's wheelchair. She reached a hand down to pet the cat affectionately.

"What any of us believes has no affect on the truth," Mrs. Lawrence explained. "Either Patrick Lawrence is alive, or he is dead. If I believe he is alive and he is actually not, that belief – no matter how strongly held – does not make him alive. And the reverse is true, too, which is why I cannot agree with Nancy and Brad and Frank's plan to have Patrick declared legally dead."

"Because what if he's really alive," Madeline said, "and he's been living all this time in a desert cave or village? Or maybe he's had amnesia and doesn't even know who he is? He could be living somewhere in the United States."

"You think like I do," the other woman said with approval. "I knew I had judged you correctly when I first read that letter you sent me. That is why I asked you to come in here now. I want your advice."

"But you hardly know me. What use can my opinion be to you? I'd feel dreadful if I told you something and you followed my advice and it turned out all wrong."

"Then let's not call it 'advice.' May I have your viewpoint on something? I assure you that you will not be held responsible for anything that might happen," Mrs. Lawrence added with wry amusement.

Madeline flushed. "Then I'll do my best to give you my view on whatever it is."

"Good enough. Here's what I want to know. Do you think I'm wrong about not selling this house? You heard what my children had to say on the subject. I know you were cornered and couldn't escape the altercation, but since you heard it, you surely formed an opinion, whether you want to admit it or not. I'm asking you to admit it now."

"Um, of course there are valid reasons for you to downsize and be some place where you can have the right medical care at hand in case of emergency."

"Stop delaying. Sell or not?"

"Stay. If you like it here as much as you say, then don't sell. It's your house and they don't have the right to take it away from you!" Madeline gave a short laugh, realizing how much she had resented the way this woman's children treated her. "Guess I did form an opinion, didn't I?"

They smiled at each other, with growing fondness.

"Thank you," Mrs. Lawrence said. "Sometimes it helps to have one's own opinion confirmed and endorsed, especially when everybody else promotes the opposite view. Even Rosa wants me to sell and move someplace newer with a modern kitchen and all the gadgets. I was beginning to waver, but now you've reminded me of something very important which none of the others have taken into consideration. Or if they have, they quickly discarded it."

"What would that be?" Madeline smiled as Calli jumped into the old woman's lap and began toying with the gold locket Mrs. Lawrence wore around her neck on a long chain.

"I really do have the right to live where I please. I am certainly old enough to pick out my own home. And if it will make everyone happier, I'll get the blasted phone connected again!"

"Why don't you..." Madeline shook her head, not wanting to interfere.

"Speak up! My feelings aren't that easily hurt, if that is what's holding you back."

"Well, I can't help wondering, if money isn't a problem, why don't you have the house fixed up?"

"But I just had the exterior refurbished and painted, and the two upper floors renovated. There were people stomping around all the time for days!"

Madeline felt indignation welling up in her. Someone had cheated this nice old lady and no one else had the decency to tell her the truth. She decided that she'd have to be the one to do it, because it wasn't right to let the deception continue. "If you've been paying someone to keep the house painted and repaired, they're not doing it. You're being cheated, big time."

"I see." Mrs. Lawrence shooed Calli off her lap and piloted her wheelchair toward a bay window. She pulled aside the lace curtain and peered out at the dark rainswept evening. "I don't go outside anymore, you know."

"Not even to go shopping or to a movie?"

"Never."

"But people in wheelchairs go everywhere! Jason could lift you into the car and put the chair in the trunk or back seat. People do it all the time. It's not... right."

Mrs. Lawrence wheeled away from the window and faced Madeline. "I had my stroke shortly after my husband died. My second husband, that is – Cyrus. Patrick's father. Nancy and Brad Junior are from my first marriage, to Bradford Calhoun. He was a tax lawyer, dealt with big corporations, made a lot of money. I realized shortly after marrying him that it was a mistake. He was too controlling. And he never took care of his health. One of those Type A go-getters you hear about. Heart attack took him when the kids were still in school. I raised them myself."

"So you know what it's like being a single mom." Madeline smiled at her. "Nobody told me the details of your stroke. Do you mind talking about it?"

"Mind? No one has ever showed any real interest in hearing the story. Except Luke, of course. He's my favorite, in case you can't tell."

Madeline blushed.

"And yours too, I see." Mrs. Lawrence reached out and patted the younger woman's hand. "But about the stroke. Two years ago, my husband caught a severe case of influenza and it led to pneumonia. Before he died, he made me promise something."

"What was it?"

"He wanted me to swear that I would never leave the house again, not even for a walk outdoors."

"That's a horrible life sentence, telling you to imprison yourself here."

"It makes sense if I tell you the whole story. I wasn't going to, but...."

"Please do, Mrs. Lawrence. I won't tell anyone about it."

Mrs. Lawrence pointed out several photos of herself with a handsome silver-haired man. "That's my Cyrus. You can see we went everywhere and did everything! I loved our life together. He helped me learn that it was okay to have an opinion of my own. In my first marriage, I got so cowed that I hesitated to speak my mind. As you can see," she added with a laugh, nodding in the direction of the living room where she'd battled her adult children, "I no longer have that problem!"

"Some day we should compare notes on 'first marriages.' I learned a lot about myself from the one I managed to escape recently. But tell me more about this promise you made not to go outside. Why would anyone ask that of you?"

"I have to back up to when Cyrus and I met. Brad and Nancy were both off on their own, and I had time on my hands so I started joining clubs, wanting more of a social life. I wasn't really looking for a man, but I guess that's the best way to meet one."

"That's what I've heard," Madeline agreed.

"We started dating, and fell madly in love. Through Cyrus, I became involved in the world of psychic phenomenon."

"You mean you weren't already, because of Luke's powers?"

"I thought that was all a big joke. A fake, to get attention. Cyrus helped me see the error in my thinking. I was narrow-minded, and I'd confused the exaggerated occult stories that are all about drama and making money from gullible victims, with the serious science of the paranormal. Sixth sense abilities, like our Luke has."

Madeline couldn't help smiling. *Our Luke.* It had a nice sound to it. "Go on, please." She was startled when Calli suddenly leapt into her lap and invited petting. This cat was beginning to grow on her affections, and she'd nearly forgotten the episode with the dead mouse.

"I was a doubting Thomas," Mrs. Lawrence said. "I felt something could not be true unless I could see or experience it in the tangible ways I was accustomed to."

"Lots of people feel that way. I think I'm one of them, frankly."

"But being skeptical blocks the messages that try to get through to you from helpful spirits. Anyway, to get back to Cyrus and the promise I made him–"

"To stay indoors."

"Can you guess the reason for it?"

Madeline shook her head. "Sounds like lunacy. Sorry, but it does."

"He promised he would manifest himself to me in some way. Somehow, he'd get a message to me that there is existence after death, that he had indeed survived."

"He planned to haunt you? And you believed it? That's why you never go out? But it's not fair for you to keep waiting here. It's been two years and he hasn't shown up yet, has he?"

"But he will. I know that. In his own time. Actually, the seance tonight has nothing to do with trying to reach Cyrus, in case that's what you've assumed in the last few minutes."

"What is the reason, then?"

"Chat with the spirits? Why else? This is a special favor Luke is doing for me. He ordinarily does not like to be the medium or channel."

"Why not?"

"Ask him. Something to do with evil spirits. When he's in a trance, something could happen."

"Like what?" Madeline asked.

"Dangerous things. Don't be afraid for him, though. He always says a prayer for protection before going into a trance. He is a wise young man, and a good man, too."

"Then why would Jason warn me away from him and say I shouldn't believe anything Luke says. He told me not to trust him."

Mrs. Lawrence chuckled. "Sounds like he's jealous, and trying to turn you away from his rival."

"Hey, look, I didn't come here to find a guy. I've got my hands full taking care of Tommy! Tell me about the seance, and then I better go check on my son before it gets any later."

The rain storm grew louder. The bedroom lights flickered a moment, then returned to full intensity.

"I'm going to try to contact my son Patrick," Mrs. Lawrence said. "Maybe I'll get proof of whether he is still alive or not. If he is alive, I'm hoping one of the friendly spirits will point me in the right direction to locate him."

"I have to admit it all sounds kind of crazy to me."

Mrs. Lawrence glanced at a bedside clock. It was nearly nine. "Almost time to begin." She wheeled toward the door.

Madeline got up to follow her, and the cat trailed behind.

With her hand on the light switch by the door, Mrs. Lawrence said, "If we reach my son Patrick tonight, or in some way receive evidence of his death, then I'll go along with what Nancy, Brad and Frank want me to do."

"I thought you said you wanted to stay in the house, instead of downsizing."

Mrs. Lawrence turned off the light. From the dark shadows of the doorway into the unlit hall, she said, "I'll have my son declared legally dead. Then I'll make out a new will, apportioning his share to the others, including Luke."

As she followed the old woman into the hall, Madeline had the sudden feeling she'd had earlier, the sensation of being watched. Swiftly, she turned her head and looked in both directions, but saw no one. Then she heard a floorboard creak a few feet away, behind a closed door. She wondered who had been listening to them.

Mrs. Lawrence seemed unaware of anything wrong. "Turn on that hall light, would you, please?"

Madeline flicked the switch and three sconces lit up at intervals along the hall. Something occurred to Madeline before she turned toward the stairs to check on Tommy. "But I thought you said you were going to leave everything to the cat?"

TWELVE

"Do you want me to turn off the lights, Luke?" Madeline asked, after everyone was assembled around the dining room table.

He shook his head, then began meditating silently in preparation for the seance.

Frankie, sitting next to Madeline on one side of the long oval table, said, "Don't you know anything?" She had just finished explaining that they would not be holding hands like in the movies, since that was a trick charlatans used to be sure everyone remained seated and did not wander around during the seance checking things out. "Only fakes do it in the dark."

"Why is that?" Madeline asked, keep her voice low to not disturb Luke. The others at the table talked quietly among themselves.

"Because that way their assistants can run around the room draped in gauzy cloth to look like ghosts. And they use wires to make trumpets dance in the air."

"Trumpets?"

"That's supposed to be where the spirit voices come from, but it's really just the medium using ventriloquism."

"All I know is what I've read in novels or seen in movies. Have you been to many before this?"

"Dozens. They're fun. I want to do them, too, but Luke says it could be dangerous. He says I have to wait until I'm older."

"Why would it be more dangerous now?"

The teenager shrugged. "Evil spirits might possess me when I was in the trance. He says it's not something to play around with. Maybe he's right." Then a mischievous look lit up her eyes. "Watch this."

"What?" Madeline followed Frankie's intent stare, and looked at the crystal chandelier. She saw the teen narrow her eyes and press her lips together as if in deep concentration. The light grew slowly dimmer. "Are you really doing that?"

The others at the table glanced at the light fixture.

The lights stabilized and remained softly glowing.

"Must be from the storm," Brad said.

Frankie chuckled softly and gave Madeline's arm a little squeeze.

Nancy Miller called across the table to her daughter, "Frances Jane! Stop your tricks right now!"

"She was being helpful. It's nicer with the lights dimmed. Now be quiet, everyone," Mrs. Lawrence urged in a low voice, and indicated Luke, who looked deep in meditation, his eyes closed and his breathing slow and even. "We're about to begin."

"Helpful?" Frank repeated. He glared at his daughter. "Showing off is what I call it. I don't know where you pick up those weird habits. Not from my side of the family!" He pointedly looked at Luke and rolled his eyes.

"Oh, Frank," his wife Nancy said, putting a hand on his arm. "Not now. We all know you haven't got an ounce of Psi in your whole body."

Madeline leaned closer to Frankie. "What's Psi?"

She was rewarded with a mildly scornful look, but the teen girl answered willingly enough, enjoying her role as teacher. "Psi means any kind of sixth sense. Telepathy. Clairvoyance. Seeing spirits. Automatic writing. Or what I've got, telekinesis, or TK."

Daphne, seated next to Luke, kept looking up at the chandelier, puzzled and out of her depth. She lit a cigarette with a gold lighter and inhaled deeply.

"Hey, Daphne," Frankie called out in a loud whisper, "need an ashtray?"

A large brass bowl below the chandelier suddenly skimmed down the length of the table, heading directly for Daphne.

"Stop it!" Daphne said. "Make it stop!" She stumbled to get up. The brass bowl shot past her and landed with a thud on the thick carpet.

Everyone but Luke stared at Frankie.

"Oops," she said, smiling. "Just trying to help."

Luke, coming out of his meditation with a tranquil look on his face, said calmly to her, "I told you that you need to develop your powers. If you were in better control, you could have stopped the bowl right in front of Daphne."

Brad got up and picked up the bowl. He set it on the buffet sideboard, got an ashtray from a drawer and handed it to Daphne. "You need to put that out. No smoking."

With a resentful glare, Daphne ground out her cigarette in the ashtray and huffed to herself as she sat down again, clearly annoyed with everything and everyone.

Nancy said to her daughter, "One more display out of you, Frances Jane, and you can excuse yourself from the room."

"Good grief, Mother! Will Luke have to leave, too? He's going to put on a bigger display!" She turned to Madeline. "He's really good. Wait 'til you hear his spirit control. That's Stephen. He was a soldier in the Civil War. You'll like him. He's pretty cool."

Madeline raised an eyebrow, skeptical but willing to sit politely with the group.

She realized everyone was staring and knew she had made a scoffing noise out loud, even though she meant to be totally quiet.

"A non-believer?" Brad asked with amusement.

"I just think that it's an easy thing to fake messages from someone who died."

Luke nodded. "That's why there will usually be one or more evidentials given." When he saw her puzzled expression, he explained. "If there is a message from a spirit purporting to be a specific individual known to someone in this room, they will give a special clue that it's really them. They'll give 'evidence' such as revealing something trivial only the two of you would know, like the name of your favorite dog in childhood. Or reminding you of something that happened when the two of you were together, that no one else here could know about. Or even telling you where to find a piece of jewelry you think is lost."

"An evidential is a way of proving it's really them and not just a general message." Frankie smiled at Madeline.

"Thanks. Sorry for interrupting. I've never been to anything like this." Madeline sat quietly, feeling bemused and wishing Luke would hurry up and start. She regretted joining the group, but Mrs. Lawrence had insisted, saying it would make her feel better knowing there was an impartial observer. The older woman expected Madeline to give her impressions, or "viewpoint," when it was over.

Luke rapped the table. "If I may have your attention, we'll begin." He folded a black cloth and tied it around his eyes. "The purpose of this blindfold is merely to facilitate my going into a deep trance."

With a nudge in the ribs, Frankie whispered to Madeline, "Isn't this exciting?"

"Daphne," Luke said, "please start the recorder."

"I'm turning it on now." Daphne set a small recording device in front of her.

He gave the date, time, their location and the first names of the seven people gathered around him at the table.

Madeline stole a glance around the room and noticed how solemn everyone looked. Even Frankie had lost her perpetual jester's grin.

The air seemed to grow cooler even though the windows were closed, and the rainstorm pelting the panes heightened the strange atmosphere.

When she checked on Tommy before sitting at the table, he was sound asleep and the windows were secure. She had no rational reason to be nervous about leaving him upstairs but still, it was with effort that she turned her attention to Luke.

"The purpose of this seance," Luke said, "is to obtain information about Patrick Lawrence. In particular, we would like to know whether or not he is still living on this side of the veil we call death. I do not know if we will get any information. And if we do, there is a chance it may be false. I have no control over what is said. Any spirit who has a message for this group will relay that message through my guide."

Putting her mouth next to Madeline's ear, Frankie said in a soft whisper, "He means Stephen. The spirit control."

Madeline nodded, even though she did not really understand what was happening. Part of her was skeptical, yet the situation was taking on a semblance of believability which she could not ignore. She resolved to keep an open mind and not make snap judgments about what she might see or hear.

"It will take a few moments for me to achieve a deep trance," Luke said, his clear voice the only sound other than the steady pounding of rain outside. "While I am in the altered state of consciousness, please do not touch me or the area immediately around me. This is very important. I repeat: do not touch me, no matter what happens. While I am in trance, my astral body leaves the physical body in order to allow my spirit guide to take control."

Madeline frowned, wondering what might happen if someone did touch him. Maybe it would be a good idea for everyone to hold hands after all, she thought.

In a low voice, Luke said a brief prayer, asking for protection against evil or malicious spirits while he was in the trance state. Then he sat very straight, very still, blindfolded and silent.

Frankie pinched Madeline's arm in excitement.

Luke's mouth opened. He began to speak, but his accent was Southern and totally unlike Luke's voice.

It must be Stephen, Madeline thought with a thrill, hearing the drawled greeting. Gooseflesh danced on her arms. Now she was glad she had not insisted on bringing Tommy downstairs. If he'd awoken in the middle of this, he'd have been frightened to hear his new friend Luke speak in such a different voice. And how would she explain it, when she didn't understand it herself?

Perhaps it was all part of the act. After all, anyone with minimal training could imitate a Georgia accent or whatever it was supposed to be.

Stephen said, "There is a person here who knows Madeline. Is there a Madeline Clark in the group?

Madeline swallowed hard. What was she supposed to do? Frankie jabbed her. "Y–yes? I'm here. I'm Madeline Clark."

"Miz Clark," Stephen drawled, "there is a woman here with me, Henrietta Stone."

"Grandma!" Madeline gasped. Her maternal grandmother had died over nine years ago, and no one in this room could possibly know about her or guess her name. She felt dazed.

"She tells me that she is your mother's mother. She wishes to give you a message. Are you listening? She says it is important."

Madeline looked around the room quickly but could get no clue as to what she should do. She hadn't thought she'd be called upon to speak. She was supposed to be an observer, not a participant. "I'm listening," she said, speaking up, wondering if the spirit heard through Luke's ears or some other method of thought-reading.

But what difference did it make, she scolded herself. Whoever, or whatever, Stephen was, he had a message from Grandma Stone. He said she was with him, presumably of her own free will, and so Madeline decided this Stephen from the Civil War was a kindred spirit.

Somehow, for reasons she didn't try to analyze, Madeline believed that the next words she heard would be a communication from her beloved Grandma, whom she'd been missing all these years.

She watched Luke's face intently. It remained impassive as the spirit who now controlled the human body began to speak. "She says to look out for the duel. She tells me that you will know what she means if you think carefully about it, but she does not wish to be more specific in case doing so at this time would place you in harm's way." After a long pause, the voice continued, "Miz Clark, she says to remember Tony Chestnut."

Frankie gave Madeline's hand a hard squeeze, excited.

Madeline relaxed into her chair, having sat rigidly forward, tensely listening the past few minutes. But she was puzzled by the whole thing. The duel? What did that mean? And who was Tony Chestnut? She felt disappointed by the cryptic message. Her skepticism flooded back.

Mrs. Lawrence said, her thin reedy voice trembling with emotion, "Stephen, I would like to know about my son. His name is Patrick Anthony Lawrence. Is he there with you? If not, does anyone with you know of him? I am trying to find out if he has crossed over."

Stephen said after a moment, "No ma'am, there is no one by that name here with us. I have asked and someone here knows of a Patricia Lauren, but not your son."

"Does that mean he's still alive?" Nancy Miller shouted, her voice grating harshly, disturbing the subdued atmosphere of the dimly lit room.

There was a long pause while Luke sat in stillness. Madeline wondered if the woman's interruption had broken Luke's trance, but then Stephen's voice filled the room. "I shall consult the akashic records."

Mrs. Lawrence asked, "How long will it take?"

"Can't you find out now?" Brad asked. "We want to know tonight whether Patrick's alive or dead."

"Shhh," Frankie warned.

Madeline realized that the teen next to her was the only one in the room aside from Luke who knew about psychic things first hand. Was all this loud and harsh interrupting of Stephen going to harm Luke in some way?

"Henrietta Stone has volunteered to check the records for you." After they waited a few minutes in silence, Stephen's voice said, "She is here with me again, and she tells me the Patrick Lawrence you wish to know about is–"

At once the room went dark as the chandelier went out. In that moment, Madeline saw the brass bowl, which Brad had put down on the buffet, rise unaided and move swiftly through the air toward Luke's head.

"Luke," she cried. "Duck!"

Daphne quickly held up her cigarette lighter and the flame flickered.

The brass bowl missed Luke's head by a hairs-breadth.

"Stephen?" Mrs. Lawrence asked. "Are you still with us?"

There was no reply.

Frankie said, "Luke! Say something! Are you all right?"

Again there was no response.

Madeline shivered, wondering why Luke didn't say something to reassure them. But what if he wasn't able to get back into his body? What if Stephen had left too abruptly, and now Luke was floating outside his own body and unable to reconnect?

She recalled last night, and the strange vision she'd had of Luke in the bedroom. Now she wondered why she could not see that glowing apparition with the blue rays bursting out of his feet.

Frank Miller flicked the light switch on the wall off and on several times. "Electricity is out. Must be the storm. Let's light some candles. Agatha?"

71

"There are tapers and candlesticks in the buffet drawer," Mrs. Lawrence said. "On the left hand side."

Madeline hurried to get the candles but, groping in the drawer, did not find matches. She realized she'd have to ask Daphne for help, but might as well get it over with. "Daphne? May I borrow your lighter?" She held out her hand.

The model dropped the cold heavy lighter into it, as if wanting to be sure their fingers did not touch.

Quickly lighting the candles, Madeline placed them on the table. Everyone gathered around Luke, who was still blindfolded and sitting erect, his breathing slow and steady.

"He looks all right." Daphne reached out to remove his blindfold.

Frankie pushed Daphne's hand back. "Don't touch him. Remember what he said?"

"He must be in a trance still," Brad said, "or he'd take it off and talk to us."

"Let's ask Stephen what happened," Nancy Miller suggested. "Get him to finish what he was about to say before the lights went out."

Frankie shook her head. "It's too dangerous. Luke told me if the seance is interrupted, we'd have to be careful not to accidentally invite evil spirits to join us."

"This is ridiculous," her father muttered.

"We were so close to finding out!" Mrs. Lawrence sighed. "Poor Luke. What should we do?"

"Wait for him to come out of it on his own," Frankie said. "And don't touch him."

"How long will it take?" Madeline asked, frightened for Luke.

Frankie shrugged. "A few hours, maybe."

"Or days?" Brad glared at her. "Will he be all right if we leave him sitting there? You said not to touch him, so we better not carry him to lie down on a couch. Will he snap out of it and be back to normal?"

"How should I know!" Frankie looked at all of them. "You ever heard of Edgar Cayce, the famous psychic?"

A few nodded. Madeline shook her head in the negative.

"Of course," Mrs. Lawrence said. "I have read many books about him. Cayce was a gifted psychic who would do health readings for people even if they lived far away from him, and he could correctly diagnose their ailments when doctors were unable to figure out what was wrong. I believe he died in 1945."

"One time this happened to him," Frankie said. "It took several hours to come out of his trance. The book called it a catalepsy. Sort of like being paralyzed, I guess."

"It's not permanent, is it?" Daphne moved away from Luke as if his condition might be contagious.

"Cayce was okay afterwards." Frankie looked at Daphne in disgust. "But I don't think we should leave Luke alone."

Nancy drained her wineglass. "Going to bed," she said, her words slurring. "The rest of you can take turns staying with him. Get me up if anything fantastic happens." She left the room unsteadily.

Frank, Brad and Daphne followed her out.

Mrs. Lawrence looked tired and upset.

"You should go to bed, too," Madeline told her. "Would you like me to help you?" When the older woman nodded gratefully, Madeline added to Frankie, "And then I'll check on my son and come back to stand watch with you."

THIRTEEN

"Who's there?" Madeline asked in a hoarse whisper when the light tapping on Tommy's bedroom door awoke her from a light sleep. The room was dark. She leaned up on her elbows and looked toward the locked door, suddenly frightened.

"It's me – Frankie. Let me in."

With a quick glance at her sleeping child, Madeline eased out of bed so the movement wouldn't wake him. Barefooted, she hurried across the cold floor and unlatched the door.

"What is it?" she whispered to Frankie, whose face was shadowed by the hall light. "Is Luke okay yet?"

Frankie had insisted on taking the first watch, promising to call her for help if needed or if she grew too tired to stay up any longer. They hoped Luke would revive quickly, but if his strange paralysis continued through the night, Brad had agreed to drive along the coast until he got a cell signal to phone for paramedics.

Frankie shook her head, worried.

"Is he any worse? What's happening? Do you need me to come downstairs?"

"He's the same. It's giving me the creeps, being there alone with him. He sits like a statue. Could you keep me company?"

Madeline understood how strange it must be for the teenager to sit alone with someone who was apparently comatose. Especially in this eerie old mansion on a stormy night.

"I guess Tommy will be all right. He doesn't wake up during the night very often anymore. Wait a minute and I'll get dressed." She went back into the room and hastily pulled on her clothes. When she came back to the hall, Frankie wasn't there.

She found her at the top of the stairs.

"I've been listening for anything from the dining room," Frankie said. "Just in case. Let's hurry. I shouldn't have left him alone but I didn't have any way to call you without waking up the whole house."

Together they went into the dining room, where Madeline saw that nothing had changed except the candles were shorter, having burned for three hours. Luke, with the dark handkerchief still around his eyes, sat rigidly at the head of the table, as if a wax figure in a tableau.

"I wish the electricity would come back on," Frankie said. "Then I could at least bring in the TV from the kitchen. You could go back to bed."

Madeline started to agree, then realized something. "The hall lights were on upstairs." She flicked the switch on the wall a few times but the chandelier did not come on. "Odd. I guess it was a fuse. Somebody can fix it in the morning."

She returned to the table where Frankie sat several chairs away from Luke, studiously avoiding him. They remained in silence several moments, and Madeline felt her eyes grow heavy. With effort she shook off the desire to sleep, but could not help yawning.

"This is no good," she said. "We'll both end up falling asleep and that's no help to Luke. I don't see how you managed to stay awake as long as you did. It's after midnight already."

"Seems later, doesn't it?" Frankie whispered. "I can't believe everybody went to bed and left us to handle this."

"Those candles don't help. I've already spooked myself a dozen times, jumping at my own shadow. Why don't we play cards? We can't go on staring into space and scaring ourselves."

Frankie agreed to the plan and volunteered to look in the closet where board games were kept. "Won't take me a minute, especially now that I know the lights are working in the rest of the house. Will you be okay?"

Knowing she was eight years older than Frankie, Madeline felt she should set a good example. "Yeah, sure, of course. I'm cool. Better take one of the candles in case this isn't the only room on that circuit that's out."

"Good idea." Frankie picked up one of the candlesticks. "I would've gone marching off and probably tripped over something in the dark and killed myself." She stopped abruptly. "Guess I shouldn't say stuff like that in front of Luke."

"You were just kidding."

"Maybe he can hear everything we say but he can't answer."

They stared at each other, each with her own thoughts.

Frankie broke the tension with a nervous laugh. "Say, do you have any gum? I'm out and it's driving me crazy. Any kind. Doesn't have to be bubble gum. I know you wince every time I blow a bubble and maybe Luke does, too. But now I'm talking too much. It happens when I get too high-strung and over-wrought. That's what my psychiatrist says."

"There's gum in my purse. Upstairs on the floor by my side of the bed. But please don't wake up Tommy."

"I'll be quiet as a mouse."

Madeline thought suddenly of that dead mouse, and her stomach lurched. She watched Frankie walk away, the candle casting unearthly shadows.

The room seemed much darker without that other light. And now the shadows distorted and contoured Luke's features. He looked strange, a monster or caricature of himself.

She wondered if his eyes were open beneath the black cloth. Shifting in her chair, she wished that Frankie had not brought up the idea that Luke might be able to hear everything. It unnerved her, thinking he might be annoyed every time she rustled in her seat.

But then she got an idea that might be worth a try. "Luke," she said in a low, calm tone. "Luke, can you hear me? It's Madeline. If you can hear me, give me some sort of sign."

In movies Madeline had seen, the person in a paralysis state would blink to signal yes and no, but with that handkerchief covering his eyes, that method was out. She thought a moment, trying to think of a way he could communicate without words, and without her touching him in any way.

Excitedly, Madeline got up and moved closer to him. "Luke? Remember when you appeared to me in Tommy's bedroom? I told you about it this morning. Or, rather, yesterday morning. You said the astral trip gave you a headache and you couldn't recall any details. But maybe in your trance you can remember. Do you?"

She watched for any sign that he'd heard, even though she logically felt it was useless to expect any kind of answer.

After a moment, she tried again. "Luke? If you can hear me, go ahead and appear to me like you did before, so I'll know you're all right. Okay?"

When nothing happened after waiting what seemed like ten minutes but was probably only one, she gave up and sat in the chair Daphne had used. At least she could do him the courtesy of sitting beside him instead of far down the table.

She wasn't afraid of Luke. There was nothing evil or scary emanating from him, and in fact it was rather peaceful sitting next to him. She had to be careful, though, not to fall asleep and slump over onto him.

Luke had warned them all to not touch him, no matter what happened. She had to wonder if this sort of thing had been in his mind at the time, or if it was a general warning he always gave before going into a deep trance.

Madeline wished she knew more about the paranormal and the things which Luke and Frankie took for granted.

"Madeline."

She looked up. Her name had been uttered in a sibilant whisper, so low and hushed as to be barely heard. It might have been the sighing of the wind. She wasn't sure if she'd imagined it, but she knew it was not Luke speaking. The voice came from elsewhere in the room.

"Frankie?" she asked, looking toward the doorway but not seeing anyone.

A sudden draft arose. The remaining candles on the table went out.

In the abrupt darkness, from a different corner of the room, the same soft voice said, "Madeline ... this is your grandmother. Do not be afraid."

Madeline looked toward that far corner but could not see in the dark. Slowly a greenish form took shape, glowing and swaying in the darkness.

She strained to see, but it was a shapeless luminescent movement with no features or human-like appendages.

"Grandma? What did you mean in that message earlier?" She glanced over at Luke but he did not move or speak. Maybe her grandmother would explain what she meant by "the duel" but if Luke was not the one channeling this spirit, then who was doing it?

"I have come to warn you, child."

Madeline shivered. "Is it something about Tommy?"

"Get out. Go home. Go-o-o-o-o...." The voice trailed off and the spirit vanished.

Madeline sat motionless, staring at the now empty corner. She realized she was trembling, and close to tears. She would really like to go home, but she felt trapped here.

When nothing more happened, she made herself get up and go to the doorway to see if Frankie was coming. The unlit hall appeared to be empty. She felt a chill breeze, as if an outer door or window had been opened, letting in the damp night air.

She pressed her shoulders against the sturdy door frame, wanting something solid supporting her. "Who's there? What do you want?" When there was no reply, she whispered, "Grandma? Was that really you? Are you still there? Please help me!"

Frankie silently approached, carrying the candlestick and a deck of cards. "Hey, what are you doing out here?" She looked in the dining room and saw it was dark. "Why did you blow out the candles?"

"I didn't. I'll explain later, but let's be sure Luke is okay."

They walked together into the dining room. Frankie held up her candlestick and the light showed that Luke was still in the same pose, unmoving.

"Know something funny?" Frankie said to Madeline. "The lights in all the other rooms down here work fine. Maybe it's just this room and the hallway."

"Let's see if you've got the magic touch. Try the switch."

Frankie went to the light switch and touched it. The chandelier blazed into life. At that moment, Luke cried out and his body jerked in a spasm.

"Luke!" Madeline rushed to him. She halted a foot away from him. Turning quickly to Frankie, she asked, "Do you think it's safe to touch him now?"

"I don't know!"

Luke yanked off the handkerchief and gasped. With a dazed expression, the spasm over, he squinted at their concerned faces.

Madeline laughed weakly and sat beside him. "You tell him, Frankie. I haven't got a clue what happened this evening."

"You've been in a trance for hours," Frankie said.

"Which explains why I feel so stiff." Luke stretched and moved around. He poured a drink of water from the pitcher on the buffet. "Everything seems to be in working order. I feel great, actually. Very well rested. I never remember what happens while I'm in a trance, so you'll have to tell me everything, starting from the time when Daphne turned on the tape recorder."

"The recorder!" Madeline looked around and found it on the floor near Daphne's chair. "She must have dropped it when things got weird. Look, it's still recording."

"Cool," Frankie said with a grin. "Then all you have to do is play it back and hear the whole thing."

Luke took the recorder from Madeline. When their fingers brushed, she felt a warm thrill and knew that Mrs. Lawrence was right about saying that Luke was a good man she could trust. A rare find, she thought, recalling the four years of her marriage. Her ex-husband Craig was the opposite of trustworthy in just about every detail.

"Let's grab a midnight snack," Luke said, turning the recorder off. "Low battery. I'll recharge it and listen to this later. You two look like you've had an ordeal. Why don't you tell me about it while we eat?"

They went into the kitchen, and Madeline realized that she felt safe for the first time this strange evening. "Nice to have you back, Luke," she whispered, not meaning for him to hear.

Walking just behind her, Luke smiled softly to himself.

FOURTEEN

At breakfast the next day, Daphne cooed over Luke. "I was so totally worried about you!" She shook a finger at him playfully and put her arm through his. "Don't do that again, okay?"

He moved away from her casually and took a plate from the buffet. Others were already seated, eating, and he joined them with a plate of fruit and toast, taking a chair next to Madeline.

Tommy looked at him with interest. "You don't scare me. I like you. More juice?" He held out his glass. "Please?"

Everyone laughed. Luke refilled the boy's juice glass. "I'm glad you're not afraid of me, Tommy." He winked at Madeline. She smiled back, then noticed Daphne glaring at her.

"Luke," Daphne said, walking over and sitting with her cup of black coffee. She settled herself after much chair-scooting and fidgeting with the cashmere sweater knotted around her shoulders.

"Yes?"

"I was wondering…" she paused, and looked down demurely. "Oh, you'll just say no, like you always do."

"How can he say anything," Frankie said from the other side of the table, "if you don't tell him what you want."

"Frances," her father said, "mind your own business and finish eating."

Daphne's eyes gleamed triumphantly. She turned away from the teenager and touched Luke's arm. "I was wondering if you'd teach me how to… you know."

"Oh, good grief," Frankie muttered.

"Don't know what you're getting at," Luke said.

Frankie whooped with laughter. "I bet I know! Here's a dollar says she wants to know how to go into a trance." She reached in her jeans, pulled out a crumpled dollar bill and tossed it on the table. "Though she's already so spaced-out you wouldn't think she'd need lessons," she added under her breath, and watched her parents slyly for a rebuke.

"Frances Jane," began the girl's mother, her jaw working tightly.

Frankie gave a little apologetic wave in Daphne's direction. To Madeline she said, "Whenever my mom calls me that, the next thing is either 'go to your room' or 'you're grounded for a week.' See why I'm such a mess? I'm the victim of a dictatorship! They tag-team me with rules, night and day."

Madeline didn't want to get in the middle of a family disagreement so she smiled, noncommittal, and tended to Tommy, wiping his sticky fingers with a napkin.

"As I was trying to say," Daphne said, "before I was so rudely interrupted – Luke, I've been wanting to ask if you'd teach me how to read a crystal ball. I think it would be loads of fun to see the future, don't you?" She waved her ring-less left hand in an all-too-casual gesture.

Her meaning could not be mistaken.

Madeline seethed, unable to prevent the jealous knot forming in the pit of her stomach. Not sure why it should disturb her so much, Madeline was annoyed. Could Luke really be in love with Daphne? She was very pretty, but they didn't seem to have anything in common.

Daphne looked like she just stepped out of a salon, and had another trendy outfit on, while Madeline was still wearing the same outfit, three days running. Earlier, Frankie had offered a spare sweater and pair of jeans but they weren't the same size and so Madeline had decided that if Luke was interested in a fashion show then he wasn't her type anyway, so why worry about it. She was clean and neat, and couldn't help it that she had arrived here unprepared for a forced stay.

"Sorry, Daph," Luke said. "Don't know anything about crystal balls." He got out his wallet and put a dollar bill on top of the one Frankie had anted up. He winked at Frankie. "Close enough. You win."

He got up, refilled his teacup with hot water and stirred honey into it. He noticed Frankie chortling over the money, and apparently felt bad about conspiring with her to mock Daphne. "Hey, Daphne, is that all you're having?" He nodded toward her coffee cup. "Can I bring you something?"

"I never eat breakfast." With a cool glance toward Madeline she added, "You should remember that by now, Luke."

Madeline flushed, hating the reference to their apparent romance. She wished it didn't bother her, but there was something special about Luke, and she felt they had a link that was beyond the ordinary attraction of meeting a good-looking guy. Maybe it was because of that late-night visitation from him on her first night here.

With a mental shrug, she decided to be more practical and stop herself from any romantic imaginings about him. He's obviously taken, she reminded herself, and finished eating her breakfast. She'd taken a full plate, stoking up for the day ahead.

With a smile, Daphne added, "Some of us keep an eye on our figures. I know if I ate like that I'd just balloon up overnight."

"Madeline's got a great figure," Frankie said loyally.

"Right again, kid," Luke said, tossing another dollar bill in front of Frankie.

"I guess I do eat a lot," Madeline said, suddenly self-conscious as everyone stared at her. "But I burn it up pretty fast, keeping up with my son."

"I'm teaching her to play baseball," Tommy said. "Can we play today?"

Mrs. Lawrence looked up from the newspaper she was reading. "It's still raining. Hear it?"

Tommy cocked his head and listened. "Yep." He sighed and looked out the window. "I see it, too." He sighed again, heavily, then pointed to Daphne, brightening. "Can I play with her ball?"

"What ball?" Daphne snapped. "I don't walk around with baseballs in my purse. That's a Louis Vuitton!" Then she noticed the look on Luke's face, and quickly changed her tone. "Sorry, little boy, I didn't bring any toys with me. If I'd known you would be here, I would have brought you a present." She looked around the room, smiling graciously. "Isn't he adorable? I love children."

"I'll bet you do," Frankie said, finishing her glass of milk. "Sautéed with onions and tarragon. Tastes just like chicken."

"Frances Jane!"

"Sorry, Mother. It was a joke. You know how everybody says frog tastes like chicken, rodents taste like chicken, I figure little kids probably do, too."

Tommy experimentally licked his arm, and shook his head. "Nope. Not chicken. I taste like soap."

"Can't you do something about your daughter's manners," Daphne said to the Millers. "She's... she's..."

"Incorrigible?" Frankie suggested, enjoying herself.

"Frances, leave the table. We'll discuss this later in private." Nancy Miller pointed to the door.

"Oh, Mother!"

"Now," Frank Miller added.

The teenager made a big show of wiping her mouth on a linen napkin then slowly getting up from her chair. She smoothed back her curly hair and carefully folded the napkin.

"Stop stalling," Frank said, after being prompted by a poke in the ribs from his wife.

"Okay, okay. I'm going. Maybe I should go get Daphne's crystal ball for Tommy to play with."

"See?" Tommy said, pulling at his mother's sleeve. "I told you she has a ball. Can I play with it? We didn't bring a ball."

"I don't have one," Daphne snapped. "Drop the subject, everyone, all right? I figured Luke had one, or Mrs. Lawrence."

"As a matter of fact," the older woman said, "I do."

Tommy perked up.

"Then Luke can show me how to use it," Daphne said to Mrs. Lawrence with a winning smile.

"No, Aunt Agatha," Luke said. "I don't want anything to do with it."

"I bet last night scared you, huh?" Frankie lolled in the doorway, technically out of the dining room but still a member of the party.

"Haven't you left yet?" Nancy asked. "Don't answer me, just do it! I'm tired of your disrupting every meal around here."

"I haven't–"

"And stop interrupting me all the time." Nancy turned to her husband. "Do something. Frances is acting up again."

Madeline observed this with amazement. To her it seemed that Nancy Miller overreacted to everything her daughter said and did. Frankie was exuberant, but surely just a normal teenager rebelling against her parents' authority. Couldn't they see that they goaded her into talking back by treating her like a puppy they were trying to housebreak with harsh methods? She felt sorry for Frankie.

The teen girl backed further into the hall, but remained in view.

"Show more respect for your mother," Frank Miller said. "I mean it, Frances Jane."

Frankie saluted formally and strode away.

With a long sigh, Nancy said, "I don't know what's wrong with that girl. She's a tribulation. Try to be a good mother, and what do you get? Sarcasm. Insults. Rudeness."

Mrs. Lawrence looked at Nancy and Brad pointedly. "I couldn't agree more."

"Mother! You can't mean that," Brad said.

In the awkward silence, Madeline felt very much the outsider. She turned her attention to her son. "Take your napkin into the kitchen, Tommy, and thank Rosa for the delicious breakfast. Can you do that? Maybe she'll let you watch cartoons again on the TV. We'll play ball when we get home again."

"Okay." He got up too quickly, and bumped his head on the edge of the table. He made a face but didn't appear to be hurt.

She rubbed his head lovingly. "That nut's hard to crack."

He giggled. "It's not a nut, it's my head!" He took the napkin and walked carefully with it toward the kitchen.

Madeline looked after him thoughtfully.

Luke watched her with interest. "Everything okay?"

"I know who Tony Chestnut is."

He looked at her blankly.

"Last night you – or that Civil War soldier – gave me a message from my grandmother who died nine years ago. And he added something about 'Tony Chestnut' but I didn't make the connection."

"So you received an evidential?" Mrs. Lawrence asked.

"I guess I did," Madeline admitted. "Tommy just reminded me of it. 'Tony Chestnut' isn't a person, it's a little game I learned when I was in kindergarten. My grandmother and I used to say it whenever I bumped my head. Then she'd tell me that my head is a hard nut to crack."

"That's a game?" Daphne looked at her, then dug into her purse for a mirror and lipstick.

Madeline noticed the others were staring uncertainly at her. "Here's how it goes," she explained, getting up. She touched her toes, then her knees, then her chest, while saying, "Toe, knee, chest..." she tapped the top of her head and finished, " – nut!"

"My pilates instructor will have to get that exercise from you," Daphne said, only loud enough for Madeline to hear.

Luke smiled at Madeline. "Tony Chestnut!"

"I haven't thought of it in years, but..."

Mrs. Lawrence nodded as Madeline sat down. "Your grandmother knew you would remember, and that sooner or later you'd realize it was indeed her personal message to you, that warning about a duel."

"Now if only I could figure out what that means." Madeline shrugged.

Daphne eyed her closely. Brad, Frank and Nancy continued to stare at her speculatively.

Madeline felt uncomfortable with all the attention and decided to deflect it. She said to Luke, "Was Frankie right about the crystal ball? Are you avoiding it because of that paralysis last night, or do you have some other reason?"

"The state of catalepsy didn't worry me in the slightest since I wasn't aware of it." Luke grinned. "Sorry it upset everyone. If I'd been able to, I would have reassured you that I'd be all right soon."

She recalled how she had talked softly to Luke, trying to get through to him so he'd give a message, begging him to give her a sign that he was alive and well. And that's when she had seen that image of her grandmother.

"Are you okay, Madeline?" Luke looked at her with concern.

"Something happened while you were in that trance, while Frankie and I were here with you."

"Yeah, what happened after we went to bed?" Nancy asked. "No more flying brass bowls, I hope?"

The cat came into the room and took a few tidbits from Mrs. Lawrence. "Another message?"

"Yes. My grandmother appeared to me and spoke."

"You saw a ghost?" Daphne rolled her eyes.

"I didn't finish listening to the recording yet," Luke said, "but it should be on there since it was in the same room." He looked at Madeline with interest.

"First it was her voice, calling my name. I thought it was Frankie from another room, because she'd left to find a deck of cards we could pass the time with. I didn't know who the voice was, but then my grandmother appeared to me and identified herself."

"Wait," Luke said. "Appeared like I did, or just a shapeless light?"

Daphne cut in, thunder in her voice, "What are you talking about, Luke? You appeared to her? When? You've never appeared to me! I demand an explanation of what's going on between you two!"

Luke studied Daphne as if with new eyes that disliked what he discovered. He directed his response to the whole table. "I had an out-of-body experience night before last, and apparently paid a brief but silent visit to Madeline while she was sleeping upstairs. Or rather, I awoke her from her sleep. I don't remember it."

"In her bedroom," Daphne said coldly.

"That's right." A laugh bubbled in Madeline's throat. If only Daphne knew how terrified she'd been when it happened, she wouldn't be so jealous now, but Madeline felt no compunction to illuminate her rival about the event. Let her stew.

Brad put down the newspaper section he was perusing and went to the buffet to refill his cup. "Anyone else want more coffee? Mother, ring for Rosa. The pot's empty."

"I'll get more coffee." Madeline stood up.

Mrs. Lawrence rang her bell. "Never mind, dear. We want to hear your story." When Rosa came in, with Tommy happily in her wake, the old woman asked for a fresh pot of coffee. After those two returned to the kitchen, Mrs. Lawrence said, "Continue, please, Madeline."

"First was the voice, from that corner." Madeline pointed.

"And it sounded like your grandmother?" Luke asked.

"It was a whisper. Actually … it could've been anyone. I was frightened when I realized it wasn't Frankie, and no one else was in the room who could've spoken."

"Except Luke and maybe he was faking that coma." Brad smiled at everyone as if making a joke.

"I assumed it was her because she said 'I'm your grandmother.' Truth be told, I don't remember exactly what she said but I had the feeling that's who it was."

"Go on." Luke gave her an encouraging nod.

"Then there was a greenish-colored glow that grew larger, until it was about five feet tall."

"About the size of your grandmother?"

"It didn't look anything like a person, it was just a floating mass of light." She shuddered.

"I'm sorry I wasn't aware or I would've been able to make it less scary."

Daphne glared at him then turned to Madeline. "Did this ghost of yours have anything interesting to say this time?" She held out her coffee cup to Brad for him to refill it. "Just black, thanks."

Madeline creased her napkin again and again, avoiding a response.

"Come on, Maddie," Luke said. "You've brought us this far, don't hold out now."

"It sounds silly in daylight. She said to go home. To get out of here."

Mrs. Lawrence looked at her a moment. "And did she say why? Or how you were supposed to leave when your car is in need of service, and we're in the midst of one of the worst rainstorms in Los Angeles history?" She idly fed the cat a sliver of cheese from her plate, and let the animal leap into her lap to be petted.

"I hope I haven't offended you, Mrs. Lawrence." Madeline hesitated. "You've been very kind to me. I was only repeating what the ghost told me."

"No offense taken, right, Aunt Agatha?" Luke looked at Madeline. "Your grandmother was kind of vague, wasn't she? A warning to get out. That's fine. But didn't she give a reason why you're supposed to leave? Apparently it wasn't scary enough of a warning to actually make you pick up your son and hitchhike to safety."

Madeline looked at him in confusion. "Maybe it was all my imagination."

"Nice going, Madeline." Brad smirked as he leaned back in his chair.

She looked at him questioningly.

"Baiting the hook for a guy interest in spooks. What better lure than a ghostly visit that no one else witnessed? Frankie was conveniently out of the room for two minutes, and during that exact time, by sheer coincidence, your granny appeared with a message. I'm curious about something no one else has seemed to question."

Madeline felt under attack. She could feel Daphne's eyes bore into her back, and she was blushing hotly. Why did Brad have to tease her so openly about liking Luke? He was making such a big issue out of it.

"How many times has your granny given you a message before last night?" Brad asked.

"Well, never, but–"

"I rest my case." Brad slurped his coffee.

"What's he talking about?" Mrs. Lawrence asked.

Daphne got up in a hurry, knocking her chair over. She didn't pick it up. Turning to Madeline, she said, "Your grandmother has the right idea. Get out. Go home! You're not wanted here."

"Daphne, stop it." Luke set the chair upright. "Don't get yourself worked up."

"I can have any man in Los Angeles with the snap of my fingers." Daphne grabbed her purse from the floor and headed to the door. "You're such a loser, Luke."

Luke started after her.

"Let her go," Mrs. Lawrence said. "She can't go far without her own car. She'll cool off. And we can all relax without that negative energy she brings into a room."

Luke sighed and rubbed his forehead as if it ached.

Unsure what to do, Madeline sat silently, creasing the folds in her napkin, mulling over something she could say to diffuse the atmosphere, wishing she didn't feel responsible for the changed mood.

Then, abruptly, the need for conversation vanished.

Madeline noticed a glass raise itself up. As she stared at it, suddenly all the dishes on the table raised up in the air and flew toward Nancy and Frank Miller. They flinched.

The dishes slammed into the wall behind them and the broken pieces fell to the floor.

"Frances Jane!" Nancy Miller bellowed. "Get in here right this minute and clean up your mess!"

FIFTEEN

Madeline dealt cards for another game of "Go Fish" with her son, sitting alone in Mrs. Lawrence's library on a thick rug in front of the fireplace where a cheery fire sparked and warmed them. The heavy rain continued to pound the roof and Jason passed by in the hall outside the open door now and then with a pan or bucket to put beneath one of the many leaks upstairs.

"But why did the ghost throw dishes on the floor?" Tommy asked, and immediately added, "Do you have a lady?"

"A queen? No. Go fish, honey. And who told you about the dishes?"

"I saw it."

She had found out from Rosa that even though the housekeeper tried to keep Tommy in the kitchen, he discovered the fun of inching the swinging door open so he could peek into the dining room and watch the adults. Unfortunately, he'd looked just as all the excitement with the flying dishes took place, and had remained in awe of ghostly powers.

"Rosa gave me a apple."

"That was really nice of her." Madeline smiled. "Do you have any twos?"

"Why did the ghost throw dishes? Didn't he like his food?" Tommy put his cards down, face up.

"Tired of the game?" When he nodded, Madeline started to pick up the cards, saw there were three "two's" in his hand and gave him a wry look. "Conveniently tired, huh?" Smiling, she put the cards away and moved to a comfortable armchair. She patted her lap invitingly and he climbed up to cuddle.

"I still want to know about the dishes," he whispered.

"Did Rosa talk to you about ghosts, honey?"

"Daphne did."

"She did? When? I didn't see you talking to her."

"After the dishes fell down. Then I ate the apple."

90

"You told me about the apple already. I bet it was yummy. But when did you see Daphne?" She remembered that Daphne left the room just before the table was cleared in such a spectacular way. "Did you see her in the kitchen?"

After patient questioning, Madeline learned that Tommy had been too frightened by the loud voices to go in the dining room and so he'd wandered down the hall, looking for the cat to play with. He saw Daphne come out of the living room and asked if he could help her look for the crystal ball so he could play with it.

"But she already told you she didn't have a ball for you."

"I know, Mommy." He sighed. "But maybe she forgot where she put it. I told her about how the dishes crashed. And she said it was a ghost. And she said forget the bargain."

"What bargain? That's a strange thing to say to you."

"Not me, Mommy." He sighed again, exasperated. "The short man."

"The–" Madeline stopped. "Oh. You mean Frankie's dad."

"Look! There's Calli!" He clambered down to chase after the cat as it went by in the hallway.

"You can play with her, but don't go upstairs. Stay where I can find you." As he sped out, she added, "And it's still raining really hard, so don't go outside either."

She stood at the window for a moment, watching the downpour, then looked over the bookshelves, hunting for something light to read such as short stories or a cozy mystery.

Tommy hurried in.

"Hey, back already? Didn't Calli want to play?"

"It wasn't Calli."

"Well, of course it was, honey. Mrs. Lawrence told me she only has the one cat. And I saw a calico cat go by."

"It was a different cat."

Madeline sighed. She knew that if Tommy had it in his mind that the cat was not the same one he played with earlier, she'd have a hard time convincing him otherwise. "Wait a minute, young man. I've got proof. An evidential," she added to herself, taking her cell phone out of her pocket.

"Pictures!" He grinned at her. "I'll get the cat."

Before she could stop him, he raced out. By the time she had the photos on display, he was back, lugging the heavy calico cat in his arms. "Here, Mommy. Look. It's not Calli."

She started to disagree, but then found herself wondering if he was right. As they looked at the photos and examined the cat, however, she wasn't convinced one way or the other. "I'm not sure, Tommy. I didn't take pictures from all sides. She wiggled, so the photos are blurry. I think it's the same cat."

His jaw set stubbornly. "No it's not! Where's Calli? I want to play with Calli!"

"Shh, honey. Come on, let's find a story to read."

Hearing the hum of Mrs. Lawrence's wheelchair, she turned.

"Finding everything you need?"

"It's not the right cat!" Tommy announced.

When Mrs. Lawrence looked at him curiously, Madeline quickly explained, "Tommy has decided you must have two cats, because this one doesn't look exactly like the cat he played with before." She shrugged to mean, *You know how kids are!*

"Sorry, Tommy," Mrs. Lawrence said, "but I only have Calli. I bet she'd like to play with you some more, though." She picked up a green feather cat toy, consisting of a few feathers on the end of a small fishing line with a pole. "She loves to play with this if you want to dangle the feathers in front of her, to bat at with her paw."

He opened his mouth to protest, but Madeline gave him a prompting look. "Thank you, Mrs. Lawrence," he said, took the toy and dashed off in search of the cat.

Madeline slipped a novel back into its slot. "I should work on a needlepoint project I brought with me. A client asked for a custom order, but he's in London on business and so I have extra time to complete it. I'm making him a pillow with a portrait of his cocker spaniel who died recently."

Mrs. Lawrence took a moment to polish her eyeglasses on the hem of her blouse. The older woman looked more vulnerable and sad without her glasses. "I've been thinking about your request to borrow

The Calico Tapestry." She put the spectacles back on and smoothed her silver hair.

"Yes?" Madeline looked at her hopefully.

"Sit down, please. I get tired of craning my neck." She smiled to soften the rebuke.

After Madeline sat in a nearby chair, the other woman went on, "I've grown fond of you and your charming son. Quite fond."

"You've been very kind to us."

"The tapestry has been in my family for generations, and it became a tradition for each new owner of it to have a living cat that looks as similar as possible to the one depicted in the tapestry."

"And so that's why your cat is named Calli, short for Calico?"

"Not very original, I'll admit, but I enjoy traditions. My children say it is an obsession of mine."

"If it makes you happy, then it's none of their business, is it?"

"You're wise for such a young woman, my dear. You're the sort I'd wish for in a granddaughter."

"Frankie is a nice girl," Madeline said. "I'll admit she has a lot of drama going on, but I think underneath all that, she's lovable and kind."

"You must agree she can be difficult."

"Aren't we all at that age?" Madeline didn't want to get into a heavy discussion about Frances Jane Miller. In her opinion, the girl's troubles were enmeshed with the way the parents treated her like a problem child.

"I'm getting old." Mrs. Lawrence held out her arthritic hands and looked at them with distaste. "I used to have pretty hands. Where do the years ago? Would it be too much of a cliche to comment on how quickly time passes?"

Madeline smiled sympathetically.

Mrs. Lawrence made an impatient noise. "I'm being morbid. Nobody likes old people to talk about age. It reminds everyone we're all going to die, sooner or later." She pressed her hands on her knees. "You've been patient, and I thank you for your good manners."

"It must get lonely living out here with not many friends nearby."

"There are two things I want to say about the tapestry and this needlework business you're so intent on setting up."

"And also custom jewelry."

"Your motives are noble and optimistic, but I don't see how you can make enough money to live on."

"I'll manage."

"Don't get your back up. My age entitles me to meddle."

Jason Malone stood in the doorway silently.

Madeline gave a start, wondering how long he'd been standing there.

Mrs. Lawrence noticed him. "I'll be with you in a moment."

"We can talk later," Madeline offered.

"This won't take long. He can wait. That's what I pay him for." Mrs. Lawrence turned to Jason. "Make yourself useful and see if Rosa needs help cleaning up the broken dishes in the dining room."

He nodded and turned away, casting a dark glance at Madeline.

She shivered, feeling he had taken a dislike to her. It was odd for a hired attendant to act like Madeline was an interloper.

Mrs. Lawrence didn't seem to notice anything amiss. "That old tapestry has hung over the fireplace in the living room in every house it has known as home. When my husband Patrick and I moved back here years ago, after living in an apartment in Westwood for five years, I held the tapestry in the car. I was afraid to let the movers touch it."

"I'm sure that gave you peace of mind."

"My children would've taken that opportunity to remind me how rigid and nervous I am."

"There's nothing wrong with being cautious with things we love. You kept it safe." Madeline smiled at her.

"Tradition. All the little rituals that make life go smoothly. I enjoy an ordered life. I like to know that if it's Wednesday, I'm going to have spinach quiche for lunch, and if it's bedtime, I'll get my glass of hot milk with butter."

Madeline glanced around the room, noting all the mementos on display with the books. "You put so much of yourself in every room of the house. I have a tiny apartment, but everywhere you look, you'd find evidence of the things I loved. There's photos of Tommy everywhere, and little things that mean a lot to me because of the memories they hold. I guess I like tradition, too."

Mrs. Lawrence was silent a moment. "And now I'm going to do something I never thought I'd do."

"What's that?"

"I'm going to break a tradition."

"You mean–?"

The older woman nodded. "You may borrow the tapestry for your exhibit."

Madeline beamed at her. "I can't tell you how much I appreciate the trust you're placing in me. I'll be extremely careful with it." Her mind filled with visions of the publicity she'd get, especially when the press found out she had succeeded where the largest museums in the country had failed.

"My horoscope today said to break a tradition and help a young person. Voila! I have done both."

They laughed companionably.

"And now for the second thing on my list," Mrs. Lawrence said. "Promise that you'll think over your response and not reply hastily."

Madeline nodded, and looked at her curiously.

"I would like you and that darling boy of yours to come live here with me." When Madeline started to interject a comment, she held up a hand. "Don't give me the first answer that pops in your head. It would be fun for me to have young people around who are easy-going instead of drama addicts."

"We're not even related. I wouldn't feel comfortable not paying you rent and I really have my small apartment budgeted carefully."

"I'd rather spend some of my money on you and Tommy, and watch you enjoy life, than let it sit in the bank and investments for my family to squabble over when I'm gone."

Madeline allowed herself the indulgence of imagining a life here. No money worries. Tommy would love it. And Madeline would be able to supervise the household so that repairs paid for would actually be made, and no one would take advantage of the vulnerable Mrs. Lawrence.

But it wasn't right for a virtual stranger to be her benefactor. Madeline knew that with the purse comes purse-strings, and she'd soon find herself obligated to Mrs. Lawrence in ways she couldn't anticipate. Also it would mean living way out here, in this old run-down mansion that looked like it might slide down the cliff in the next big storm.

"Please, Madeline," Mrs. Lawrence said, watching her closely. "Consider it from all angles before you turn it down."

Madeline got up. "I'll do that. And now I really must see what Tommy is getting into. He wanted to play with Calli, but I need to be sure the cat doesn't need to be rescued from his love."

Jason was once again in the doorway, silent and hulking.

"Now as for you, Jason," Mrs. Lawrence said briskly, "Why is it that you don't join us for meals? My whole family is here and one more at the table is no burden. Rosa tells me you always eat after we do. You're welcome to eat at the big table."

"I'm just an employee," he mumbled. "I'll eat in the kitchen with Rosa."

Was it Madeline's imagination, or did she detect surliness in his tone? She didn't like Jason, and found it hard to believe Mrs. Lawrence willingly allowed him around her.

After Jason left, she blurted out, "Wouldn't you rather have a female attendant or nurse?"

"After my stroke, I did have a woman nurse."

"Did she quit because it's too far to work out here?"

"No," Mrs. Lawrence said. "She died."

SIXTEEN

"Did you apologize to Luke for last night?" demanded Nancy Miller of her sulking daughter.

Frankie slouched in a chair in the living room. Nancy stood over her with an angry frown.

Madeline looked up from her needlepoint, wondering what Nancy was talking about. Apparently it was no private matter since they were all gathered by the fire, and everyone could hear. She was glad that Tommy was upstairs taking a quick afternoon nap, tired out from running after the cat.

When she had asked him about playing with Calli, she braced herself for another argument that it was a different cat, but he agreed that the cat did like to play with the feather toy, and apparently had forgotten his insistence that there was a second cat lurking somewhere.

"I told you already, Mother," Frankie shouted. "I didn't do it! Why should I apologize?"

"What's this about?" Luke asked, a bishop in his hand. He was playing chess with Brad at a small game table.

"We all know Frances made that brass bowl fly across the room, barely missing your head, Luke. That's when you gave us all a fright by pretending to be dead."

"Nancy, why do you have to put things in a negative context?" Mrs. Lawrence asked, wheeling closer. She held a book on numerology in her lap. "He was in a trance. Something went wrong so that he could not return to consciousness."

"Can't you stay out of this?" Nancy asked her. "You always nitpick. All I meant was it looked like he was dead. Do you have to take everything literally?"

"Calm down, Nance," her husband cautioned.

Nancy hurried to the wet bar and refilled her drink, clutching the bottle with such intensity that her knuckles showed white. "I am calm! You're no help, Frank, so why don't you go somewhere and watch TV or get out of my hair?"

Frank shrugged and stayed where he was, in a comfortable rocking chair with the crossword puzzle from the morning paper.

"Frankie says she had nothing to do with last night," Luke said. "Let's not assume it was her doing."

"I suppose the breakfast dishes weren't her fault either?" Nancy said. "Then why did it happen as soon as she left the room in a huff? And why did the dishes slam straight for me and her father? Scared the living daylights out of me."

"We could have been killed," Frank added, with a stern look at his daughter.

"Why does everybody pick on me all the time?"

"Stop whining," Brad told her. "Why not confess so I can get on with this chess game. I'm winning."

"Yes, Frances Jane," Daphne said, "admit it. We all know you did it. Has everybody forgotten how she made the lights grow dim? And what about me? I'm the one she tried to hit with that brass bowl she called an ashtray. It almost killed me!"

"Didn't even come close," Frankie said. "My aim was a bit off."

"That's enough, Frances Jane." Her father's tone was enough to silence Frankie.

Nancy Miller said thoughtfully, taking a long swallow of her drink, "If Frances didn't do all these things, then who did? Luke, any ideas?"

He shrugged. "Maybe the old house is haunted."

Daphne glanced around uneasily.

"We shouldn't automatically blame Frankie every time something moves," Luke said.

Madeline smiled at Luke, glad he was being fair-minded and equable.

"But this kind of thing has happened before," Nancy said. "You've all seen she is capable of moving stuff around with that weird power of hers. I still say she owes Luke an apology. And as a matter of fact, she owes all of us one for putting us through such trauma."

Frankie's face reddened. She leapt to her feet. "Have it your way. I'm sorry. Okay? Did everyone hear me? I apologize!" She ran toward the door then stopped and turned to face them. "I apologize for living!" She fled down the hall.

Madeline put down her needlepoint and got up.

"Where are you going, Nervous Nelly?" Daphne asked. "Afraid she'll wake up your precious son?"

Luke looked at Daphne with distaste.

"I want to be sure Frankie is okay," Madeline said and left. She was afraid the girl might do something foolish to teach her parents a lesson. Even if she didn't actually kill herself, she might do more harm than she intended in this agitated state.

Madeline caught up with Frankie on the stairs. "Hey, hold on, let's talk."

Frankie slowed her pace but didn't stop. "Did my parents send you?"

"I came on my own."

"You sure?" The teen stopped at the top of the stairs.

"I'd like to know your theory about who else has telekinesis besides you. Somebody's trying to make you look bad. Let's talk about it. In your room?" Madeline gestured to a nearby door. She had been in there when Frankie tried to loan her clothes to wear.

"You afraid of heights?" Frankie asked abruptly.

"Depends how high you're talking about."

Frankie laughed and led the way up to the third floor. Madeline glanced toward that door which had been locked her first night here, and wondered if it was still locked.

There was no time to investigate because Frankie led her past buckets catching drips from the leaky roof, and up another short flight of stairs to the wrought iron belvedere perched at the top of the house. It overlooked the front entry, and had a magnificent ocean view.

The teen opened the door leading out to the roofed gallery. Wind and cold rain swept in.

"Forget it, Frankie. We'll get soaked. We can watch the rain from here."

Frankie went out and scurried to a corner with an overhang protecting it from the worst of the rain. "It's dry enough over here. I'm not going back. Not yet."

Madeline didn't like the sound of that. They were high up, four stories above the ground. If Frankie meant to do herself harm, she might vault over the railing onto the stone path below.

Reluctantly, Madeline closed the door and approached the younger woman, hurrying to reach the dry corner. In her haste, she didn't notice a broken weather vane someone had leaned against the house. She tripped and stumbled, but righted herself.

Hurrying to Frankie, Madeline shivered and clutched her sweater. "Cold out here. Let's not stay long, okay?"

"Don't you like the rain? I do. It's coming down hard."

Each time the wind shifted, the girls were sprayed with cold drops. Much longer out here, and they'd be drenched, Madeline realized. She needed to convince Frankie to go back inside the house.

"I wanted to be sure you're okay," Madeline said, "after that scene with your mother."

"Yeah, I'm used to it."

"Have you tried–"

"Everything. No way to please either of them. They think I'm a freak." Frankie huddled in the corner, squatting with her back against the wall of the house. "They wish I'd go away. Life would be easier without me in it."

"I bet they don't really think that."

"They could adopt a normal daughter. Or maybe they want a boy." Frankie shrugged.

Madeline sighed to herself. What could she say? The teenager's depression was contagious. Shaking off the dark mood, she said, "I'm getting soaked. Let's go check on Tommy. He really likes you." She held out a hand to Frankie.

"You're real nice and everything, Madeline, but it's nothing to do with you."

"So I should walk away and let you mope?"

"Come or go. Stay or not. I'm not moping. I'm thinking."

"Well then, what are you thinking about?" Madeline squatted beside the teenager, knowing she couldn't leave her out here alone. It was far too dangerous on this open gallery so high above the ground, even for the short time it would take to run downstairs and get Luke to help convince Frankie to come indoors.

A peal of thunder rolled across the sky. Even though it was mid-day, it was dark and gloomy as if the sun had set early.

"They don't want me," Frankie said, her voice low.

Madeline had to strain to hear despite the storm.

"I heard them talking late last night," Frankie said. "Their room is next to mine and I put my ear to the wall." She looked at Madeline defiantly.

"I can't blame you for eavesdropping."

"They were fighting about money. As usual."

"I thought you guys must be well off, the way your mother dresses and the way you talk about therapists and going away to a private school."

Frankie shook her head, not getting sidetracked. "It was after Luke revived. Mother was saying that if Daphne didn't hurry up and get Luke to propose, we'd have to sell our house and totally downsize."

Madeline knew Daphne had arrived with Frankie's family, but she hadn't questioned their connection. Now she was beginning to get an inkling.

"Daddy said that it was all her fault in the first place and her idea better work. He said it was too expensive to keep me and they'd have to find another way. I think maybe I'm not even their child."

"Oh come on, Frankie. You look just like your mother. Don't let your imagination go crazy here. Parents fight about bills and it's easy to think it's all your fault. I remember one time when I was a kid I heard my dad complaining about the water bill. I started taking cold baths in one inch of water, feeling guilty that I was too big an expense."

Frankie laughed grudgingly. "It's obvious Daphne's trying to catch Luke, but I never knew there was some kind of plot about money." She thought a moment, standing to stretch. "Her father is a producer. About a year ago, my parents invested heavily in one of his films. It was my mother's idea to put the money in it, but the movie was a flop. I guess that's what Daddy meant about it being my mother's fault."

"But how does Daphne marrying Luke fix all that?" Madeline frowned, thinking. "Unless Daphne has some kind of old-fashioned dowry they want to get?"

"I hope Luke doesn't marry Daphne. You're more his real type. It'd be cool if you two hooked up."

"We're just friends."

"Yeah, because you don't want to be related to me."

"It's not that at all, Frankie. I'd be happy to have you as a relative."

"You don't think I'm a weirdo?"

"I think you're a teenager with a lot of potential." Madeline could see that her prompt answer was the right one.

"Do you believe I did that to Luke last night? Made him go into that catalepsy mode?"

"You did make that brass bowl move earlier, shoving it at Daphne, so I don't know. All this is a mystery to me. I don't know enough about those kinds of things." As soon as she spoke, Madeline realized she should've lied and said she was positive Frankie was blameless. "I'm sure you didn't mean to–"

"Forget it. What you mean is that subconsciously I wanted to hurt him. I've heard all that stuff from my psychiatrists and therapists and parents enough times to know what you're thinking."

"Frankie, please–"

"Don't lie because you feel sorry for me. I know I'm a freak. I'm used to being pitied and scorned. Suicide watch is over!" With that she flung open the door and ran into the house.

When Madeline followed, she was delayed by having to close and lock the gallery door against the stiff wind. She hurried to go downstairs but the teen was nowhere in sight.

SEVENTEEN

"When can we go home, Mommy?" Tommy rubbed his eyes sleepily. "I don't like it here anymore."

On her way back downstairs, having given up trying to find Frankie, Madeline stopped in Tommy's room to see if he was ready to get up from his nap and go downstairs. He sat up as soon as she walked in the door.

"But I thought you loved it here. You told me earlier that you want to stay here forever." When that happened, she'd suspected that Mrs. Lawrence must have talked to Tommy about moving in, but as usual it was difficult to pinpoint the truth when talking to him. He tended to get more vague the more she pursued an issue, so she'd learned to be casual in her questions.

"I don't like ghosts," he whispered. He held out his arms for a hug. As soon as he was in the security of his mother's embrace, he added in a braver tone, "I'm not afraid of ghosts. I just don't like them."

Madeline didn't want to tell him about Mrs. Lawrence's offer to live here until she'd had more time to consider it, and then only if she decided to answer in the affirmative. It seemed cruel to burden a child with the ramifications of such an important decision.

"We'll go home as soon as the car is working," she promised, glad to be able to speak the truth. After all, she reasoned, even if she did agree to come live here, which she doubted, she would first have to go back to the apartment in Hermosa Beach to pack their few belongings. When she'd left her marriage, she'd taken only their clothes and personal items, leaving behind furniture and anything bulky that would impede a smooth departure.

Sometimes she regretted having done things that way, but it was over and done with, and there was no chance now of changing it. She had no intention of asking Craig to ship any of the things she'd left behind, because she'd have to give him an address. Her peace of mind and Tommy's safety were more important than material goods.

"Now let's go down and join the party, okay?" She smiled at him.

"I like parties!" He wriggled free and jumped to the floor. He tried to put his shoes on by himself, but needed help.

She obligingly lent a hand. "Wait. How did your shoes get muddy? Did you go out when I told you not to?"

"No."

"Tommy?"

"Really."

"Then how did your shoes get mud on them that wasn't there before? Are you going to tell me they went outside by themselves while you were taking a nap?"

Waiting for his excuse, she worriedly cleaned the mud off with a tissue.

"Really," he repeated, sounding less certain of himself.

"You know I don't like you to make up stories unless you tell me it's just for pretend. So is this a pretend story?"

"It's a secret!"

She looked up sharply. "What do you mean, a secret? Tell me about it."

"I can't. The ghost told me not to."

She sighed. Sometimes it was a challenge to be patient. As charming as he could be most of the time, Tommy was exasperating when he confused truth with fantasy. "Please tell me the whole story, honey. Okay?"

"You saw a ghost," he accused.

"You're right. I did." She finished putting his shoes on and straightened, holding back a sigh. Whenever Tommy had heard about ghosts on television or from playmates or even in a storybook, she had reassured him that they were make-believe and nothing to be afraid of.

So now what could she say without losing her credibility?

She took his hand and led him out of the room. "Why don't you tell me about your ghost."

"Okay. He was real tall. And he came in and did this." He put his fingers to his lips.

"He told you to be quiet. And then what?" She looked down at him as he skipped at her side. "Tommy? What did he look like?"

She was beginning to believe that he had seen something strange. Whether it was actually a ghost or not remained uncertain, but for now she was assuming that a man had come into Tommy's bedroom, the boy had woken up and the man had indicated he should be quiet.

"He was tall."

"And what did his face look like? Was it anybody you know or have seen already?"

"No."

"You don't sound too sure. Why is that? Do you think maybe you've seen him before?"

"He didn't have a face."

"I see." Madeline realized the man had worn a mask.

"And I was scared. But he said don't be scared. And we went outside."

"Where? Where did he take you? Did you go out the front door?"

"We didn't go nowhere." He lifted his small shoulders as if unsure how else to explain it. "It was a tiny door and you crawl to go out it. I'm little. The ghost said that was good."

"Okay, what did you do when you crawled out this tiny door?" She was feeling skeptical again. He probably saw a cartoon in the kitchen earlier and then dreamed this adventure of ghosts and crawling through hidden doorways. But she wanted to see what else he remembered.

"I don't know."

"Try to think!" She took a breath and relaxed. As he started to go down the stairs, she held him back, wanting to finish this conversation before they joined the others. "Sorry. Please, honey. Try to remember. For me, okay?"

He looked up at the ceiling thoughtfully. "I know! I saw kitty. And he played with me."

"Who did? The cat or the ghost?"

"Ghost? He left."

"And then you came back upstairs and went to sleep? Or you waited for me?"

He looked at her, confused. "Can we get a kitty, Mommy? Can we?"

She laughed helplessly, giving up. It looked like Tommy had simply had a vivid dream. Probably the mud had been there earlier and she just didn't notice it with all the other things on her mind.

No doubt all the talk in the household about ghosts had fired his imagination. But she decided to have a little chat with Daphne about putting those ideas in his head. He was at an impressionable age, and what Daphne had done was irresponsible.

She'd set her straight, Madeline decided, her eyes glinting in anticipation of the confrontation.

"How dare you tell my son there are ghosts in this house?" Madeline stood between Daphne and the television show she was watching in the living room.

Daphne craned to see past her. "For heaven's sake, Nervous Nelly, I'm not the only one talking about ghosts around here. And you're the only one who claims to have seen one."

"I didn't talk about it in front of Tommy. He told me you had a conversation with him about ghosts."

"Cartoons are full of ghosts." She lit a cigarette and blew the smoke in Madeline's direction. "Give your kid a chance to grow up normal. You're making a sissy out of him."

Madeline fanned the smoke. "Frightening a child into having nightmares is hardly under the classification of good judgment."

"Talk about over-reacting. He's not going to have nightmares."

"For your information, he already has."

Daphne shrugged. "Kids have bad dreams all the time. Probably something he ate. So why don't you sue Rosa, instead of harping on me?"

"From now on, if you feel the need to talk to my son, either stifle the impulse or–"

"Or what?"

"Stick to ordinary topics like the weather. Don't mention ghosts or goblins or things he's too young to understand."

"Tell you what," Daphne said idly, "I'll make a deal with you." She picked up the remote and randomly channel-surfed, even though she could barely see the TV screen.

Madeline waited, wondering how she had so easily lost control when she'd started off assertive and in command.

"I'll stay away from your precious Tommy…" she paused to blow smoke and then tap the ash into a porcelain Chinese bowl which Madeline was sure was an antique, not an ashtray.

"And? What's the condition?"

"And you, dear Madeline – you see, I do know your name isn't Nervous Nelly – you stay away from Luke. I recall you have a compulsion about shaking hands to seal a bargain." She held out her beautifully manicured hand.

Madeline remembered how Daphne had rebuffed her offer of friendship the night they met, and had refused to shake hands. So now she pointedly ignored the manicured hand.

Another thought came to mind: Frankie had said her parents felt it important for Daphne to marry Luke. Apparently Daphne was not motivated by love. But Madeline was, she realized abruptly. She was falling in love with Luke and was not about to hand him over to Daphne as if she'd won him in a contest.

Daphne let her hand drop. She ground out her cigarette in the Chinese bowl. "Deal or no deal? Do I stay away from your son or not?"

"I'll tell him not to believe anything you say."

"You won't stop flirting with my boyfriend? We're practically engaged!"

Madeline smiled sweetly. "Haven't you noticed the way he's been looking at you? Hardly the look of a man in love."

"Why you little b–"

"More name-calling, Daphne? What is this, junior high?"

Daphne jumped up. "You haven't got a chance with him. You're not his type."

"What makes you so sure that you are? So I don't have the clothes and jewelry you do. Can't afford it. But I happen to believe Luke is the kind of guy who appreciates the quality of what's inside."

"You saying I'm stupid?"

"I'm talking about heart and spirit and feelings. Never mind. I can see from your face that you don't follow me."

"Spirit? Let's not get into that mumbo-jumbo."

"You want to marry a man whose whole life is 'mumbo-jumbo' to you?"

"That's a small part of his life. We have so many other things in common."

"Like what?" Madeline leaned against the back of a tall chair and crossed her arms.

Daphne brushed past her. At the doorway, she turned. "Don't waste your time trying to compete with me. I always win. Luke doesn't care anything about you."

"Why don't we let him decide?"

Daphne sputtered in outrage but turned on her heel and strode away, in the direction of the stairs.

Grabbing the remote, Madeline turned off the television and hurried out as well, suddenly fearful for her son. She'd left him with Rosa in the kitchen, but she couldn't expect the housekeeper to guard him like the crown prince.

What if Daphne went upstairs to Tommy's room, found he was not there and began a hunt for him? She'd love to torment Tommy with scary stories, just to get back at Madeline. But could Daphne really be that heartless, or was Madeline overreacting?

Madeline hesitated, then hurried to the kitchen with all speed, knowing that Daphne was an unknown element, and should be treated as dangerous.

EIGHTEEN

Madeline heard her son laughing from inside a room further down the hall. She'd assumed he was still in the kitchen with Rosa, but maybe he was following the housekeeper around while she did chores.

Still, she wanted to be sure Daphne did not discover him first and say something upsetting to Tommy out of spite.

Jason stepped out of a doorway and blocked her.

She stopped, startled.

"You're always in such a hurry," he said. He was dressed in a drab shirt and faded jeans.

She tried to go around him but he moved each time so she could not pass. "Let me by, please. I don't have time for games."

"Can't you spare me a minute?"

"Actually, I can't. Sorry."

He grabbed her arm.

She twisted away. "You're hurting me. All it'll take is one yell from me and the whole household will come running. Your employer is right down the hall." She broke off as he picked her up bodily and hurried toward a closed door. She was too startled to scream after all.

He carried her into a room she hadn't seen before. He shut the door and clapped a hand over her mouth. "I just want to talk to you. Promise you won't yell?"

She nodded quickly, and he removed his hand. She glared at him. "All right. Talk."

"Why don't you like me? You're cute. I like your hair." He stroked her silky brown hair.

"Don't touch me."

His face grew dark. He raised a fist as if to strike her, then his hand trembled as he exercised control over his impulse. The arm dropped to his side. "Why didn't you leave when you had the chance, the first day?"

"My car is broken." She backed up toward the door. Quietly, with her hand behind her back, she twisted the doorknob, hoping he wouldn't notice her movement.

"I haven't kissed a girl in a long time."

She opened the door. "That's your problem, not mine!" As he lunged for her, she backed into the hall.

"Wait. It's about your boy!"

Madeline stopped. "If that's a trick to get me back in here–"

"No. I promise. Don't trust Luke. Don't let him near your kid."

"You're being ridiculous. Luke loves kids."

Jason scowled and tugged at his scraggly beard. "Go away before it's too late."

"Too late for what?"

"At the seance, strange things happened. Right?"

She nodded.

"Who do you think caused them?"

"Everybody's saying that Frankie–"

"I know who really did it."

"Frankie and Luke are the only ones here with powers like that. You're saying Luke did all that to himself? He could have been seriously harmed."

"Ever been to a magic show? Think the magician lets them padlock chains on him without first practicing how he'll get free?"

"Luke's not a fake."

"You like Mrs. Lawrence?"

"Of course I like her."

"Luke plans to murder her."

"That's crazy!"

"You think you're so smart," Jason said. "I'm warning you as a favor. Go away. Don't get involved with these people."

"Why would Luke want to kill her?"

"Money. What else?"

Madeline heard Tommy's laughter, faintly, from down the hall. She wanted to go to him and be sure he was okay. "You say Luke did all that to himself at the seance. But you didn't say why."

He looked confused. "You find out."

"Me? How?"

"Get him talking. Find out how he goes into trances. Then tell me."

"Why don't you ask him? I don't want to be stuck in the middle. In my experience, that's always a bad place to be."

"If I ask him a list of questions, you think he'd answer?"

"I've got to go."

"But you'll do it." It was a statement, not a question. Jason smiled at her, a tight, small smile that was more the grimace of someone in pain than it was a friendly grin.

She started to refuse, but then reconsidered. "If it will help Mrs. Lawrence."

"And remember everything he tells you, so you can repeat it to me."

"Why?"

"I know this family better than you do," he said, then quickly added, "Mrs. Lawrence and Rosa gossip. I'm invisible to them. A fly on the wall. He might say something that would make sense to me. Don't you want to help Mrs. Lawrence? She's done a lot for you and the kid. Not everybody would let complete strangers stay just because they claim their car won't start."

"But it won't! The battery is dead and it needs a fan belt. If there was a phone or I could get cell service, I'd call the auto club and be on my way. You can't expect me to walk out of here carrying my son in this storm?"

He chuckled softly. "So you'll do it," he repeated, more confidently this time.

She studied him a moment. There was something about him that made her want to draw back to protect herself, but now she attributed his gruffness to an unpleasant personality rather than anything sinister.

He didn't have any social skills, but that didn't mean he was out to get her. He'd impressed her with his concern for his employer's safety.

Noticing a dead leaf in his coarse dark hair, she reached up and brushed it off.

He pushed her away. "Don't touch me."

"Now you know how I felt!"

He rearranged his hair over his forehead. "Don't do it again."

"There was a leaf in your hair. Good grief, you overreact."

"Me?"

She started to go, but remembered something else. "Why did you put that dead mouse on my bed?

"What?"

"Don't act like you don't know what I mean. The first night I was here, there was the head and tail of a mouse on my pillow. I'd like to clear up the mystery."

"Why are you so positive it was me? Probably the cat did it."

"Cats always leave three trophies. Head, tail and pancreas. The pancreas wasn't there."

He laughed. "Who told you that?"

"Frankie said–"

"She spouts off misinformation to sound superior."

"Sorry I accused you. It was that nasty cat, after all."

"Don't you like cats?"

"Not ones that leave unpleasant gifts on my pillow." She turned to leave.

"Besides," he said, "if I did that to scare you away, the plot failed, didn't it?" He abruptly walked past her and hurried to the stairs.

She watched him go. Had he meant that as a confession? Or was he being enigmatic for the sake of confusing her?

Madeline sighed, wishing she could simply drive off with Tommy and go home to Hermosa Beach, away from all this drama and the complications her wayward heart was raising in regards to Luke.

Miles away, she reflected with another sigh. Home might as well be on the other side of the ocean, because she still had no means of getting there.

As she headed toward the sound of Tommy's giggles, she decided to ask Brad if he'd drive her and Tommy home, and then she could deal with the car later. She'd offer to pay him for gas and his time, and hope that he waived the expense. Funds were painfully tight, but it would be worth it to get away from here even if she had to pay a taxi. But now, having come to a decision, she walked with a lighter step.

NINETEEN

"Look, Mommy. A Christmas ball!" Tommy gripped the glass globe in his small hands.

"That's a crystal ball, honey. Not Christmas. But where did you get it?" Having followed the sound of Tommy's voice, Madeline found him in a small room off the library, visiting with Mrs. Lawrence. "Thanks for keeping him out of trouble, Mrs. Lawrence. I didn't mean to be gone so long."

"No problem. And I gave him that ball to play with. I knew I had one around here someplace."

"I found it, Mommy!"

Mrs. Lawrence smiled indulgently, and explained to Madeline, "I let him look through that antique trunk. As you see, it's full of tarot cards, my Ouija boards and old books. I have a rune collection as well, and most of the tiles are bagged up in there. Tommy had fun poking around and then he came across the box with the crystal ball. It's an old one, but not valuable."

"Still… Tommy, be careful with it. Make sure you don't break it. It's glass, not plastic."

"I doubt if it will break even if he drops it on the carpet." Mrs. Lawrence smiled as Luke tapped on the door and then joined them. "Consider it a gift for Tommy."

"How's Frankie?" Luke asked Madeline. "You didn't come back to report any new catastrophe, so I hope we can assume everything's all right?"

She nodded, suddenly feeling it difficult to speak to him with the affection and warmth she'd been feeling the past couple of days. Jason's words had wormed into her mind and planted seeds of distrust and suspicion. But she should make an effort to keep up appearances. "Actually, I'm not sure if she is all right or not."

"But I thought you were going after her when she ran out of the room earlier." He looked at her with an odd expression.

Had he sensed her coldness? "I did," she explained, deciding to leave out the "suicide watch" in the rain on the upstairs gallery, "but then after we talked for a while, she hurried away and I guess went to her room."

"I'm fine," Frankie said from the doorway. Her eyes were puffy as if she'd been crying. She burrowed into an overstuffed armchair near the window and hid behind the pages of a magazine.

"I wish she could get along better with her mother," Mrs. Lawrence said in a whisper to Luke and Madeline, "but then I don't know why she should. My daughter never got along with me, either."

Luke squatted beside Tommy and played with him for a few moments.

Madeline hoped Luke would leave the room soon. She couldn't bring herself to chat easily with him or even meet his eyes.

Turning her shoulders to exclude him, she said to Mrs. Lawrence, "I'm glad Tommy can't break the ball, but I don't know much about these things. Is it all right for him to look at it? Is there any risk?"

"You want to know if he'll see the future while he's playing with the crystal ball?" Luke joined them.

"Something like that," she said coolly. Madeline caught the surprised look on Mrs. Lawrence's face. The older woman was too observant! Madeline hoped she would not probe. It would be embarrassing to discuss her mixed-up feelings about Luke.

"Your fears are groundless," Mrs. Lawrence said, her bright eyes darting back and forth between Madeline and Luke as if trying to figure out what had gone wrong between them.

Luke had a similar look of puzzlement. "You see, Madeline, crystal balls are like tea leaves or colored sand, or any other device a psychic might use to—"

"It's for show?" Madeline cut in. "A gimmick?" She thought cynically about last night, and the very real probability that Luke had rigged his so-called disaster, as part of the entertainment.

"Don't be bitter, child," Mrs. Lawrence said. "I once was a skeptic. Let Luke explain."

"Sorry," Madeline said crisply. "Please continue. I won't interrupt again."

He stared, and then when he spoke his voice matched some of her coolness. "A crystal ball helps the medium to concentrate. It gives a focal point so they can ignore outside distractions. A plastic cup would work just as well as that," he added, nodding toward the crystal ball which Tommy was rolling around on the floor between his outstretched legs.

"Oh, I see."

"You're right, though. It is a gimmick." He looked at her with a challenge in his gaze.

She tilted her head defiantly.

Without another word, Luke turned and left.

Mrs. Lawrence watched Madeline for a moment. "Care to explain?"

"I don't know what you're talking about."

"What happened between you and my nephew? I thought you two were shaping up quite nicely."

Madeline colored. She glanced toward the doorway, exhausted and sad. "I thought so, too, but I was wrong." Not wanting to be so transparent, she tried to backpedal. "It's nice of you to have Tommy and me here, but I'm going to see if Brad or Frank would be willing to drive us home. I'll get a mechanic out here to take care of my car. It's ridiculous to impose on you, because of a dead battery."

"Do you see how your heart spoke the truth before your brain could try to censor the message? Listen to your heart, Madeline. All too often we try to use logic to determine our course. But listen to your heart," she repeated slowly with emphasis on each word. "If you're worried about Daphne, forget it. He's no fool. He'll never marry her. She's so obvious about her yearning for what money can buy, as if it buys happiness."

Briskly putting things back in the trunk that Tommy had taken out, Madeline picked up the crystal ball, against his protest. She held it out to Mrs. Lawrence. "Daphne is welcome to him."

When Mrs. Lawrence didn't take the crystal ball, Tommy snatched it and carefully moved out of reach to play with it again.

"So something else has happened in addition to Daphne," Mrs. Lawrence mused. "Could it be that you found last night's seance so distasteful that you want nothing more to do with a psychic?"

"I was worried about Luke last night! That's why I stayed up with Frankie, at least part of the time. And I was there when he came around." She stopped, then went on in frustration, "I changed my mind, that's all."

Mrs. Lawrence looked at her carefully. "We rarely do an about-face without impetus. Perhaps when you feel like confiding in someone, you will choose me? I am a good listener. And don't forget," she added with a twinkle in her eye and a coaxing smile, "I've had two husbands. I kept both of them happy, each in his own time of course, for a total of fifty-two years. I do know a little about what makes romance tick along smoothly."

Madeline knew she was being difficult. She couldn't get her thoughts away from the hurt look that had been in Luke's eyes when he abruptly left a few moments earlier. Could it be that he did care for her?

There had been a warm, easy, developing relationship between them. And now it was gone, replaced by a chilly distance.

Why couldn't Jason Malone have kept his mouth shut? she thought angrily. It was his fault that Madeline now viewed Luke from a less flattering angle. If Jason had not said those things to her about Luke, she'd probably be flirting happily with Luke at this moment, trying to push Daphne far from his thoughts.

Daphne.

Madeline had momentarily forgotten her flippant vow to compete with Daphne for Luke, and let him choose for himself which girl he preferred. She couldn't let the other young woman win by default! And what better way to give Daphne something to think about than to win Luke's love and then reject it as if the prize had not been worth fighting over in the first place.

"Well," Mrs. Lawrence said, having watched the changing expressions that flitted across Madeline's face, "I see you've come to some sort of conclusion. About Luke? Or are there other things troubling you?"

"I thought you were–" Madeline began angrily, planning to tell the woman to mind her own business. She stopped short, recollecting her manners. "I'm sorry, Mrs. Lawrence. I had no right to snap. I guess I do have a lot on my mind today, but that's no excuse for rudeness."

"I suppose I was meddling. I care about you, dear. And I love Luke. Nothing would please me more than to see the two of you straighten things out and get back in harmony. Get in the groove." She smiled. "I grew up in this house. And I was married here, both times. So was my daughter Nancy. The grand staircase seems to have been designed with a bridal procession in mind."

"Don't play matchmaker, please. You seem to hear wedding bells. Keep them ringing until Frankie is old enough to need them, because I'm out of the picture."

Frankie spoke up, reminding them of her presence. "I'll never get married." She tossed aside the magazine. "Not if I have to go to that all girls' school! How can I meet boys? I'll end up an old maid."

Madeline smiled, remembering how hard it was to be a teen. "Don't forget a lot of those girls will have brothers and cousins. Probably they go to an all boys' school and will be dying to meet you."

Grabbing a pack of gum from her pocket, Frankie popped two pieces in her mouth, then handed the package to Madeline. "Thanks for the gum. I forgot to tell you that I found it in your purse, like you said."

"Keep it if you want."

"Thanks!"

The cat hovered around Mrs. Lawrence. As she petted him, the old woman said to Madeline, "Do you have any pets? Calli is such a good companion. I can't imagine a house without a cat."

"No pets allowed in my apartment," Madeline said.

"What a shame. A boy needs a cat or dog to play with."

Madeline laughed to herself at the obvious ploy. Mrs. Lawrence might as well have said: *If you come and live here, Tommy will have this cat to play with all the time.*

Feeling bad about having been sharp earlier, Madeline said, "I told you I need some time to think about it, okay?"

To his mother, Tommy said accusingly, "I do so have pets. I got goldfish."

"Fish are nice pets," Mrs. Lawrence said.

"We made a mobile with paper cutouts for his room," Madeline explained.

Tommy held out his arms to Calli, and to his delight the cat went to him readily, rolling over on her back and offering a fat stomach to be rubbed.

"That cat is so friendly. I know my son has enjoyed the chance to play with her."

"Calli is a good cat. She likes everybody." Abruptly, Mrs. Lawrence looked saddened. She removed her spectacles and began polishing them on her sweater.

Frankie got down on the floor to play with Tommy and Calli. Time stopped for Madeline for a moment as she watched Mrs. Lawrence, wondering what the woman was thinking. Obviously what she'd said about Calli liking everyone had triggered another thought, or a memory. And just as obviously, not a pleasant one.

Brad came into the room and rubbed his hands together. "Where's the rest of the happy gang?"

"In their rooms, I guess." Mrs. Lawrence put her glasses on, seeming distracted.

"How goes the romance with young Luke?" He winked at Madeline. "I see Daphne isn't here, either. If everybody is in their rooms, as you put it, Mother, maybe I should do a bed check and be sure each one is in his or her own room."

Madeline flushed.

"Leave her alone, Bradford. And don't be crass. That sort of talk is vulgar."

"You're an old fuddy-dud, Mother. But I refuse to be put down. I went in the living room and no one was there yet. You said to regroup at four. I'm a bit early, but what difference does time make on a day like this?" He glanced out at the pouring rain. "I'm going to stir up a batch of dirty martinis. Can I interest anyone?"

"I'll take one," Frankie said.

"Me, too!" Tommy said eagerly, not wanting to be left out.

Laughing, Brad left the room.

"Come on, Tommy," Frankie said, "let's go in the kitchen and get a soda or something. Maybe Rosa has some sandwiches left from lunch. It's tea time!"

After they left, Madeline took the opportunity to speak in private with Mrs. Lawrence. Knowing they might be interrupted, she got to the point. "Who is it that Calli doesn't like?"

The cat wandered over to strop her back against Madeline's legs, purring throatily.

Mrs. Lawrence shook her head. "Help me with my sweater. And let's go into the living room."

Madeline assisted the woman, then they headed down the hall toward the voices coming from the front of the house.

"It must be someone important to you," Madeline persisted. "Or you wouldn't have looked so sad and troubled. Won't you tell me? I'm a good listener, too, you know. Who is it that the cat doesn't like, even though she likes everyone?"

"My son."

"But I sw Brad playing with the cat more than once. Calli seems to like him just fine. Why do you say—"

"You've forgotten I have two sons."

"Patrick," Madeline said softly. "Calli didn't like Patrick?"

They reached the living room.

Nancy Miller perched on a tall stool at the wet bar area, talking to Brad. "Don't bruise the gin this time."

Her husband Frank entered behind Madeline and Mrs. Lawrence. "Make mine a double! I need the strength to get through another evening of family conviviality." With a laugh, he joined them at the bar and grabbed a drink while Brad was still pouring.

Madeline felt dismay that she would probably not get a response from Mrs. Lawrence now that others were around. However, she'd forgotten this family's love of strife and drama.

Mrs. Lawrence looked up at her, and raised her voice for all to hear. "Calli <u>doesn't</u> like my son Patrick," the old woman corrected with sharp emphasis. "We have not yet established whether Patrick is alive or not."

All eyes were suddenly on them.

"Don't start again, Mother." Nancy drained her martini glass and held it out to Brad for a refill.

"Why not?" Mrs. Lawrence said loudly. "As far as I'm concerned, we have no conclusion yet, so we're not finished."

Madeline hoped this didn't mean they'd have another seance today.

She saw Frank Miller exchange a long-suffering look with his wife, and guessed that she was not the only one who thought of that possibility.

TWENTY

"Lookit," Tommy said, pointing to the cat. "His tail is broke."

"Where?" Frankie asked, pulling the reluctant cat closer.

Madeline commented to Mrs. Lawrence, "I suppose I should correct his grammar. And gender."

"Leave him be," the older woman said, agreeing with a smile. "Aren't those two sweet together? Your son is good medicine for young Frances. The girl needs a healthy outlet for her emotions. She keeps everything so pent up inside." Mrs. Lawrence studied Madeline for a moment. "You're good for her, too."

Madeline smiled, knowing the woman was building bricks to create the structure for her and Tommy to live here.

Brad and Frank had retired to the other side of the room to watch a football game on TV. Nancy was still perched on a bar stool, idly humming show tunes. Madeline couldn't help noticing the absence of Luke and Daphne, and tried not to think about what they might be doing together.

Frankie called out to Madeline and Mrs. Lawrence. "He's right! Calli's tail has a kink in it. When did that happen? Did she get her tail caught in a door?"

"Bring her to me, please." Mrs. Lawrence held out her hands. In an aside to Madeline, she said, puzzled, "Do you suppose the cat could have hurt herself without my even knowing it?"

"Wouldn't a broken tail be painful? If it was me, I'd be crying and moping, and making the problem known."

Mrs. Lawrence laughed. "I don't think so. You'd bravely carry on, with a stiff upper lip and a smile for everyone."

"See?" Frankie held the cat and let Mrs. Lawrence examine the tail. "Look how it's bent."

Tommy pressed against the side of the wheelchair to get as close as possible. "It's bended," he said gravely, imitating Frankie's gesture toward the tail.

"I've had this cat thirteen years. The one in the tapestry had a kinked tail, also. That's why it's doubly odd I never noticed Calli's tail."

"You probably just forgot about it, Gram." Frankie looked at her sympathetically.

"So maybe it's not broken. Is a kinked tail common?" Madeline asked.

"Perhaps Frances is right and I am losing my memory."

"I'm glad you're finally admitting it," Nancy said, walking unsteadily toward them. She drained her martini glass and waved it in the air. "Bartender! Another round for my friends! Drinks are on the house."

"You've had enough," Mrs. Lawrence said.

"If you think so, then I must need another." Nancy returned to the bar and clattered through the assortment of bottles before grabbing one at random. She put down the shallow martini glass, grabbed a tumbler and then splashed two inches of scotch into it.

Frankie watched nervously. "Take it easy, Mom."

"Siding against me, sweetie?" Nancy took a gulp and shuddered. She ate a few small pretzels in a bowl at the bar. "Would you deny me fortification to get through another evening in this creepy old place?"

Brad glanced over, annoyed at the loud voice. "Slow down, Nance."

With a defiant toss of the head, Nancy finished her drink then began dancing, kicking her legs in the air while humming. "I haven't had so much fun in this house since... since never!"

Frankie cringed. "I hate when she gets like this."

"Do you, daughter dear? Then leave! This is one little mother who's going to have a good time tonight. Otherwise? Boooorrrrrrring!" Nancy dropped onto a couch.

Frank looked at his wife. "Maybe we should have an early dinner."

Daphne walked in. "I read an article that says time is the only way to sober up. It takes a certain number of hours for the alcohol to leave your system. Maybe if she'd eaten before drinking, the food would've slowed the absorption. But afterwards won't do anything. Except maybe make her throw up."

"Thanks for the 4-1-1." Frankie tipped an imaginary hat.

"Frances Jane. Nobody likes a smart-aleck." Nancy struggled to her feet. "Isn't that right, Frank?"

With a shrug, Frank turned back to the football game.

Madeline noticed that Tommy was quietly examining the cat's tail, and hoped that he was not upset by all the tension in the air.

Mrs. Lawrence asked Madeline, "Would you get me a glass of ginger ale, please?"

"I'd be glad to." Madeline went to the wet bar and fixed the drink.

Brad opened a can of nuts and offered it. "Sorry about my sister. She's been through detox a couple of times but has no intention of sobering up. She claims a drink or two... or ten... makes life easier. But it's not easier for the rest of us."

"It must be difficult."

"She's not an alcoholic," Frankie said, grabbing a soft drink can from the small refrigerator and popping it open. "She just needs to cut back."

Daphne sat at the bar and smiled at Brad, waiting. He held up one bottle after another, offering her a drink. She finally nodded when he held up a bottle of white wine. "You're a mind reader."

"Runs in the family," Frankie muttered.

"Happy New Year!" Nancy Miller pretended to blow a party horn.

"Not yet." Brad handed his sister a glass of plain club soda. "Drink this. It'll make you feel better."

She took a suspicious sip of the water. "What is this poison? Plain fizzy water? Put something decent to give it some color. Mother always kept Chivas Regal for her darling second husband. Nothing was too good for Cyrus, right, Mother? For Patrick either!"

Mrs. Lawrence looked pained, but said nothing.

Brad held the glass of club soda below the bar and poured a tiny splash of scotch and then a bigger splash of cola into it. "Don't anybody tell her it's not Chivas Regal," he said to the girls with a wink. "Why waste the good stuff on her? In her condition, she'll never know."

"What's the cola for?" Madeline whispered.

"You are the naive one, aren't you?" Daphne lit a cigarette. "Otherwise she'd know by the color that it was a weak drink. If she's as drunk as she seems, she won't notice the taste is mostly cola."

Brad handed her an ashtray, seeming happy to wait on her. He gave the drink to Frankie to give her mother.

"Tonight, everybody!" Nancy clapped her hands for attention. "Listen to me, everybody! Where's Luke? Go find Luke," she added to Frankie, taking the drink.

"What for?"

Tommy looked up from the cat. "I like Luke." He dashed for the door.

Madeline caught him up and swung him in the air. "Hey. Stay with me, okay? Someone else can find Luke."

"Why do you want Luke?" Brad asked his sister.

Nancy held up the glass, admired the dark amber color and took a long drink. "That's more like it, bro'!"

Daphne shot Madeline an amused look as if to say, *See? I told you.*

Mrs. Lawrence sagged, clearly distressed by all the undertones. "Why do you want Luke, Nancy?"

"He'll do a seance. And we'll finally find out if my other bro' – Patrick– has gone to his just reward." She giggled and took another swallow. "I hope so. Then I'll get MY just reward! Whee!"

In the stunned silence, Brad slowly clapped his hands in mock applause. "Dear sister, I would advise you to limit your intake of alcohol henceforth. It does indiscreet things to your tongue."

Nancy finished her drink in a long gulp, then belched. "At least I'm honest!"

"What about those things you told me, Mother?" Frankie stepped closer. "About how sad it is my Uncle Patrick is still missing. I believed you. Stupid me. Wow, you really wish he's dead."

With a sway, Nancy sat abruptly.

"Frances Jane. Apologize to your mother!" Frank hurried to the couch and sat beside his wife, putting an arm around her shoulder as if to present a solidified front to their child.

"No one asks her to apologize for her version of the truth. Why do I have to apologize for mine? Just because you're too blind to see, Daddy–"

"That's enough, young lady. Please remember that we are not alone."

Nancy started crying noisily.

"Is that all you two care about?" Frankie looked at his angry face, and then at her mother. "What kind of impression we make?"

"Here's Luke," Madeline whispered to Mrs. Lawrence. "Maybe he can help."

"Luke!" Nancy struggled to get up.

Everyone turned to stare as the young man walked in to join them. His amiable smile changed to wary puzzlement when he saw all eyes were on him.

"Mother wants another seance," Frankie said.

"Count me out." Luke held his hands up in a staying motion. "I don't want to take the risk again so soon. And not here."

"Why not here?" Brad asked. "I'll have to admit Nancy does have the right idea, even if she did express herself crudely. Don't you agree, Mother?"

Mrs. Lawrence seemed drained, but she rallied to reply. "Yes, Brad. I do agree. I would like to get the answers I seek."

"But Aunt Agatha," Luke said, hurrying to her side, "you can't mean that. You know the danger–"

"It's the only way I can be sure about Patrick." She looked around the room, letting her gaze rest on her two children and her son-in-law, grouped by the couch. "And isn't that what you want? For me to be sure he's dead? If I get proof that he is, I will rewrite my will, just as you wish." She sighed, defeated.

Madeline frowned, drawn into the family drama despite her resolve not to get involved in their lives and problems.

She looked at Tommy, and saw he was watching everyone with wide eyes. He was tugging the hair at the back of his head, something he only did when he was nervous or upset. This wasn't the type of scene she wanted him to witness at this young age but she'd waited too long to leave.

The damage, if any, had been done. She would explain later to him that some families argue a lot, and they don't always handle things the right way.

"I'm not doing another seance." Luke shook his head. "What happened last night might have been caused by evil spirits in this house. I don't want to find out what they'll do if I ignore the warning.

"If you won't do it," Frankie said, "then I will."

"I forbid it," her father said.

Frankie looked at him a moment and let the silence stretch. "Seance, anyone?"

TWENTY-ONE

"Don't be a fool." Luke grabbed Frankie's arm as she started to leave the room. "If I think it's too dangerous for me – and I've been doing sittings for over ten years – can't you see how foolish it would be for you? You've never even gone into a trance!"

"Always the first time." She broke free.

"Listen to him," Brad said. "Be realistic, Frankie."

"You saw how I looked when things went wrong last night, Frankie." Luke sighed. "You said I looked dead, or in a coma. And you said you'd never been so scared. But now you want to take a chance the same thing will happen to you?"

"It won't."

"How can you be so sure?" Madeline asked, then fell silent, knowing she should stay out of a family quarrel.

"I said I'd do it," Frankie said, looking around the room as if trying to marshal support, or perhaps defying anyone to contradict her. "And I will."

Luke touched her arm gently. "No one will criticize you for changing your mind. It would be the smart thing to do. Too many things can go wrong."

Nancy Miller announced, "I'm going to be sick."

Her husband leaped. He got his hands beneath her arms and tried to pull her up, but she was a dead weight. He called to Brad, "Give me a hand, will you? She's a ton of bricks."

Together the two men hustled Nancy out of the room.

Mrs. Lawrence ran a hand over her brow, as if trying to compose her anguish. "Why don't the rest of us go into dinner? Brad and Frank can join us. No doubt Nancy will want to skip this meal." When no one moved, she said, "I asked Rosa to prepare her famous corn chowder. We'll start with a bowl of that."

Madeline picked up Tommy. "We'll wash up and be right there."

When she entered the dining room with her son a little later, Jason Malone was there, replacing the electric switch plate. The cat was curled around the toolbox, dozing. Jason did not appear interested in the dinner party.

"Did you find that short in the chandelier?" Mrs. Lawrence asked, stopping her wheelchair next to Jason.

"Must've been the storm."

Madeline couldn't help noticing that he didn't look at his employer when he spoke. He didn't smile. He didn't stop what he was doing to converse with her. When he finished his task, he bent to collect his tools.

The cat started to follow Jason out of the room, but when Tommy asked if the cat could have dinner with him, Mrs. Lawrence snapped her fingers and the cat turned. To her surprise, the cat continued after Jason.

Mrs. Lawrence frowned. "Well, that's odd. Since when does Calli snub me!" Laughing, she turned to Tommy. "We've been 'dissed' by the cat."

"Why is your nurse trying to fix the electricity?" Daphne asked the old woman.

"He's not a nurse. I hired him as a handyman to keep up repairs around the house and help with heavy work that's too much for Rosa."

"But then he ended up as your attendant?" Madeline asked, buttering a roll for Tommy. "That's quite a leap, isn't it?"

"My aunt is notorious for strange leaps." Luke grinned.

Frankie looked up from her soup, interested.

Madeline was glad to see the teenager had dropped the notion of conducting a seance by herself. It looked like Luke had managed to convince the girl it was a bad idea. She hoped no one would be thoughtless enough to bring up the subject.

Now that Frankie had calmed and was showing interest in other topics, it would be a shame to get her excited by mentioning her threat to play at being a medium.

"Just to clarify," Mrs. Lawrence said, "Jason is not my nurse or personal attendant in the way most people mean that. I can take care of myself and my own needs. But it's comforting to have a strong man around if I were to fall out of bed or need carrying."

"Notice how she diverted us from Frankie's question." Luke went around the table, pouring wine or mineral water depending on each guest's preference.

"What Luke means about the strange leaps," Mrs. Lawrence said, "is that I've been known to literally leap when I see a ghost."

"Ghost?" Tommy craned to see the woman.

Madeline squeezed his arm reassuringly.

"But–" Frankie began, staring at her grandmother's wheelchair. "You can leap?"

The older woman ran her fingers lightly over the tops of the wheels at either side of her frail body. "I used to. Now I jump up in my mind."

"Sorry, Gram. Didn't mean to remind you that you can't walk."

"Remind me? It's something I've lived with for two years, but each morning it is still a surprise that I can't get out of bed and stand up."

Madeline spoke without thinking. "Mrs. Lawrence, you told me that your late husband has communicated with you. Is he the gho–" She broke off abruptly, recalling Tommy's presence. To her son, she said, "Why don't you finish your dinner in the kitchen with Rosa?"

"I like it here."

"But–" Madeline faltered. She hated to use the phrase "Because I said so" but she didn't want her son to be exposed to another discussion about ghosts. It wasn't fair to the adults to avoid the topic to protect Tommy when the obvious solution was to remove him from the conversation.

"Hey, Tommy," Luke said. "When I was in the kitchen, Rosa was trying to figure out what to do about dessert. She baked a carrot cake this morning, but she didn't know if it's a good idea to serve it or not. But maybe you don't care about dessert. You probably can't give her any advice."

Tommy slid off his chair and wriggled underneath it to get out. "Mommy, can I eat in the kitchen? Please?"

Amused, she took him to Rosa.

Upon returning to the dining room, she said to Luke, "Thanks. I don't know how you do it, but you always seem to know the right thing to say." She smiled warmly at him and sat down.

Glancing across the room, her eyes met Mrs. Lawrence.

She saw the expression of surprise in the older woman's gaze, and remembered all at once that she was supposed to hate Luke. She looked at her plate, troubled that she was so easily swayed. All it took was a nice gesture on his part, and she was in love with him again. With effort she steeled her heart against him, reminding herself of the facts Jason had told her.

As the meal progressed, Luke chatted easily about a wide range of subjects, and Madeline decided she could see through his hypocrisy. Of course he had to be nice to everyone! If he was going to kill Mrs. Lawrence and get away with it, he couldn't let anyone suspect that he had murder in his cold heart. He had to play the game cleverly. But she wouldn't be fooled again.

She dug into the creamed scallops with more fury than the delicate dish required.

"Should we get back to what you were saying about ghosts, Madeline, before you took Tommy out of the room?" Mrs. Lawrence asked, amused.

Madeline stared blankly. She'd forgotten that she had been mid-sentence when she left for the kitchen, and that had been fifteen minutes ago. Everyone must think she was an air head. Quickly picking up her prior train of thought, she said, "I was curious if your husband is the ghost you were referring to when you said that ghosts make you leap, or if there have been others."

"He has appeared to me on a number of occasions since his passing."

"Cool." Frankie was impressed.

"Mother, you're not going to start that business again, are you?" Brad looked at her in disapproval. "The doctor agreed it was a case of hallucination brought on by the heart medication you were taking at the time."

"Doctors don't know everything. I know what I saw. Hallucinations do not speak."

Madeline frowned to herself, recalling that Mrs. Lawrence had confided that Cyrus had not yet appeared to her as promised. She wondered why the old woman was lying but decided it would be best to go along with the story. "But you had your stroke after he died, right? And yet earlier you said you leap at the sight of ghosts. So that means there are other ghosts, ones that appeared to you before your stroke. Right?"

"Trust Nervous Nelly to be afraid of ghosts."

Madeline looked across the table at Daphne, and controlled the urge to say something sarcastic. "I didn't say I'm afraid."

"And I suppose you're not, Daphne?" Frankie waved her arms wildly in the air and shouted, "Boo!" then laughed when Daphne jumped, startled.

"Enough, Frances," Mrs. Lawrence said, the corners of her mouth twitching with a repressed smile. To Madeline she said, "I have also seen Calico's ghost. The last occasion was a few months ago."

"But Calli isn't dead," Madeline said. "Unless you believe every cat has nine lives."

"Not this Calico," Frankie said.

"Oh, right. I forgot there have been more than one with the same name. But didn't it startle you to see ghosts?"

"Startling," Mrs. Lawrence agreed, "but a welcome message that brings comfort."

"How many times have you seen a ghost, Luke?" Daphne leaned closer to him. "I bet you're never afraid."

"You've never seen fear until you've seen my face after I've seen a ghost. Ghost hunters agree. Each time is like the first. It never gets to be so ordinary that you take it for granted."

Madeline noticed that he didn't respond to Daphne's question about the number of times he'd had ghostly encounters. She wondered if it was a large number.

"Say, Madeline," Frankie called out. "Did you ever figure out what your grandmother's message meant last night?"

"That thing about a duel? No, it's meaningless."

"Maybe it is a warning for a future event, and it will make sense to you one day." Mrs. Lawrence rang the bell for Rosa.

Luke looked at Madeline. "You're not convinced."

Rosa came in to clear the table, with Tommy helping as he was able. Seeing her son in the room, Madeline was careful to sound ambiguous. "But if it's something to do with a later event, why appear a couple of hours later with another warning? Either the whole thing is a fake or the messages are related."

"I'm tired of talking about G-H-O-S-T-S all the time," Daphne said, with a smirk for Madeline. She tousled Tommy's hair as he passed her. "It's odd that Madeline is the only one who got a message. Don't you agree? She's a stranger. And the whole point was to find out about Patrick."

"We need a seance," Frankie said quietly.

Her father came in, carrying a tray with the remnants of his meal on it. Earlier Brad had explained that Nancy was in bed and Frank planned to have dinner on a tray with her. Now he glared at his daughter as he set the tray on the table. "Forget it."

"You don't know what you're talking about!"

Trying to be helpful and offer Frankie support, Madeline said to Frank, "We were rehashing last night's message, trying to make sense of it."

"Keep out of this," Frank said. "It's a family matter. You have no business even being here."

"Frank." Mrs. Lawrence voice was firm and steady. "She is here at my request. And I will thank you to treat her politely."

Without speaking, the short man dipped his head toward Madeline in a gesture that could be taken as an apology, no matter how grudging.

"As a matter of fact," Mrs. Lawrence said, "you should all know that I have invited Madeline and her son to stay."

Tommy looked at his mother curiously.

Madeline felt dismayed, wishing that the older woman hadn't said anything. She could sense all eyes on her, in varying degrees of interest and distrust.

Brad gave her a cool look. "Fast work," he said *sotto voce*.

Mrs. Lawrence went on, blithely unaware of the reaction building in the room. "I hope they'll come and live here with me. And I plan to include her in my will!" She beamed at Madeline.

TWENTY-TWO

The big old house was still and quiet. Madeline had grown accustomed to the various creaks and other noises. The steady rain continued, part of the background soundtrack. She finished tucking Tommy into bed and kissed him good night.

She felt bone-tired and even though it was earlier than her usual bedtime, she decided to turn in now. Maybe the bedside light wouldn't bother Tommy if she angled it away from him. She'd borrowed a novel from Mrs. Lawrence's extensive library earlier, and was looking forward to starting it.

Perhaps the book would take her mind off not only the question as to why she had chosen to stay instead of getting Brad or Frank to drive her and Tommy home, as had been her avowed plan, but also the unpleasant scene in the dining room following Mrs. Lawrence's announcement.

Brad had let Madeline know his opinion that she was a gold digger. No one paid attention when she said she was as surprised as they were to hear she'd be in Mrs. Lawrence's will, even though the older woman agreed it was news to Madeline.

"I'm sorry I said anything," Mrs. Lawrence had said afterwards. "I had not planned to." Her eyes pleaded with Madeline to understand and forgive.

Madeline knew it would not be fair to punish her hostess. If their places were reversed, she too might have reacted to Frank's rudeness with an outburst.

After trying the light by the bed and finding it too bright, she decided to track down a spare lamp or a lower wattage bulb in one of the vacant rooms. She tiptoed toward the door. A floorboard squeaked.

"Where are you going?" Tommy sat up.

"Shh, honey. Go back to sleep. I want to get a reading light. I'll be back in a sec."

He yawned. "Going downstairs?"

"Maybe. But if you're going to ask for another dessert, forget it. You had too much already."

"Rosa said I can have more *manana*. I want my Christmas ball."

She went back to him, abandoning the need to tiptoe. She smoothed the covers around his shoulders. "Where did you leave it?"

"Downstairs."

"I figured that. Which room?"

"Dunno," he mumbled drowsily, closing his eyes.

She smiled, turned off the light and left.

The hallway was vacant but adequately lit and so it was not until she was partway down the stairs that she remembered she would need a flashlight or candle and matches. But since she had neither, she'd have to rely on memory and groping to find light switches. The stairs grew dim the further she went from the upstairs hall light.

At the bottom of the stairs, she was glad to see a triangle of light coming from a partly open door in the near distance. She wondered idly who the other night owl might be. The house was so silent that she'd assumed everyone was asleep or tucked in.

She felt a chill draft, and knotted the borrowed robe tighter, grateful now for its bulky warmth. Recalling that she'd last seen the crystal ball in the living room, she headed in that direction and realized that's where the light was on.

Stopping short of entering, she heard voices and crept closer. The wide hallway was furnished only with a few paintings on the high walls. There were no plants or credenzas she could duck behind if someone came, and in any case that position would be hard to explain.

When her glance rested on the closed door next to the living room, she quickly opened it and slipped inside. Recalling that the room had tables and chairs set up as if for card games, she gingerly moved forward in the dark, afraid of making a telltale noise.

Each time she brushed against a chair or table, she steadied it to avoid making noise, and kept moving toward the wall shared with the living room.

At the wall, she pressed an ear against the paneling. She could hear everything Brad, Frank and Luke were saying. They were the only three voices she distinguished, and after a moment of listening, she doubted that Frankie, Daphne and Nancy were silently in the room.

"You have to help us, Luke." It was Frank Miller's voice, close to panic.

"I should have walked out as soon as I realized what you two were up to."

"Nancy's in on it, too," Brad said, "and let's keep it in the family."

"I wondered how long it would take you to get around to her."

Madeline frowned, and listened more intently, but the men seemed to be walking away from the wall.

"Get her out of the picture and keep her out," Frank said. "She's trouble."

Brad said something Madeline couldn't understand.

Luke said, "I saw your faces when Aunt Agatha said she's putting her in the will."

So they were talking about her.

"Incompetent action," Brad said. "We can use that in court, if needed."

"Contesting a will could get expensive," Luke said.

"Worth it," Frank put in. "We can't let her pick up strays and leave her money to them."

"Or to the cat," Brad added.

"Think what the money could mean for Frances when it's time for college. We've got an eye on an Ivy League name for her."

Madeline tried to stretch without moving her ear from the wall. It was uncomfortable standing, but she had to hear what else they said. She sat on the floor and leaned against the wall. It was an easier position to maintain.

Hopefully, Tommy would not awaken and come in search of her and the "Christmas" ball. He'd give away her listening post in a shrill cry of "Found you!" as if they were playing hide-and-seek.

She pressed her ear to the wall again.

Luke was talking. "… when she's eighteen, so that means you've already decided Aunt Agatha will die and leave you money within the next two or three years. Since when are you psychic, Frank?"

"She's old and sick," Brad said. "Don't make a big deal. Frank was talking off the top of his head."

"Or else one of you – at least – is planning to speed up her departure."

Madeline held back a gasp. She closed her eyes tightly, trying to send Luke an ESP message to be more careful.

"I don't mind letting Mother Nature take the reins," Brad said smoothly. "What I do object to is sharing with more people than I have to."

"Why should we have to divvie it up more than necessary!" Frank's voice was heated and the volume went up. He giggled nervously. "Not that I begrudge you two your shares."

"Stop laughing," Brad said. "You're getting on my nerves."

Madeline listened hard for Luke's response, but he made none. It was frustrating, not being able to see their facial expressions. Was Luke too angry to speak? Or perhaps he was amused by Frank's greed. After all, he was no stranger to these men, and had no doubt heard their talk before.

She was tempted to sneak into the hall and watch through the crack in the living room door, but it was a momentary impulse and she saw the danger in it.

She shifted her weight carefully, trying to get more comfortable, thankful she didn't have on earrings that might make a sound. She recollected the time she tried to eavesdrop at that locked door on the third floor, and her earring had scraped, making a loud noise. It was hard to believe she'd been here three nights now, and had sunk so low as to eavesdrop on the people who had a right to be here, by virtue of being related to Mrs. Lawrence.

"I don't think Aunt Agatha was serious about including Madeline in the will." Luke's voice was fainter than before. "Anyone else for brandy?"

The sounds of glasses and bottles rattling at the wet bar came to her, and she hoped they wouldn't stay there long. Their voices were harder to hear.

"She's not the main concern," Brad said. "Or at least not mine."

Frank said, "It's Patrick."

"Aunt Agatha said she's willing to split his share as soon as she has proof he is dead and not MIA."

"It's been seven years and we haven't heard a word," Frank said. "What else can he be?"

"A prisoner of war," Luke said. "Or disabled mentally."

"Amnesia?" Brad said scornfully.

Madeline nodded. That was one of her own theories.

"It can't hurt to leave him in the will," Luke said. "If he's dead, he can't inherit. He never married so the money would go to the other heirs."

"But what if he's alive?" Frank asked.

"If you have him declared legally dead, and then he turns up," Luke said, "the court would have to reverse that decision."

"Granted," Brad said, with a long pause. "But we don't know that he's not married."

Madeline visualized him sipping brandy as if the camera was on him for a commercial.

"But moneywise," Brad continued, "he'd be out in the cold as far as the will goes. We wouldn't have to share if he's not in it."

"And you'd do that to your own brother." Luke sounded disgusted.

"My half-brother. You were just a kid when he left for Iraq. You can't possibly remember."

"There was a big farewell party here," Luke said. "A couple of people kept bugging me to make a prediction about what would happen to him in the war."

"But you wouldn't do it." Frank spoke with derision.

Madeline wondered if Frank had been one of the people who urged Luke to make a prediction. If not, then he might have been behind the scenes, getting others to ask on his behalf. That was more his style.

"It's what he did to my wife," Brad said.

"His second wife," Frank corrected.

Luke asked, "What did Patrick do to Melanie that you're still so bitter all these years later?"

"He raped her! And then he told her that I put him up to it. Told her other lies about me." Brad sounded broken. "He destroyed my marriage. She never believed in my love again."

Madeline grew tense waiting in the silence. She didn't dare leave the room until they went upstairs. If she walked into the hall now, she took the chance that one or more of the men might come out and see her on the stairs.

She didn't want anyone to find out she had overheard this sadly personal conversation.

"What's the verdict, Luke?" Brad's voice was back to his normal persuasiveness.

"There's no danger," Frank said. "Fake a trance. Then imitate that Stephen guy."

"I don't know what he sounds like."

Madeline frowned, knowing Luke was lying. He was looking for excuses. Although Luke never remembered what happened during his trances, she knew about the recordings.

He could play the latest one to hear Stephen's accent.

"Listen to your recording," Frank said, as if he'd read Madeline's mind. "Practice the guy's Southern accent, and then say that Patrick is there with the happy spirits and sends love and hugs to his dear mummy."

Brad said something Madeline couldn't hear.

"And then you'll drop it?" Luke asked.

"There's no reason a seance has to be at night, is there?" Brad asked, coming closer to the wall.

Madeline nervously backed off, then pressed her ear to the wall again. She heard a glass being set down loudly on a table, and then nothing more.

After a moment's confusion, she realized they were walking out of the room together now that the main issue had been settled, possibly with nods and a hand shake.

She got up and sped toward the door, listening for their voices in the hall. She was shocked that Luke had agreed to their deception. Now she could believe the things Jason had told her about him. Before this, she'd been ambivalent. But no longer.

In a moment, she heard the men passing, talking quietly and then going upstairs, no doubt to their separate rooms. She waited a couple of minutes, with time passing slowly in the dark, then turned the doorknob and left stealthily, fearing she'd be discovered after all.

But to her relief, the hall was empty.

Her eyes were accustomed to the dark, so it was not a problem that they had turned off the living room lights. There was no light in the hallway, either, but she knew the way to the stairs and headed in that direction without mishap.

She was halfway up the stairs, moving toward the glow of the upstairs hall lights, when she remembered that her original errand had been to get a reading lamp and Tommy's "Christmas" ball.

As she hesitated, deciding she might as well give up the idea of reading and get the ball in the morning, she heard footsteps approach the stairs from below. In a panic, she noticed how much further she'd have to go to get to the top of the stairs and scurry to Tommy's room. She might not make it in time. Or she might make too much noise.

Apparently only two of the men had gone upstairs. She'd be discovered by the third.

Thinking fast, she turned and started walking down, not trying to be quiet. She mentally rehearsed her story. She was on the way downstairs to get the lamp and the crystal ball. No one but Tommy knew how long ago she'd left on that errand, and he was not the best judge of time anyway.

No one would suspect she'd already been downstairs... eavesdropping, yet again.

The sound of heavy footsteps continued to advance up the stairs.

Decided to be completely aboveboard about her mission to get a reading lamp, she called out, "Hello? Somebody there?"

No one answered.

"Hey, come on," she said, forcing a brave laugh. "Is that you, Jason, trying to spook me out again?"

The steps came closer.

She stopped on the stairs, and stood stock still, straining to see who it was in the dark.

The steps came nearer, and nearer.

"Who is it?" she asked, whispering.

And then the steps passed by her.

Madeline whimpered.

There was no one on the stairs except her.

The phantom footsteps continued upwards.

She stood there a long time, in the solitude, too shaken to move in either direction. And then she snapped.

TWENTY-THREE

"What was all that screaming about last night?" Daphne asked, coming in to breakfast late. She looked stunning in a white tunic with plum leggings and boots. Taking her customary cup of black coffee, she sat at a corner of the table and lit a cigarette, using her saucer as an ashtray.

"You mean something actually woke up the princess?" Frankie asked, amazed. "You didn't join us on the stairs so I assumed you slept through it."

"Madeline saw a ghost." Brad rolled his eyes.

"Heard one," Frankie corrected.

"Another ghost?" Daphne smiled tautly. "Aren't you the lucky one."

This time, Madeline had come into the dining room prepared for a discussion about ghosts, knowing it was inevitable. She'd already deposited Tommy in the kitchen with Rosa, and more importantly the "Christmas" ball she'd found in the living room.

The housekeeper was already working on individual pot pies to serve the party for lunch, and had good-naturedly told Tommy she needed his help in rolling the dough. Rosa had winked at Madeline and shooed her off to eat breakfast.

"Next time," Madeline said to Daphne, "I'll ask the ghost to wait for you."

"Any more messages from your dear departed grandmother?"

"Not that kind of ghost this time." Frankie enjoyed her superior knowledge.

"I suppose you saw it, too?"

"Nothing to see," Madeline said. "I'm sorry I disturbed everyone's sleep. I hope you'll forgive me?"

She glanced around the table. Mrs. Lawrence smiled at her, but seemed bemused.

"You said there was a ghost." Daphne ground out her cigarette. "I don't appreciate being lied to."

"She heard one, Daphne. How many times do I have to say it?" Frankie glared at her. "Heard a ghost! Like with these things called ears." She flapped her earlobes. "Footsteps on the stairs. In the dark. Nobody there. Not even feet." She shuddered involuntarily. "Glad I wasn't there."

"Then how are you such an expert on what happened?" Daphne looked at the others. "So Madeline screams and tells you she heard a ghost walking on the stairs and everybody gets all excited." She made a dismissive scoffing noise.

Now that it was morning and Madeline was safely surrounded by lights, people and normal everyday noises, it was hard for her to recapture the terror she'd experienced the night before. It seemed now to have been a bad dream. She recalled being so afraid she couldn't move.

Luke had reassured her that happened to even the most seasoned ghost hunters and psychics, at least sometimes, but thinking about the event made her uneasy. She wished she could go home and put it behind her, along with the nagging suspicion that she'd actually imagined the footsteps.

Daphne watched her in amusement. "Isn't it strange that the ghosts are only interested in Madeline?"

"Jealous?" Frankie asked.

Madeline darted her a look, wondering briefly if the teenager had read her thoughts. There was enough tension here without adding fuel to the fire.

With a meaningful glance toward Luke, Daphne said to Madeline, "You're clever to use that kind of bait."

Brad laughed. "I already suggested that." He got up and refilled his plate from the serving dishes on the buffet.

"That's a rotten thing to say," Frankie said.

"You don't even know what we're talking about." Daphne crossed her long legs.

"What are you talking about?" Frank Miller asked, baffled. "Is someone going fishing in this kind of weather? Forecast is for more rain into next week."

Luke turned to Madeline. "Don't let them upset you. Just because you didn't see anything doesn't mean you imagined what you heard. Manifestations can be aural without being visual."

"Thanks for taking her side." Daphne gave him a long, measured look.

"I didn't know there were sides," Luke said, then addressed the table. "It's normal for ghosts to make an appearance when only one person is around. That's what makes it hard to verify a haunting. Difficult to get witnesses, though it can be done."

Frankie looked up from her plate. "How?"

"Don't start, Frances Jane," her father said. "Finish your breakfast. I promised your mother you'd go sit with her."

Nancy Miller was still feeling unwell and had declined coming down to eat with the others. The housekeeper had taken up a tray of hot lemon tea and buttered toast but came back moments later with it untouched, and a message that Mrs. Miller didn't want anything.

"Oh, Daddy! Why do I always have to leave when things get interesting?"

Daphne got up. "I've had a few hangovers. I know to tiptoe and talk softly."

Frank seemed mortified by the open discussion of his wife's drinking. "She's probably picked up a stomach bug. But you don't have to expose yourself to it, Daphne. It's Frances Jane's responsibility. Her mother is looking forward to the visit."

Madeline didn't realize she'd said anything, but since everyone was staring she knew that she'd snorted in disbelief.

"See, Daddy? Even Madeline agrees. It's ridiculous to say Mother even knows I'm alive and in the same house with her."

"I never said all that–" Madeline began, then dropped it. Nancy had displayed no maternal joy whatsoever, and Madeline couldn't imagine she'd welcome seeing her daughter when her head was pounding with a hangover. She wondered why Frank wanted the teen girl out of the room.

"It's no trouble," Daphne said. "The change of conversation would be refreshing." With that barbed comment aimed in Madeline's direction, she sauntered out.

"Don't mind her," Frankie said to Madeline, whispering. "She's jealous because Luke pays more attention to you. I bet she wishes you'd drop dead."

Madeline blanched. She started to reply, but felt it would be better to ignore what Frankie had just said.

"Well, my dears," Mrs. Lawrence said, "here we are at December thirty-first. Where did this year fly away to? What say you to planning this evening's festivities? We can't let the new year come in unheralded." She pushed a button and her wheelchair backed away from the table.

"I should get home," Madeline said, knowing she should have done this much sooner. "Maybe someone could drive me? And I'll arrange for a mechanic after the holidays are over."

"Nonsense! You're one of us now," Mrs. Lawrence said. "Anyone who can see ghosts is a welcome addition to this oddball family. Besides, you can imagine how much squabbling there'd be without you here as a buffer."

Frankie looked at Madeline pleadingly. She mouthed, "Please stay!"

Madeline nodded. "But you must let me help if there's to be a party tonight."

Mrs. Lawrence smiled. "It looks like everyone's finished eating, so let's go in the card room and start planning. Maybe we could do tarot readings to see what the coming year holds in store for each of us."

"Or," Brad said as if it was a spur-of-the-moment idea, "how about another seance? The first one wasn't completely successful, but it wasn't a total disaster. Madeline did get a message, and Luke's 'Stephen' seemed eager to help. Let's go for it!"

Madeline intercepted the nodding glance shared by Brad and Frank. She quickly looked to see Luke's expression but his back was turned.

She wondered if that was deliberate, but then remembered that, even when she was screaming about ghostly footsteps, she'd retained her presence of mind and firmly established the story that she was heading downstairs to get a reading lamp when she had encountered the unearthly nightwalker. They didn't know she'd overheard their secret conversation in the living room.

So Luke had nothing to hide from her, at least from his viewpoint.

After checking on her son, who was happily patting strips of pastry with his hands, Madeline joined the others in the card room. She couldn't help a nervous glance at the wall where she had eavesdropped last night on Brad, Frank and Luke.

Perhaps the ghostly encounter immediately afterwards had been a not-so-subtle injunction to stay in bed where she was supposed to be, instead of wandering around the house.

With a measure of relief, she pulled up a chair and became part of the group, chiding herself for believing the old adage that there's safety in numbers. After what Luke had said about ghosts usually visiting a solitary person, she decided to keep with the others as much as possible from now on.

Tomorrow was the start of a new year. A new beginning for her and Tommy. And soon they would be putting fifty miles between themselves and the misadventures here.

She had no intention of living here, no matter how much money Mrs. Lawrence might tempt her with. Not with ghosts wandering freely.

A chill washed over her as she thought about Tommy hearing footsteps or seeing a ghostly apparition. She would not subject him to such things, and to stay here would be to risk just that.

Frankie touched Madeline's arm, startling her. "Jason is in the hall. Wants to see you."

"Tell him to come in," Mrs. Lawrence said. "We don't stand on formality here."

"Since when?" Frankie said. "Anybody got gum? I'll go nuts if I don't find some. Can't believe my dear mother forgot to pack it."

Madeline realized that was a good excuse for leaving, and finding out what Jason wanted as well. "There might be some in Tommy's backpack. I'll go up and see."

She found Jason Malone leaning against the balustrade. With a glance back toward the open door and the voices discussing what to do tonight, she said in a low voice, "You wanted to see me?"

"Yeah. Report."

"Pardon me?"

He looked at her impatiently. "What did you find out from Luke?"

"I haven't had a chance to talk to him alone."

"Better find time. If he kills my– Mrs. Lawrence, it'll be your fault."

"Did you follow me up the stairs last night in the dark? From the first floor to the second?"

"I heard about your ghost. Wasn't me." He patted himself all over. "See? Solid mass."

As he started to leave, she hurried after him. "Wait. I... I did learn something. I don't want anything bad to happen to Mrs. Lawrence."

"Haven't got all day to gossip."

The cat strolled by, then returned and rubbed against his legs. He picked up the cat and stroked her. The animal purred contentedly.

"The others are planning a seance for later, but it's going to be a fake to say that her son Patrick is dead, so she'll stop waiting for him to turn up."

"And then they'll get her to change her will," he said. "She can do it without a lawyer. A holographic will–"

"I know what that is. You write the will by hand and sign it. That's legal. But she'd probably want to see her lawyer, make it official. With that arthritis of hers, I bet it's hard to do much writing."

"Brad's a lawyer," Jason said.

"He's an actor."

"A man of many talents. As soon as she writes Patrick out of the will?" He made a wringing motion with his hands.

She unconsciously touched her throat. "You're her attendant. Be her bodyguard. Prevent it."

"You can help."

Their heads drew closer as their voices dropped to the barest whisper.

"She'll never believe me if I warn her," Madeline said. "And then she'd be terrified of every noise and shadow. We have to protect her without her knowing."

"Stop the seance."

"Stall? Okay, I get it. They won't try to kill her until she rewrites her will to omit Patrick. As long as she thinks he's alive, then she's safe from them." Madeline looked at him, wanting confirmation that she was on the right track.

"Good for you." There was no praise in his voice. He walked away, toward the kitchen.

For a moment, Madeline was afraid for her son. Then she relaxed. It wasn't Jason she had to watch out for now. Tommy was safe with him. It was those others.

I'm battling The Unholy Trio, Madeline realized.

Brad. Frank. And Luke. Especially Luke. He was the one with the power to set their wicked plan into action, and therefore, he was the most dangerous.

TWENTY-FOUR

As soon as she had settled Tommy for a short nap, Madeline returned downstairs. There had been no further discussion of another seance, at least not that she was aware of, so she felt safe in pursuing an errand of her own. In repayment for Mrs. Lawrence's hospitality, she'd decided to make the woman a needlepoint cushion for the back of her wheelchair.

She went into the library and pulled out the oversized art book she remembering seeing there. Flipping idly through the pages, she sought inspiration for a design to use. It would be fun to start a new project, even though she'd just be working out the preliminary needlework chart that would show her what color yarn to use in each square of the needlepoint canvas.

Perhaps getting involved with such a soothing and engrossing pastime as selecting colors and patterns would relieve some of the pressure she had felt ever since Jason placed the burden of keeping Mrs. Lawrence safe squarely on her shoulders.

"What're you doing?" Frankie asked, wandering in, eating a cupcake.

"I couldn't help noticing how utilitarian your grandmother's wheelchair is. And yet throughout the house, you can see how much she loves and admires things of beauty. So I'm going to stitch a needlepoint cushion for her to lean against. I'll sew on tabs so it will hang from the back of her wheelchair and won't slip down."

"Hey, that's cool. Gram'll love it. You're really thoughtful, aren't you?"

"She's been very nice to me and my son. There's got to be a motif that would have more meaning to her than the typical flowers." She closed the art book and put it back on the shelf. "Do you know if your grandmother has any hobbies that might inspire me?"

"Horoscopes and stuff like that." Frankie sat in a reading chair and swung her legs over one arm. "Do a zodiac design."

"I was thinking of a simpler design that won't take too long to create."

"How about a picture of Calli? She loves that cat."

"She's already got a cat portrait." Madeline thought of The Calico Tapestry which had drawn her into this morass in the first place.

"Sorry I butted in." Frankie swung her legs around and started to get up. "Nobody ever likes my ideas."

"That's not true, and you know it. I need your help. Let's brainstorm."

Grudgingly, Frankie stayed, and they bandied ideas back and forth. None sparked an idea which excited Madeline until Frankie said, "I still think she'd like something to do with cats. What about that old poem? You know the one I mean?"

Madeline shook her head.

"About the calico cat. And some dog. The checkered dog?" Frankie shrugged.

"Wait! I know the poem you mean. My grandmother taught it to me when I was a little girl."

"Yeah, me too. I guess it's a tradition for grandmothers! They haven't changed the curriculum in a long time."

"I'm not that much older than you are." Madeline laughed good-naturedly. "Let's see if your grandmother has any poetry books. She doesn't have a computer or we could look it up quickly. But the old-fashioned way will have to suffice."

They scanned the bookshelves for poetry books.

"I think it starts off 'The gingham dog and the calico cat...'," Madeline said, "but I don't remember what comes next."

Giving up, Madeline sat with another art book and paged through it. "I was looking forward to starting the drawing now. I'm not usually this lazy all day, every day. Then I'd transfer it to a blank canvas later. Obviously it's not something I can stitch today. I have to finish a project for a client and anyway I don't have the supplies with me, but–"

"Here it is!" Frankie held up an old book. "Look."

Madeline glanced at the page. "Wow! You're brilliant!"

"This book has a section in back where poems are indexed by their first line." Frankie shrugged, but the proud shining in her eyes belied the nonchalant pose.

Madeline couldn't help wondering how rarely the teenager was praised for anything. From what she'd seen, Frankie's parents were more interested in criticizing and critiquing.

"You solved the mystery," Madeline said, pointing to the poem's title: "The Duel" by Eugene Field.

Their eyes met and they couldn't stop grinning.

Madeline read the opening lines of the poem, "'The gingham dog and the calico cat, Side by side on the table sat....' No wonder her message about a duel didn't make sense. I kept thinking in terms of the Three Musketeers or pirates."

"But what does it mean?"

"I guess it means to look out for Calico. There's a cat here by that name, and there aren't any dogs. So I guess Calli will give me the next clue."

"Stephen said your grandmother didn't want to tell you anything more, in case it was too dangerous. There has to be more to it than this, Madeline. What's dangerous about a fat old pussycat who likes tummy rubs?"

"But this poem must be what my grandmother was talking about. The only thing Calli has done that could be considered a danger was leaving that mouse on my bed, but that happened before the seance. Maybe the cat is going to do something else?"

"There's plenty of mice around here, I guess. Maybe she's going to bring you another dead one."

"Even so, that isn't dangerous. Didn't you get the feeling during the seance that it was real danger and not just something creepy?"

"Maybe it doesn't have anything to do with that poem after all."

Madeline put all the books back on the shelves. "Do me a favor? Don't mention the poem to anyone. I don't need to look like a fool if we're wrong about it having anything to do with my grandmother's message."

With a shrug, Frankie agreed.

In the living room, most of the party had gathered to watch a holiday movie on the DVD player. Nancy sat stiffly in a corner of the couch, nursing a cocktail. She looked pale and weak. Suddenly she put the drink down and got up. "Daphne! I'm going to be sick again!"

The blonde groaned, but got up and hurried to help Nancy out of the room.

Frankie looked at Madeline. "I guess that stomach flu is lingering."

Madeline didn't feel it was appropriate to bring up Nancy's drinking problem. If the teen couldn't deal with it, it wasn't Madeline's responsibility to force an intervention. "I hope she gets better soon."

The teen girl coaxed Madeline into playing a game of backgammon. While Frankie set up the board, Madeline decided to talk to Mrs. Lawrence about The Calico Tapestry.

Before she could broach the subject, the older woman asked, "What do you think of Brad's idea about having another seance tonight?"

"I don't think it's a good idea."

"You don't have to attend if you are afraid of getting another personal message. By the way, did you decipher your grandmother's message about a duel?"

"Luke said it would be dangerous to do another one, after what happened. Don't you think it's unwise to take a chance that he'd have another catalepsy, or that it would last longer the second time?"

"He's exaggerating the danger to keep Frankie from trying it. We could set up a screen around him, to protect him from flying objects. Or we could take insurance to make sure that wouldn't happen again."

"Insurance?"

"Keep Frankie out. Lock her upstairs and don't tell her what room we'll be using down here."

"So you think she was responsible?"

"Her telekinesis powers have been validated by independent experts. You saw the display she put on with dimming the chandelier lights and shooting that bowl at Daphne."

"Luke said–"

"What did I say?" Luke joined them.

Madeline stiffened, on guard.

Mrs. Lawrence cast her a curious look, but said to him, "We were talking about Frankie." She nodded toward the teenager, who was out of earshot.

"And?"

"You tell him, Madeline, why don't you?"

Knowing it would seem strange to refuse, Madeline gave a quick summary of their conversation, then added, "I was going to remind your aunt that you said the fault might lie with evil spirits in the house. It's not fair to blame Frankie."

"So she's found a champion," he said, looking pleased. He pulled up a chair to join them. "I agree with Maddie," he said to his aunt. "And as for me doing another seance...." He shook his head. "Not here. I know how much it means to you, but I don't feel right about it."

"You don't?" Madeline asked quickly. Could it be this simple? Her job for Jason was easy, if the medium wouldn't put on the show Brad and Frank wanted.

"Getting tired of repeating myself, but no, I won't." He looked at her curiously.

"Hey, Madeline!" Frankie waved at her. "Want to play or not?"

"I'll be right there." Madeline suddenly had a new worry. If Luke told Frank and Brad that he wouldn't do the seance they wanted, maybe the Unholy Trio planned to use Frankie instead. The teenager was willing, and would need little encouragement. Maybe Luke had decided it would be all right if he supervised.

But what about Frank Miller? He'd been dead set against it earlier. Still, he might change his mind if it became apparent his daughter was the only means to the end. He wanted Patrick Lawrence struck from Mrs. Lawrence's will, no matter what it took. From what she had overheard last night, Frank would not give up that goal easily.

Madeline and Frankie began playing the board game, but Madeline found it difficult to concentrate. Her thoughts kept spinning with conjectures about how Brad and Frank would react when Luke refused to conduct the seance they wanted so badly tonight.

Daphne returned, without Nancy, frowning as she walked in.

"What's up, Daph?" Frankie called out. "Frowning? Aren't you afraid of getting wrinkles?"

The model hastily smoothed her brow with her fingertips. "Don't call me Daph. You know I dislike nicknames, Frankie."

"Yep," the teenager agreed, rolling the dice and then making her move on the board.

Daphne perched on the arm of Luke's chair. "I'm worn out. Complain, complain, complain."

"You must be referring to my daughter," Mrs. Lawrence said. "Still got a hangover?"

"That's what I think."

"But she doesn't?" Luke asked.

Daphne laughed. "It's classic, straight out of one of those old movies she loves to watch."

Madeline looked at her with interest.

"Why?" Luke asked. "What does she say it is?"

Daphne laughed again. "Nancy claims that she's being poisoned."

TWENTY-FIVE

"One more game, Frankie. Then I've had it." Madeline rolled, then moved three of her pips.

Tommy, who was up from his nap and ready for action, danced at his mother's elbow and watched the backgammon game with interest. "Can I play next?"

"Sure," Frankie said. To Madeline she added, "It'll be a relief to win, after playing with you. You're such a stickler for the rules."

"And you like tricky maneuvers when you think I'm not looking."

"Calling me a cheater?" Frankie laughed. "I've learned to take every advantage when playing with people who are better than me. My dad says I'm a practical joker. Maybe I was wanting to see if you'd catch me at it."

"Practical jokes? Like what you told me about cats and mice?" Madeline nodded toward Tommy to explain her vagueness. "You said cats leave three things. You said there was a third thing that should've been there."

Tommy was busy stacking discarded black and red pips, and didn't seem interested in their discussion, but Madeline didn't want to pique his curiosity by mentioning dead mouse heads and tails.

"Oh, yeah! The pa–"

"Right. That other thing." Madeline mouthed the word "pancreas" for Frankie to see. "You know it's not something cats leave behind."

"Who told you different?" Frankie looked angry all at once.

"The point is, your joke about it put me through a lot of worry, wondering who did that, if the cat didn't."

"What did the cat do, Mommy?" Tommy looked at her with interest.

"Nothing much, honey. Why don't you get your backpack. I see it over on the couch. Find your Go Fish cards and I'll play with you."

"But Frankie is going to play this game with me."

155

"Go on." She gave him a love pat and pointed to the couch. The moment he scampered off, she turned to Frankie. "It was a rotten trick, making me believe—"

"I had a cat. They leave all three things. Ask my dad if you don't believe me. No, never mind." Frankie stood up in a hurry. "I thought we were friends. But you're looking at me like everybody else does, like I'm a freak. I wouldn't be friends if you paid me."

The teenager fled the room.

Madeline sighed. She didn't know what the truth was anymore. But first off, she should mend fences with Frankie.

"Tommy?" she said to him. "Get your game set up on the coffee table and I'll be right back. Okay?" As soon as he nodded agreement, she sped out in Frankie's wake.

She caught up with the teenager on the grand staircase. "I'm sorry, Frankie! Please?"

The girl stopped on the stairs and turned grudgingly.

"I never had a cat, and I'm sure you're right since you've been around them. Come back and play cards with Tommy and me."

Madeline hoped the teen wasn't headed for that upper belvedere again. It was unnerving the way Frankie immediately went from being amiable to a high-strung reaction of flight.

"Going to my room. If that's okay with you." Frankie glared, then unbent a little. "Come if you want." She turned away, with the air of not caring what Madeline did next.

"Sure, I'd love to join you for a few minutes."

Inside Frankie's bedroom, Madeline said, "Jason told me you were pulling my leg."

"So he's the one who said I was lying?"

"But I guess that means <u>he</u> was." Madeline grew thoughtful. It seemed clear now that Jason had been the one to leave the dead mouse's head and tail on her pillow. When she'd told him that cats leave the animal's pancreas as well, he had covered his error by claiming that Frankie made it up.

"He's really weird," Frankie said.

Madeline nodded. "He told me to go away, and not trust Luke."

"Luke is the one person in the world I'm sure about."

Madeline looked out the window at the driving rain. As a new thought came to her, she turned back to Frankie, excited. "I know a way to find out more about Jason."

"How?"

"He tried to keep me out of a locked room upstairs. I bet he's got something in there he doesn't want me, or anyone else, to see."

"Like what?"

Madeline shrugged. "I have no idea. But I'll have to figure out how to pick that lock."

"You don't have to." Frankie grinned.

"You know how to pick locks?"

"Even better," Frankie said, getting up. "I know where all the keys are kept."

Fifteen minutes later, with Frankie in the lead, the two young women tiptoed up to the third floor.

"We don't have to be quiet," Frankie said. "Jason's in the kitchen helping Rosa polish silver for tonight's dinner party. I saw him when I sneaked around to see if he'd be a problem."

Relieved, Madeline told Frankie about her first night in the house, when Tommy had been missing for a while. "I thought he was in the locked room, but then I found him back in bed, asleep. Your grandmother told me he probably went downstairs for a drink of water. I asked him about it later but he didn't remember anything."

"Unless he really was in that locked room."

"But—"

"And while you were downstairs talking to my grandmother about it, Jason snuck Tommy back to bed, figuring it wasn't worth the trouble after all."

"But why bother in the first place? I don't have any money, if he thought of holding him for ransom." Madeline grew thoughtful.

Maybe Jason was working on Craig's behalf? But how could the two men know each other? Madeline had come here about the tapestry. It's true that Jason might have learned her name from Mrs. Lawrence a few days before she arrived with Tommy, but it was a stretch to imagine that Jason instantly deduced an ex-husband in the wings, managed to locate Craig and asked if he could help with a dirty deed, for pay.

And if Jason had hidden Tommy to scare Madeline, then why had he returned the boy so quickly? None of it made sense. Why would Jason go to all that trouble to frighten her? And yet now he was so friendly, enlisting her aid to save Mrs. Lawrence from greedy relatives.

Giving it up for the moment, Madeline sped up the stairs.

On the third floor, Frankie flung open a linen closet. It was bare and dusty within, but a row of keys hung inside one of the double doors. "I used to play up here when I was a kid. These were the servants' rooms a long time ago. Nobody uses them anymore. I bet Gram doesn't know that Jason has been hanging around up here."

All of the bedroom doors up and down the hall were shut. The windows at either end of the long corridor did not admit enough of the gray light from outside to be of much help. Frankie pulled a penlight out of her pocket and shone it on the keys.

"Are they marked?"

Frankie grabbed a key ring.

"He probably just has girly magazines in there."

"Chickening out, Madeline?"

"I don't want to drag you into danger."

"I can take care of myself," Frankie said as they walked toward the room Madeline indicated. "I've been taking judo lessons for three years. My mother says a girl living in L.A. has to be able to protect herself." At the door, she tried one key after another. "Maybe it's not on this ring. But there are plenty of others."

"We'd better hurry."

"He's got a lot of silver to polish. Rosa is making a special assortment of canapes since we won't eat dinner until ten."

"I'd nearly forgotten it's New Year's Eve." Madeline watched as Frankie tried a long brass key with notches on the end.

"I tried this first, but maybe I didn't wriggle it enough."

"Let me try?" Madeline used the key but the door remained locked. She studied the key. "I underestimated Jason," she said, giving the teen a sharp look. "This key fits, but it won't turn. I think he either changed the lock or did something to the key so it doesn't fit right. Let me see the flashlight." She examined the key under the beam. "See the marks here? Someone filed the notches. That's why it won't turn the lock."

"Why not just take the key?" Frankie asked, puzzled.

Madeline hesitated. "I don't... yeah, I do know. Because what if your grandmother hired a worker and they needed to open a door, and maybe she thought of that linen closet and the old keys. She might know how many keys should be on each ring. Jason was being extra cautious, to be on the safe side. She might have a list of the keys tucked away. He couldn't take a chance that she'd notice a key missing, and send for a locksmith."

They looked at each other, and then the locked door.

"I guess we might as well give up." Frankie turned to put the key ring back.

Madeline's jaw set stubbornly. "I want to find out what he was so determined to prevent me from seeing."

Frankie glanced around uneasily. "Maybe he's on the way." She turned to go.

Madeline grabbed the teenager's arm and held her back. "Shh. Don't move!"

"What's wrong with you?" Frankie twisted away.

"Look," Madeline whispered, pointing.

Frankie followed her gesture. Her jaw dropped. Trembling, she whispered, "Oh my god...."

They clung to each other as a glowing apparition approached them. It was a cat. But not a cat with a solid body. As the creature padded silently toward them, its eyes took on a reddish gleam.

Chills coursed through Madeline's veins.

The ghostly animal walked within a foot of them, then disappeared through the closed door of another room.

When the tip of its kinked tail was out of sight, Madeline took hold of Frankie's hand and yanked her toward the stairs.

"Luke's right," Frankie whispered, awed. "This house is haunted."

"That's what I've been trying to tell everyone." Madeline clattered down the stairs, anxious to leave the third floor behind. Jason could keep his secret room locked and bolted.

Satisfying her curiosity wasn't worth another ghostly encounter.

TWENTY-SIX

Madeline burst into the living room with Frankie at her heels.

Mrs. Lawrence and the other members of the party looked up.

"Ghost – upstairs!" Frankie gasped for air.

"Your grandmother again?" Daphne asked Madeline, bored.

Frankie told Mrs. Lawrence, "It was Calico. Just like you described."

The older woman paled. "I'm sorry this happened. Please sit and relax."

Luke looked at the girls. "Tell me about it when you feel up to it. Can I get you something to drink?"

"Anything soft," Madeline said. He brought them sodas. "Like Frankie said, it was a cat. But not this one," she added, petting the big patchwork colored cat that came up to her now. "You could see through it, and it didn't make any sounds. No purring and no noise when it walked on the floor."

"She saw it first," Frankie added. "When I looked, there was this cat ghost walking toward me."

"Did it go through you?" Mrs. Lawrence was interested in the details. "That has happened to me."

"No. And I'm glad Tommy was in the kitchen with Rosa. It'd be hard to explain this to my son."

"I wish I'd been in the kitchen with him," Frankie said.

"But don't you see the importance?" Luke asked. "Madeline has a witness."

"Where did all this supposedly happen?" Brad asked.

Madeline shot Frankie a warning look. "Upstairs," Madeline said.

"In your room, Nervous Nelly? Or Frankie's?" Daphne smiled without warmth.

Madeline tried not to show how annoyed she felt by that stupid nickname. She wished Daphne would go away somewhere. A commercial she'd seen came to mind, and she nearly laughed out loud. In the ad, a brand of rodent poison promised that mice would go away and die. Too bad she felt murder was ethically wrong, or it would be tempting to slip some of that poison into Daphne's dinner.

That thought leapt to another. That dead mouse in her bedroom. "But that was before!" she cried out involuntarily. It didn't make sense to believe Jason put the mouse's tail and head on her pillow to scare her away from the locked room on the third floor. When she had found the mouse, she hadn't even been on that floor yet.

"Before what?" Luke asked. Seeing her startled expression, he added, teasing lightly, "Talking to yourself?"

She laughed it off, and moved closer to Frankie, who was telling a few other details of the cat ghost.

"But what were you doing on the third floor?" Mrs. Lawrence persisted. "No one uses those rooms. Playing hide and seek?"

"Oh, Gram!"

Madeline saw the possibility in that story. It would get them off the hook. "I know we're a bit old for the game, but we were just fooling around. But then the ghost chased us away. Game over!" She was grateful to see Frank Miller come in and fix himself a drink at the bar. "How is your wife? Feeling any better?"

He shrugged. "She's turned into a hypochondriac. Won't eat anything."

"Still claims to be poisoned?" Daphne asked.

With a casual glance around the room, Madeline took in the various reactions she hadn't been able to notice before when this topic was raised. Brad looked uneasy, but Frank seemed impassive. What if her suspicion about the Unholy Trio was correct, and they wanted Nancy out of the way to avoid a further split of Mrs. Lawrence's money?

She wasn't sure about the legalities. Since Nancy and Frank were married and living in a community property state, Frank would get the money intended for his wife, the same money he'd get if Nancy remained alive. But what if Nancy had been threatening divorce lately, in one of their fights? Divorced, he'd be out of the line of inheritance. But if his wife died, and then Mrs. Lawrence died… she sighed to herself.

Puzzling it over as the others talked about Nancy's tendency to drama, Madeline raised the possibility that Frank didn't know Nancy had been poisoned. What if Brad and Luke were plotting to increase their own shares? That made more sense, and it also meant that Frank would be the next to go, as soon as Nancy was out of the way.

With a glance at Frank, she felt sorry for him, and decided to keep an eye on what everyone did from now on. As her glance fell on his daughter Frankie, however, a new worry popped up. Even if Nancy and Frank died and couldn't inherit, there was probably a provision in California law that meant their own heir – Frankie – would get the money.

That meant, she thought with a chill, that the entire family would have to be eliminated in order for that money to revert to other heirs of Mrs. Lawrence. Madeline felt confused. She wished she knew a lawyer she could ask about all this.

She stared at Brad, remembering that Jason said the actor was an attorney. But how could she ask him? He'd know at once that she was on to their scheme, and she'd place herself and Tommy in jeopardy.

"You look like you're trying to solve the world's problems," Luke teased, taking her empty glass from her hand. "You were about to drop the glass," he explained when she looked at him.

"Just thinking about a, uh, new needlepoint project." She dragged her thoughts from the subject of murder to the gift she wanted to make for Mrs. Lawrence. In a whisper, she added, "I'm going to make something special for your aunt and I haven't been able to come up with a design for the cushion. I want it to be meaningful."

"Nice."

She couldn't think of anything else to say to him. In the awkward silence, she eavesdropped on what the others were discussing.

"My wife insists somebody put poison in her drink," Frank said, enjoying the spotlight. "Trouble is, which drink? She's had so many!" He laughed loudly.

Madeline noticed the pained look on Frankie's face, and knew that Nancy's drinking problem affected the whole family.

"I'll ask Rosa to make her a tray," Mrs. Lawrence said. "Nancy always liked tapioca pudding when she had the stomach flu. I'll sneak an egg into it the way I used to. She'll never get well without sustenance. Frankie? Please go ask Rosa to fix a tray for your mother."

As Frankie left the room, Brad shook his head. "You coddle Nancy too much, Mother. What she is craving right now isn't tapioca with an egg in it. It's a stiff drink!" He moved to the wet bar.

"No," Madeline cried out. She jumped up. When everyone stared, she stammered, "I'll do it for her. Mrs. Lawrence is right. Nancy could use some nutrition. What about an orange juice?" She filled a tall glass with juice.

Chuckling, Brad took the glass from her, dumped half the juice into the wet bar sink, and poured in vodka. "That'll be more to her taste." He held out the glass to Madeline.

Hesitating, knowing she had to take it or risk suspicion, she took the glass, then grabbed a cocktail napkin and straw.

Upstairs, Madeline tapped on Nancy Miller's closed bedroom door. When she heard a thin reply to come in, she entered with the glass of juice and vodka. "How are you feeling?"

"Ghastly. How do I look? No, don't answer that." The middle-aged woman passed a hand over her brow and moaned softly. Her curly hair was matted and unkempt. She wore no makeup. Dark circles under her eyes made her appear older and more tired. The sheets were tangled, as if she'd been sleeping restlessly. She spotted the drink in Madeline's hand. "That better be a screwdriver and not plain orange juice."

"It is."

Taking the glass, Nancy brought the straw to her lips. "Wait. Who made this?"

"I did." Madeline felt that was close enough to the truth because she saw Brad pour from the vodka bottle and not add anything else.

She endured the assessing look, feeling uncomfortable, and hoping now that the woman wouldn't ask her to sit and stay. What had started as a noble plan to keep Brad from poisoning his sister now seemed foolish. No one else took it seriously that Nancy claimed to have been poisoned. *Why did she feel the need to meddle?* Madeline scolded herself.

Nancy drank thirstily. "What are they saying downstairs about me?" She reached under her pillow and brought out a bag of chocolates. She ate a few quickly, and offered the bag to Madeline.

Refusing, Madeline thought at least they didn't have to worry about Nancy starving. Madeline noticed a pile of fashion and gossip magazines scattered on the bed and realized the others could be right in discounting Nancy's claim of being poisoned. It looked like she was enjoying her solitude.

Still… the woman looked ill, and it might be true about the poison. *Stop making snap judgments*, Madeline warned herself.

"Frankie is bringing you a tray. Your mother thought you'd like tapioca pudding so Rosa is making some."

"Build my strength up? They'd all be happy if I died. You don't have to tell me what they're saying. I can hear it."

"You can?" Madeline looked at her uneasily.

A weak laugh came from Nancy. "Not with psychic powers. I can imagine it, though, can't I? Brad is scornful that I'm faking it to get attention and he got mad when my mother suggested a tray. I can tell from your face that I'm right. I usually am, about this family. And my dear husband is calling me the drama queen, or something equally dismissive." She waved a hand airily.

"One of them could drive down the hill and get a cell signal to call for a doctor. Would you like that? At least find out what kind of stomach flu it is? There's probably some medication you could take to feel better."

Nancy indicated the bedside table, littered with over-the-counter digestive aids. "I wasn't sure which to take, and then I realized I'd better not take anything at all." She looked at Madeline meaningfully.

"Because there might be more poison in any of those." Madeline decided she might as well go along with Nancy's idea, and thus be in a position to learn more. If she dismissed the possibility of a deliberate poisoning, then Nancy would lump her with the others who disbelieved.

With a sage nod, Nancy finished the vodka drink.

"I saw a ghost," Madeline said.

"Yeah, I know. Your granny."

"Another one. A cat. It happened just a little while ago, and Frankie was with me. She saw it, too."

"Mother's cat ghost? I don't believe it."

"Well, of course I have no way of knowing if it was the exact same ghost, but it was a cat that looked like the Calico in the old tapestry."

"I don't like cats. Never have."

"But you grew up here," Madeline said. "And I thought there were always cats, ones that look as close as possible to the original, with all the right color patches and markings."

"When I lived here, when I grew up here, it was a beautiful house. The gardens were well-tended and the house was a showplace. Now look at it – a disgrace! No wonder the ghosts hang around. It's straight out of a Hollywood production for a 'Psycho' remake."

Madeline felt at a loss. The other woman was right to describe the house as falling down, but she didn't want to get into a session of criticizing Mrs. Lawrence for not taking better care of it in her old age.

After learning that Mrs. Lawrence had paid to have the house repaired and painted, and had been cheated, Madeline knew that not everything that happened here was as it might seem at first.

"I've been trying to convince Mother to sell this old dump and move closer to us. But you know all about that, don't you?"

"I didn't mean to overhear. But she obviously doesn't want to move, or she'd agree to it."

"She'd better change her mind fast. I'm sick of coming all the way out here to see her. And now this business of ghosts and footsteps when nobody is there. You're a bad influence."

"Me?" Madeline gave a start.

"Well, duh. You're the one who sees ghosts. I don't. My husband doesn't. My brother doesn't. Daphne doesn't. But you waltz in here with your little boy, seeking a handout and looking the place over to see if it will suit your needs–"

"I came here on business. To borrow–"

"Yeah, yeah. Whatever. As soon as you got here, you started claiming to see ghosts here, there and everywhere. Now the cat ghost. Your trump card."

"I'm not making these things up."

"Don't get all hot and bothered. My daughter sees that stuff, too, so I'm not sure what I believe. And she saw the cat ghost?"

"It walked toward us, and then turned and vanished through a closed door."

"I don't like to bring Frances Jane here. It sets her off. You saw what happened with the brass bowl, and those dishes. The atmosphere is wrong for her. She's delicate."

"And she does have a tendency to change moods quickly."

"Yeah, her psychiatrists say it's a problem. That's why we're going to send her to that expensive boarding school. For her own good."

Madeline remained silent. She didn't believe boarding school was the answer, but had not been asked her opinion.

Nancy set the empty glass on the bedside table, shoving medications aside heedlessly. "I'm going to tell Mother we won't come here again. Not until she moves someplace nicer that's convenient to get to. Driving all the way out here to the county line and a mile up a winding hairpin road that needs re-paving is not my idea of a relaxing country drive."

"She'd be sorry to not see you."

"That's how we'll get her to change her mind about selling. We'll boycott her!" Nancy nodded, pleased with her new plan.

Madeline picked up the glass and tried to neaten the bedside table but gave it up as hopeless. She needed to stop interfering in the lives of these people.

"I need to get back to my son and make sure he's not getting into mischief."

"His mother does enough of that for the both of you." Nancy chuckled to herself and settled back on the pillows, looking drained.

"Want me to leave the light on?" Madeline asked from the doorway, her hand hovering over the light switch. "Or are you going to rest now?"

"I don't care."

Not sure what that meant, Madeline quietly left without turning the light off, and eased the door shut behind her. In the dark hallway, she frowned, trying to remember if the hall lights had been on when she came up with the drink.

Due to the rainstorm and the short winter days, they needed lights in the big house most of the time just to see where things were and not stumble into furnishings. She thought the light had been on before, but supposed she was mistaken.

As she turned toward the stairs, a long trumpet danced above her head and moved around slowly in front of her face. No one held the instrument.

Her eyes widened in fear.

The trumpet floated without support. It glowed with a soft golden light.

"Madeline." A hushed unearthly voice came from the trumpet. "Madeline Clark."

Chills washed over her. The sibilant words sent gooseflesh racing up her arms. She shrank against the wall.

The trumpet moved in closer. "Go home," the voice said. "Get out. Go home!"

She inched toward the staircase leading down to the first floor, desperate to escape. The trumpet followed, repeating its warning.

"This is my imagination," she whispered out loud. She closed her eyes, willing the trumpet to disappear. She concentrated hard, praying the eerie voice would stop talking to her, and that the glowing trumpet would vanish or go back into the dimension from which it came.

Madeline knew she couldn't stand there all day, trembling, so she bravely opened her eyes.

The trumpet was gone. She was alone, but not at peace in her solitude. She was shaking all over. And she knew that if she opened her mouth to scream for help, she would not be able to stop.

"This is ridiculous," she muttered under her breath.

TWENTY-SEVEN

"Where's Tommy?" Madeline asked, racing around the living room, picking up her son's playthings and stuffing them haphazardly into her needlework bag. "Where's my son? Is he still in the kitchen?"

Luke picked up a stuffed toy that dropped out of the bag and handed it to her. He placed a soothing hand on her shoulder but she jerked back as if scalded. He looked at her steadily.

"I'm taking Tommy," she said to his unasked question, "and we're leaving, even if we have to walk all the way back to Hermosa Beach."

"That's fifty miles." Brad looked at her. "Guess my sister put the fear of the devil in you."

With shaking fingers, she picked up the crystal ball and handed it to Mrs. Lawrence.

"I told your son he could keep it," the older woman said. "Please let him enjoy it."

Impatiently, Madeline shoved the ball into her bag.

Not taking his eyes off her, Luke said quietly, "Another ghost?"

"Yes!" Tears filled her eyes. "No. I don't know what it was. A big trumpet talked to me and told me to get out. I'm not going to stick around and see what's planned for an encore."

"You have to stay," Brad said, coming closer. He looked around at the others. "We all do."

She slumped into a chair, overwhelmed. "Could someone drive me, please? I'll pay for the gas. At least take me somewhere that I can call for a cab."

"The canyon road is out. Mudslide." Brad seemed to be pleased by the situation. "If one of us had four-wheel drive, we could make it. Rosa told me. You can see it from the kitchen window. I hoped it wasn't as bad as it looked, that maybe it was drivable, so I ventured out and took a look. It's a mess out there."

"And that's all my fault, isn't it?" Mrs. Lawrence looked smaller than ever in her wheelchair.

"That's right, Agatha," Frank said, taking advantage of her guilty feelings. "We've been telling you for years to have that road paved properly. Now look what's happened! The rain has got us trapped here."

"But I've got to leave," Madeline said, more to herself than the others. "There has to be a way out."

"Walk already." Daphne shrugged.

"Even if I could make it, my son couldn't. But I'll figure out something." Full of determination again, Madeline got up. Leaving the packed bag on the floor, she hurried into the kitchen.

"Rosa?" she called out, approaching. "Is Tommy with you?"

"No, missus."

Luke spoke from behind Madeline, having followed her. "I'll look around upstairs." He gave her a reassuring smile and touched her shoulder.

This time she forced herself not to flinch. He was trying to help. The least she could do was be polite to him, and put aside her suspicions for later. "He does like to play hide and seek. Maybe...."

"I'll find him," Luke promised.

"I'll look in all the rooms downstairs." She hurried out and began her search.

When she ended up in the living room, again, the others looked at her expectantly. She shook her head. "Luke is searching upstairs, but I don't understand why Tommy doesn't come when I call."

"But he did, dear," Mrs. Lawrence said.

"You saw him?" Madeline asked, baffled. "I thought you said–"

"Not just now. Earlier, when he came in from the kitchen looking for you. I wouldn't let him wander off by himself. But you called to him from the hall, so I told him to go with you."

Madeline's heart raced. "Someone tricked you, pretending to be me." She looked around the room, wondering who had been in here at the time, and thus was safe to trust.

She didn't think it would help to interrogate Mrs. Lawrence, because people had been freely coming and going. It would be nearly impossible to create a list of who was in the room at any particular time.

Luke hurried in, seeking Madeline. As soon as she saw his face, she knew he hadn't found her son.

"Brad," he said, beckoning, "let's check the third floor."

The two men left.

Frankie caught Madeline's eye, and seemed to transmit a question: *Is Tommy locked up in that room on the top floor?*

Madeline nodded, accepting the possibility. She hurried out, calling, "Luke! Wait, I'll go with you."

As she passed the grandfather clock in the hall, the tiny door opened and Tommy's head popped out. "Boo!"

"Oh, Tommy! What are you doing in there?" As she pulled him out of his hiding place, she called out, "I found him. Luke! Brad! Come on back!"

"I win!" Tommy was delighted.

Her relief was so great that Madeline didn't have the heart to scold him. She hugged him tight, then picked him up and carried him into the living room.

"Look who I found in the grandfather clock," she said, keeping it light.

"What were you doing in there?" Mrs. Lawrence asked. "You could have been hurt, or gotten stuck."

"He's fine, and the clock is still working." Madeline set Tommy down.

Brad and Luke joined them.

"Hey, young man, you gave us all a chase," Brad said, heading for the bar and another drink.

Luke smiled at Madeline. "Glad you found him."

"Thanks for helping." She couldn't help smiling back at him.

"Where's my coloring books?" Tommy looked around and under the chairs.

"Here, honey." Madeline grabbed the needlework bag she had stuffed hastily with his toys. She got him set up with a holiday coloring book, crayons and stickers. "Why did you hide in the clock?"

"You told me to." He picked out a red crayon and began coloring Santa's beard. "You said, 'Come here, Tommy' and so I did. But you were hid already." He concentrated on his project.

"Okay, so you heard me, but you didn't see me. And I know you like hide and seek. So then I told you to get inside the clock? Are you sure?" She knew it wouldn't be productive if she explained someone had been imitating her voice. That might frighten the boy, so it was better to play along teasingly, and see what else she could find out.

"You told me to hide and be quiet," Tommy said. "So I did. I won. Didn't I, Mommy?"

"You did indeed." She looked at him, grateful for his safety. "We both did."

Later, in the kitchen, Madeline boosted her son up onto a kitchen stool and tied a dishcloth around his neck, bib-fashion. "Thanks, Rosa. I really appreciate this. You've been a big help."

"No problem."

"Some of the talk in there isn't meant for little ones."

"Tommy is good company for me." She set a plate of holiday cutout cookies in front of the boy and poured him a mug of milk.

"Tommy?" Madeline hugged him. "It's okay if you want to go to sleep. I brought down a blanket you can curl up on, as long as you don't get in Rosa's way."

"I want to see the big Christmas ball. Daphne told me it will be on TV at midnight."

"The crystal ball at Times Square? If you fall asleep, I'll wake you up for a Happy New Year kiss."

"You look pretty." He smiled at her.

Madeline had been resigned to wearing her same casual outfit yet again, even though everyone else was going to dress up for the holiday dinner party, but Frankie had taken charge, talked to her grandmother and led Madeline by the hand into an old dressing room.

The upshot was that Madeline was dressed in a long slinky silver evening gown, her hair twisted up in a knot with a few jewels shining in it, and she wore elegant dangling earrings and high-heeled satin sandals.

At the door, Madeline turned. "One more thing, Rosa. Don't let him leave the kitchen, all right? Even if you hear me call to him from outside. When I want Tommy, I'll come in here personally and get him from you. Don't let anybody else take him, okay?"

Rosa chuckled. "It is always that way with the first one. Relax. I won't let nobody steal this precious child."

Madeline was the last to take a chair at the dining table.

Even Nancy Miller was there, looking tired but festive in a heavily sequined emerald-green dinner suit. Her grayish pallor was gone, hidden by heavy makeup.

Frankie looked uncomfortable in a gown of burgundy velvet and grumbled about its oversized bows every few minutes. "Going formal for a family dinner is ridiculous."

"We have a guest," Mrs. Lawrence said with a smile, nodding toward Madeline. "And she looks very pretty in that old dress of mine. It fits you better than it ever did me," she added to Madeline.

"Smashing." Luke winked at Madeline.

Daphne's eyes narrowed. The model was in a designer gown of ivory silk, and her jewelry was from Beverly Hills. She pointedly looked at herself in satisfaction and then cast a disdainful glance at Madeline's outfit and hair.

Ignoring the taunt, Madeline decided she would enjoy herself this evening. Tommy was safe in the kitchen, and tomorrow they would be home again, somehow.

She accepted a glass of wine from Brad and began eating.

Dinner conversation flowed easily, as if everyone had tacitly agreed to avoid the sensitive subjects of wills, ghosts, seances and apparitions.

Toward the end of the meal, Jason Malone came in. He kept his head lowered and stood next to his employer as if he hated to be there. "Rosa said you wanted to see me?" His voice was a gravelly mumble, difficult to understand.

"Yes, Jason. Thank you for staying up. I know it's late, so I won't keep you." She rang the bell for Rosa, who came in at once with Tommy. The boy ran to his mother's side.

Mrs. Lawrence lifted her glass in toast. "I wanted to gather everyone to wish you a Happy New Year."

"It's not midnight, Gram." Frankie sounded like she was sorry for her grandmother.

"I do know that, Frances. Thank you all the same. I'm not senile. Although sometimes I think that state must be a blessing in disguise."

"What is that supposed to mean, Mother?" Nancy looked at her sharply.

"Rosa?" Mrs. Lawrence got the housekeeper's attention. "Please take Tommy back in the kitchen and see that he's got all he needs to be comfortable."

Rosa nodded. "Happy New Year."

A few people replied "Happy New Year," but all eyes were on Mrs. Lawrence.

The tension in the room increased, and Madeline was glad to give her son a quick hug and then indicate he should go with Rosa out of the room.

Mrs. Lawrence set her glass down and lined it up with the water goblet in a studied motion. When the silence was nearly unbearable, she looked at Nancy. "To answer your question, darling daughter, I meant that it would be a relief to be unaware of all the scheming and intrigue that goes on around me." Her lips twisted in a bitter smile. "Money. It always comes down to that, doesn't it?"

Barely moving her head, Madeline tried to gauge everyone's reaction. Frankie and Luke seemed equally curious. Brad, Frank and Nancy leaned forward, their interest obvious. Daphne yawned, but Madeline wondered if she was faking boredom so no one would realize how interested she was in the older woman's wealth and how it would be dispersed.

"Happy New Year," Jason mumbled and turned to leave.

"I'm not through with you," Mrs. Lawrence said, her voice calm and cool.

He turned, staying near the door.

"You came to me some time ago, seeking a job," she began. Her words addressed Jason, but she did not look directly at him. She divided her attention between her wineglass and the lit candles in the center of the table. It seemed she was having difficulty with what she wanted to say.

Madeline watched, wondering if Mrs. Lawrence was too tired to handle all this stress and emotion.

The older woman went on. "I hired you to do odd jobs, and I've been pleased with your work. You've been useful to have on hand in this old house that's starting to fall apart. You're handy with electrical gadgets." Her smile was sad and wistful. "So was my son Patrick."

Brad nodded. He looked at his mother as if hoping she would declare Patrick dead and get on with the business of the will.

Madeline noticed how intent the Unholy Trio became, and she imagined they were all thinking about Mrs. Lawrence's youngest child. Was she going to agree to have him declared legally dead? She'd held out this long, but was she going to abandon the idea of a seance to get evidence of Patrick's death before making a decision?

"I didn't make the connection until now." Mrs. Lawrence turned to Madeline. "It was something you said."

"Me?" Madeline faltered, and shook her head in confusion.

"It was your question about how Jason came to be my attendant. I told you I had a female nurse, but she died. Remember?"

Madeline nodded. She noticed that Luke was staring at her with a puzzled expression.

To Jason, Mrs. Lawrence said, startling all of them, "You killed her, didn't you? That fall she had wasn't accidental, was it?"

Jason blinked, but remained silent.

"He murdered that nurse?" Frank dropped his fork with a clatter. "Somebody do something!"

"What do you suggest?" Brad asked.

"Tie him up!" Nancy cried. "We could all be murdered." She leaned into Frank for protection, and he put an arm around her shoulder.

"Is this guesswork, Aunt Agatha?" Luke seemed to be the only one who was taking the news calmly. "Or do you have proof?"

"I know it's a grave accusation," she replied. "I heard a description on the radio today of an escaped convict. A murderer at large. The description fits you, Jason. And the timing is right, because he escaped

175

weeks ago but they lost his trail. I have no doubt the police will be happy to ask you a few questions."

Madeline studied Jason. He didn't seem worried. She had the feeling there was a reason why Jason felt untouchable, but she couldn't figure out what it could be.

"You're guessing all this, Mother?" Brad looked at her in disgust. "What kind of game are you playing? I suggest we forget this outburst and finish dessert." He picked up his fork, took a bite of cake and waited to see who would follow his lead.

Daphne carefully scraped the rich frosting into a pile on the side of her plate, then took a nibble of cake, no doubt counting calories.

Mrs. Lawrence was undaunted. "Eat if you want, everyone." She looked at Jason Malone. "As soon as the road is dry enough to travel, I'll pack you off to the police. They'll know how to handle you. And in the meantime, you can explain why you kept the money I gave you for hiring a painter."

"You mean he's been cheating you?" Frank's face turned an angry red. "Kick him out. Let him walk to the police himself. Maybe he'll drown on the way in this wretched storm."

Throughout, Madeline noticed that Jason stood like a dark statue in the door, silent and glowering.

"No wonder this place is such a disaster." Brad shook his head. "Mother, I hope this episode changes your mind about selling."

"And you call me senile!" Mrs. Lawrence laughed softly. "Look who's dim-witted. Get it through your heads, all of you. This is my home. And here I stay. Nothing you can do or say will budge me."

"You're being ridiculous, Mother." Nancy drained her wine glass and reached for the decanter.

Frank and Brad joined in with complaints and comments.

Ignoring the outcries, the older woman said to Jason, "Need I add that you are fired? Consider yourself under house arrest."

She looked at Brad and Frank. "It will be up to you two to guard him. Be sure he doesn't get away."

"Why me?" Frank complained. "Can't Luke do it? My wife needs me."

"We should discuss the legality of this," Brad said. "We can't hold him here against his will, on the grounds that he matches a description on the radio. Be sensible, Mother. Don't open yourself to litigation."

Was it Madeline's imagination, or did Jason wink at her? In any case, she was reminded that Jason was the one who'd told her Brad is a lawyer. She felt confused. Why wasn't Jason trying to run away? Why didn't he protest? He stood passively accepting it. She couldn't figure him out.

Mrs. Lawrence gave Jason her best polite-hostess smile. "Before they lock you in one of the rooms upstairs, please take down The Calico Tapestry in the living room, roll it in brown paper and then in heavy-duty plastic, and put it in Miss Clark's room. She'll be taking it with her when she goes."

No one moved.

Jason straightened, gave a small salute as if tipping a servant's hat to Mrs. Lawrence, turned on his heel and left.

Frank looked around uncertainly and started to stand.

Brad motioned him to remain seated. "We don't have the right to hold him."

TWENTY-EIGHT

"If you're going to sit and let a murderer escape," Mrs. Lawrence said, "then I'm going to bed." She pushed a button on her wheelchair and backed away from the table.

"What about the party, Gram?" Frankie asked. "You told me you've never missed ringing in the new year."

"I never have. But if I don't take a nap now, I'll be fast asleep at twelve. Come along, Brad. You can help me get in bed."

Madeline got up. This would be the perfect opportunity to measure the invalid's wheelchair for that needlepoint cushion she wanted to make. "I'll help you."

"Thank you, dear girl. But I'm afraid you're not strong enough and I'm feeling worn out."

Turning to Frankie, Madeline sent a beseeching glance and tilted her head toward the door.

"I'll go, too," Frankie said quickly.

As they left together, Madeline whispered an explanation to Frankie, then made a quick detour into the living room for the tape measure in her work bag.

When Madeline caught up with them, Frankie was turning on the lights in Mrs. Lawrence's bedroom. The older woman wheeled toward the large four-poster bed which was high off the ground.

"It's really the main thing I need a nurse for," Mrs. Lawrence explained. "I'm afraid of falling out of bed and not being able to get up again. Of being helpless. Everything else I can manage by myself or with Rosa's help. My arms are stronger than they might look to you. I'm just tired right now."

"Why don't you get an adjustable hospital bed?" Madeline suggested. "You'd be able to lower it and get in more easily."

Mrs. Lawrence shook her head. "Another of my traditions." She patted the bed. "I was born in this bed, and I'll die in it."

"Oh Gram, don't start talking like that."

"Why not, Frances? I'm not afraid of death. It will be like walking through a doorway. I have friends and loved ones waiting for me on the other side." They helped her get into bed. She put her eyeglasses on the nightstand and then settled back against the pillows. "But I'm in no hurry to join them." She smiled, then grew thoughtful. "I wonder if Patrick is waiting there with his father." Her eyes slowly closed.

Thinking Mrs. Lawrence had fallen asleep, Madeline whipped out the measuring tape and got the dimensions she needed for her project.

"Frances," said the girl's grandmother, opening her eyes. "Are you still here?" She lifted her head off the pillows and blinked.

"Yes, Gram. You need something before we go?"

The old woman groped for her spectacles and put them on.

Madeline concealed the tape measure. "Would you like a drink of water?"

"No, no." She pointed toward the table of family pictures which Madeline had noticed the first time she came into this room. "Bring me Patrick, will you please, Frances? Maybe if I sleep with his photo beneath my pillow, I'll find out if he is still alive."

"Think you'll dream about him?" Frankie asked as she looked over the assortment of photos.

"Or maybe Cyrus will come and tell me what I want to know." Mrs. Lawrence sighed heavily. "If Patrick himself comes, that might answer my question."

Frankie brought a large framed photograph of the blond young man in uniform to her grandmother. As she passed, Madeline glanced at the picture curiously. While Frankie and Mrs. Lawrence chatted, and Frankie helped her grandmother slide the frame under her pillow, Madeline wandered over to the table of photos and looked them over.

There was a smaller snapshot of that same young man. She studied it, not sure why it was intriguing. In it, Patrick stood in the shade of an oak tree and next to him was what looked like an old television set. He held up a medallion with ribbon streamers, an award of some kind.

Seeing that Mrs. Lawrence was still awake, Madeline took the snapshot to her. "What's this?"

Frankie grabbed it. "It's just Patrick with one of his gizmos."

"His what?" Madeline laughed.

"He won first prize in the science fair with that gizmo," Mrs. Lawrence reminded her granddaughter with mock severity. "You were just a little girl, so I'm not surprised you don't remember." Including Madeline as she pointed to the photo, she said, "It's a movie projector. Don't ask me how it works. He didn't get his mechanical genius from me! As I recall, you put film in the back and then watch home movies. It was his own version of a DVD player."

"Did he patent it? Sounds like a clever idea."

"I agree, Madeline, but he went to Iraq about a year after that. I never dreamed he'd be gone so long. He always had so many ideas and inventions."

"When did you get that letter from the army, Gram?"

"It's been seven years. He'd been in the war about eight months when he was declared MIA – Missing In Action." The older woman sighed deeply.

"Why don't we let you take your nap now," Madeline suggested, taking the snapshot from Mrs. Lawrence's fingers. "Do you want us to come back at a certain time and help you get up?"

"She's got a buzzer Jason hooked up." Frankie pointed to a small box attached to the bedpost near Mrs. Lawrence's pillows. "It rings in the kitchen and in Jason's room."

"Don't let me sleep past eleven thirty. I don't want to miss the fun."

"Did you get Mother tucked in, girls?" Brad asked when Frankie and Madeline joined the rest of the party in the dining room.

Madeline nodded, and accepted the cup of tea which Luke handed her with an affectionate smile. Her heart skipped a beat and she returned a dazzling smile.

Daphne's eyes narrowed dangerously. "If it isn't our little candy-striper and her helper. Tell me, Nervous Nelly, do you also enjoy tucking men into bed?"

"Of course not," Madeline said without thinking. As soon as she spoke, she regretted it, but it was too late. Comments like that didn't deserve a reply.

"Leave her alone!" Frankie frowned, her hands clenching into fists at her sides. "And stop calling Madeline names. I told you to stop before. You better listen."

"Butt out, juvenile delinquent." Daphne looked at her derisively. "Nice try, telling us you're going to an exclusive girls' boarding school. It's a teen rescue residence for 'troubled' girls. Guess I'll have to call you 'Frankie the Freak' from now on. Or 'Troubled Tilly' – that goes with Nervous Nelly better, don't you think? And you two are quite the team now."

"I think you've called my daughter enough names," Nancy Miller said to Daphne. "Cut it out."

Frankie glanced swiftly at her mother and seemed shocked yet pleased that her mother had come to her defense.

"Hey, Daffy Duck," Frankie said to Daphne, her eyes gleaming with mischief, "want some more wine? Red would go nice with that white dress."

"No, Frankie!" Luke seemed to know at once what Frankie had in mind.

As Madeline saw where he was looking, she gasped. She watched helplessly as a carafe of red wine shot across the table and emptied itself into Daphne's lap.

Daphne sat in stunned silence. She grabbed a napkin and futilely swabbed at her ruined gown. "You can pay for a new dress even if you have to sell your mangy little body to do it!"

"Frank!" Nancy's cry drew all eyes to her corner of the table. "Look!" With quivering fingers, she pointed toward the window.

Drifting through the closed window from outside was a puff of smoke which took form as it approached the dining table, and became the holograph of a silver-haired man in a business suit.

"It's Cyrus!" Brad whispered, awed.

Luke, standing next to Madeline, was the closest to the apparition. He walked nearer to it.

Afraid for him, she grabbed his arm.

He stayed with her, as if realizing caution was a good idea. "What do you want here?" Luke asked in a soft, non-threatening voice.

The luminescent apparition swayed. The man's eyes glowed and he stared directly at Madeline.

"Another one of Madeline's ghosts," Daphne said bitterly.

Frankie shushed her.

Madeline was glad when Luke put a reassuring arm around her shoulders and held her in the safety of his embrace. She felt a little braver.

"What do you want?" Luke repeated. "Is there something you need to tell us?" He waited. When there was still no reply, he yelled, "Then go away and don't bother us again! Begone!"

The apparition glided closer. Its arm moved up, and the hand pointed to Madeline.

"Say something," Luke commanded it. "Speak, or leave us in peace."

Slowly the ghost's mouth opened. Words came out as if with great effort. "Go. Sell house. Tell Agatha. Sell house. Now. Danger. Go!" The apparition began fading, like smoke in a breeze.

"Wait," Luke cried. "Tell us what danger you mean." He stepped nearer to the ghost, but it abruptly vanished.

Frankie and Madeline escorted Mrs. Lawrence into the living room. The television was on, tuned to a New Year's Eve countdown celebration with music, dancing and celebrity appearances.

"Thank you for waking me immediately," the older woman said. "Are you sure it was Cyrus?" she asked Brad and Frank. "Without a doubt?"

"Yes, Mother." Brad finished stirring a large bowl at the wet bar, and ladled out cups of eggnog for everyone. "Positive identification. Looked just like him, down to the Rotary Club pin in his lapel."

When they were gathered by the coffee table, Mrs. Lawrence said, "I am sorry that I missed it. He promised to come to me... and when he did, I was napping."

"It can't be helped, Aunt Agatha. These things happen." Luke smiled at her.

"Cyrus never gave me a bad piece of advice in all the years we were together. If this is the message he wanted me to have, then I must heed it. I always listened to him when he was alive. And I'll listen to him now."

"Does that mean–" Brad began hopefully, trying to dampen his elation.

"Tell that realtor friend I'm ready to sell."

Brad, Nancy and Frank shared a look. Madeline wondered what was going through their minds, but she could guess at the general nature of it. They'd be pleased by this turn of events.

"We'll call her in the morning as soon as one of us manages to get down the hill and use a phone," Brad said. "This calls for a celebration." He set down the glass of eggnog and hurried to open champagne. "It's close enough to midnight." He filled a glass and took it to his mother. Handing it to her, he bent and kissed her cheek. "You won't regret this."

She touched her cheek, smiling wryly. "You haven't kissed me in years. This must be an exciting occasion for you."

He poured champagne for the others, then lifted his glass. "To this house." A loud thunderclap drowned out his next words. He shrugged good-naturedly.

Madeline looked out a window. "We don't usually get thunder and lightning. I hope the storm doesn't wake Tommy before midnight. He needs the extra sleep." She returned to the couch. "I've gotten so used to the sound of rain that it's going to seem blessedly quiet when it finally stops."

"If it ever does," Frankie added. "I heard on Gram's radio there are mudslides all over the place."

"This house may be old," Frank said, "but it's sturdy. We're perfectly safe."

As if the house heard and wanted to voice its disagreement, the room trembled beneath their feet.

"Earthquake!" Nancy cried. She grabbed the nearest champagne bottle, filled her glass and drank hastily.

The rumbling and shaking stopped.

Madeline ran from the room. Although Tommy had fallen asleep on a blanket in the kitchen, she'd taken him up to his bed so he could be more comfortable. Now she raced up the stairs, taking them two at a time.

She flung open the bedroom door.

The bed was empty.

Reeling with the sense of *deja vu*, she cried out his name. No reply.

She searched under the bed and in the closet. He wasn't there.

With a frightened gasp, she sped into the hall and made a systematic search of the bathroom and each bedroom on the second floor. She found nothing. Not a sign of her son.

She started down the stairs, knowing she should alert the others and get them to help her look for Tommy.

Jason Malone stepped out of the shadows and blocked her passage. "Where you going in such a hurry?"

She tried to get past him, but he would not allow it.

Glancing at him in the shadowy light from above, Madeline realized the reason that snapshot of Patrick had bothered her so much when she saw it in Mrs. Lawrence room earlier.

"You're Patrick Lawrence!"

The man's nose was different, flatter and broader, as if it had been broken and then badly reset. His blonde hair was dyed or else he wore a dark wig. And he didn't have blue eyes now, they were brown, probably due to colored contact lenses.

But in the snapshot Patrick had been standing with shadows from the oak tree on his face, and in the same stance Jason had now. Patrick was slimmer, but in eight years the young man had grown into a stronger physique with the right exercises. He'd bulked up, making his face fuller as well. And the beard disguised his features, too.

Jason was clever with electrical devices like the bedside buzzer in Mrs. Lawrence room, and repairing the chandelier switch. Patrick won an award for his electronic invention, and was known for devising 'gizmos,' as Mrs. Lawrence and Frankie called them.

All the pieces fell together and she intuitively identified the imposter.

Jason Malone was actually Patrick Lawrence, the MIA soldier who had been missing for seven years. He was the half-brother Brad and Nancy wanted to declare legally dead.

But why had he decided that Madeline was his enemy? "Listen," she said, trying to stay calm, "I don't blame you for being angry at them. But I'm not part of it. Please give me my son and I'll get out of the way."

He clamped a big hand over her mouth. When she tried to escape, he gripped her waist like a vise. "Walk up the stairs," he said in a voice so low it was barely above the hiss of a snake.

She struggled.

"If you want to see your little boy," he said in her ear, his breath hot and unpleasant, "keep walking."

Her eyes grew wide. *Jason has Tommy!*

Knowing she had no choice but to comply, Madeline put one foot in front of the other and kept walking up those stairs.

TWENTY-NINE

"Mommy!" Tommy barreled into her legs and clutched her. "My mommy mom-mom!"

"Hello there, my Tommy tom-tom," she whispered, trying not show how afraid she was.

"I want to go home!"

"I know, honey."

"Shut up." Jason shoved Madeline into the room with her son, and shut the door, remaining inside with them. "Sit down," he said, indicating two straight back chairs. "No talking."

Tommy whined.

"It's okay, honey," Madeline said quickly, squeezing his hand for comfort. She sat down and nodded toward the other chair, so that he reluctantly sat, too.

Jason had brought them to the room that she and Frankie had tried to unlock. A quick glance around didn't give her any understanding of why Jason had been so afraid she'd gain entry. It was an ordinary small bedroom, furnished with odds and ends of discarded furniture and mismatched chairs.

But perhaps there were secret things in the closet or dresser drawers.

She slowed her breathing deliberately, hoping to transmit calmness to her son. If she tried to run with Tommy toward the door, Jason would easily catch them. It would be safer to go along with what he wanted, and hope to escape as soon as he left them alone.

Madeline thought with dismay of her needlework bag, downstairs. Now was the time to have Frankie's telekinesis powers, she thought, because she'd transport her sharp tapestry scissors up here in an instant. With those scissors in her grip, she wouldn't feel so helpless.

Jason grinned as he methodically tied them to the chairs with nylon cord.

"What are you going to do to us?" she asked, hardly recognizing her own voice, and hating that her fear of him was so obvious.

186

He did not answer.

The sound of the rainstorm was loud up here, with the rain pounding on the rooftop.

Without thinking, she screamed.

Jason slapped her. He grabbed a bandanna and tied it tightly around her mouth.

"Don't do that to my mommy!"

Madeline tried to get Tommy to look at her, and convey with her eyes the need to be silent.

Without a word, Jason gagged the boy.

Tommy began to cry.

She looked at him, wishing she knew more about all the ESP methods that Frankie had rattled off. She'd heard about things like good vibrations, and tried now to send positive thoughts to her son, to help him feel braver and more at ease.

His sniffling seemed to get softer.

She smiled at him, difficult to do with her mouth bound, but she knew her eyes would crinkle up in the way he loved, and that would tell him to stay strong and keep on smiling.

Her only consolation, and it was a minor one, she realized, was that her guess about Jason's true identity had been correct. Even though he hadn't admitted to being Patrick Lawrence, why else would he have reacted the way he did?

When he had brought her to the third floor, she'd resisted as much as possible, sensing he would take her to the locked room. But he was too strong for her, and she was unable to escape and run for help.

She knew it would be a while before anyone downstairs would notice she'd been gone a long time. Probably they would each assume she was busy with her son, telling him a story, perhaps, to calm his fears about the thunder and crashing rain. Or that she had decided to go to sleep and skip the festivities at midnight.

Jason checked his knots, straightened and without a backward glance at his victims, went out the door. The sound of the key turning in the lock filled Madeline's heart with despair.

When she saw the same emotion mirrored in her son's eyes, she tried to get her own fears under control so she would not increase his panic. She nodded, trying to look reassuring.

He wiggled and strained against the cords, but it was useless.

She shrugged her shoulder up and tried to push the bandanna off her mouth, but it was tied tightly. If she could only get the cloth off, then she could talk to Tommy and tell him everything would be all right.

But will it? She couldn't help thinking her options were limited. *How will we get out of here?*

With persistence, she kept working at the bandanna gag, scrunching against it with one shoulder, and then the other when she tired. It seemed the cloth was loosening, and she gained hope.

Then she heard footsteps approach. She'd wait to hear a key in the lock – that would warn her Jason was returning. But if she heard the person walk by, it might be Frankie or someone in search of them. In that case, her plan was to rock her chair and make noise to draw attention.

Her worst fears were realized when the door was unlocked and Jason walked in. He'd only been gone a few minutes. She saw that he carried her purse, her needlework bag and Tommy's backpack, as well as their jackets, her casual outfit and a few other things. She wondered how he'd been able to do all that without being noticed, but no doubt he was adept at moving quickly and staying hidden when necessary.

He dumped everything on the single bed. Then he went back in the hall and brought in a long rolled-up object wrapped in plastic. She knew at once that it was The Calico Tapestry.

He set it against a wall, then shut the door and locked them in with him. He studied her. "You didn't wear that dress here. It must be my mother's. Take it off."

She glared and wriggled her arms, clearly saying, *How can I, with these cords wrapped around me?*

As he untied her, he said, "Don't try anything clever. Get undressed and put on the clothes you came in." He nodded to the heap on the bed.

She remembered what Mrs. Lawrence had said about the female nurse, who had died in what looked like an accident. Had Jason really murdered that woman?

She needed to stop thinking of him as Jason, and remember that his real name was Patrick. He had just confirmed it, by referring to Mrs. Lawrence as his mother.

Once the bonds were off, she leaped up, wishing she could overpower him, but knowing that was pointless. Guessing her thoughts, he held a knife to Tommy's neck and asked her, "Will you be good?"

She nodded, and reached up to remove the bandanna. Patrick slapped her.

"Leave it on. Just hurry and change your clothes. I haven't got all night."

Madeline glanced at her watch. The others were probably gathered in the living room, eagerly waiting for the countdown to begin at Times Square. Tommy would miss seeing the big "Christmas" ball drop at midnight.

No time to think about it, she scolded herself, and hurriedly grabbed her things. She opened the closet door.

"Hey–" Patrick began.

She shot him a cold look and ducked behind the closet door to change clothes, dropping the slinky evening gown and quickly pulling on her corduroy jeans and the sweater she'd been wearing the past few days.

She'd been right to tell Frankie that "Jason" was hiding something in this locked room. In the closet, she saw evidence of his criminal intentions, including sleeping pills and poison. In addition, there were books on how to develop your telekinesis powers and other psychic volumes.

She came back into sight, carrying the dress, and neatly folded it. She looked through the things he'd brought up, but didn't see her boots.

"Got everything you had on when you first got here?" he asked.

Her mind raced. It was clear that he wanted to make it appear she and Tommy had left the house. She decided there might be some small advantage to still be wearing the borrowed high heels, instead of her soft-soled boots, which she knew were in Tommy's room, where she had changed for the dinner party.

Patrick must not have seen the boots on the floor by the bed when he surveyed the room for all their belongings. So now his haste would be to her advantage.

Nodding, she slid a hand into her needlework bag and hid the small pair of sharp, stork-shaped scissors in her jeans pocket.

"What are you doing?" he snapped suspiciously.

She grabbed a lip gloss tube and held it up.

"Useless," he said, indicating the bandanna gag. "Unless you're hoping I'll take it off."

She nodded eagerly.

His laugh was harsh. He did not untie the gag. Instead, he handed her a notepad and a pen. "Write what I tell you."

Her heart sank. She sat on the edge of the bed, taking the opportunity to brush near Tommy and give him a loving pat on the back.

Patrick dictated the note she was to write.

After hesitating, and getting yelled at for it, Madeline wrote what he said. She tried to figure a way to add her own secret message but he watched her carefully.

"Don't try anything funny." He took the paper from her and read it out loud, to be sure. "Dear Mrs. Lawrence, I am too afraid to stay here any longer. I took Tommy and we are going to call for a cab as soon as I get a cell signal. Don't worry about us. Thank you for everything, and for the tapestry. Madeline. P.S. Thanks for loaning me the dress."

Madeline inched her fingers toward the scissors in her pocket, but as Patrick loomed over her, she realized she didn't know how to defend herself, and would probably make matters worse for her and Tommy.

She didn't want to anger Patrick to the point that he would separate them. At least they were together, and surely she would figure a way to escape.

After he tied her to the chair, he picked up the evening gown and the note, and then left, once again locking them in.

She was thankful he left a tabletop lamp burning. It would be much harder to bear this in the dark.

Madeline heard Tommy's heartfelt little sigh. She tried to scoot her chair closer to him, and managed to scrape the legs an inch or two on the bare floor. With a wink, she willed him to understand she was trying to figure out a way to get them out of this predicament.

She tried not to keep checking the time on the bedside alarm clock, but found herself glancing at it again and again.

As time steadily marched onward, Tommy grew tired, and his head slumped on his chest as he fell asleep sitting up. She felt grateful for that, and wished she could sleep, too, and then wake up to the noise of rescuers pounding on the door.

Given that, in her experience, wishes did not come true without at least some action on her part, she forced herself to think of practical steps they could take to gain freedom. The first step would be to cut her bonds. She glanced around the room, taking inventory.

On the dresser, she saw a box of black hair dye among other items. Now she knew why he'd been so angry when she touched his hair to get out that dead leaf. She might have seen his blond roots. How many days ago had that been? He had to prevent her from realizing he colored his hair, because she might mention it to Mrs. Lawrence.

She guessed he'd given himself some other kind of hair treatment as well, to make the texture seem coarser and less silky than Patrick's hair appeared in those photos she'd seen.

Noticing a bottle of wetting solution for contact lenses, she realized she'd been right to guess he had disguised his distinctive blue eyes by wearing brown contacts.

But why had he tricked his mother into hiring him under an assumed name? None of it made sense. After being missing for seven years, you'd think a normal person would run to the door and fling it open, expecting to be welcomed.

Normal. That's the problem, she thought. What if he had been injured in the war or endured so much stress that he had returned with a heart full of rage against his family instead of love?

He's a madman. The word came to her, and she shivered. If he had killed that nurse, he would not hesitate to kill her and Tommy. She had to escape.

Looking around, she didn't see anything that would help. Her only chance was to free her hands, untie herself, untie Tommy and get the door open somehow. Then run downstairs, screaming for help. Luke would help, if only he knew she needed him.

She sat morosely for long minutes, thinking. Every once in a while, she strained against the cords, but he had tied them tight and the only result was chafed skin.

Luke... Luke... She wondered if she could get a mental message to him. He was psychic, after all, and it couldn't hurt to try.

Frankie said that everyone had latent powers. Well, now was the time to develop hers. She closed her eyes and tried to focus, but her mind kept wandering. She was worried about Tommy, and distracted by guessing what Patrick was doing now.

Probably he had joined the others for a midnight toast, his disguise still in place as the handyman and hired attendant. No wonder he always ate his meals alone or with Rosa, spoke little, and ducked his head all the time. He was afraid his true identity would be discovered!

She recalled that he had said Tommy would be in the kitchen with "Mrs. Doyle" and later she found out from Mrs. Lawrence that Mrs. Doyle was the name of the prior housekeeper – no doubt that slip of the tongue had plagued "Jason" but she had not seen the significance of it. Not until now.

He had probably counted on his beard, and the changes in his size, coloring and other small details to prevent anyone from even imagining he might be the prodigal son, returned home.

Again, she wondered the reason for his charade.

And then she thought of Nancy, and that woman's claim that she'd been poisoned. From what Madeline had seen in the closet, that was probably true, and not just more of her high drama. He might have poisoned the chocolate candy that Nancy stashed in her room. That way he would not have needed to risk doctoring a drink, and being caught in the act, or having the wrong person drink it.

Madeline recalled hearing that once a person had committed murder, the second time was no big deal. If that was true, then what if Patrick's plan was to kill off the heirs, then disappear as "Jason Malone," wait briefly, reappear as Patrick, the long lost son, then kill his mother and inherit everything?

It was an audacious plan. But she knew that she was right. Why else would he pass himself off as a stranger? There had to be an ulterior motive worthy of all the trouble he'd gone to.

And she'd gotten in the way. By chance, she'd turned up in her quest to borrow The Calico Tapestry, just when Patrick thought he had everything lined up perfectly.

She realized now that his timing was scheduled for these few days when the whole family was gathered. Perhaps he planned an explosion, or something of that nature that would appear to be of natural causes and kill the entire family. He would be the lucky handyman who managed to escape without harm, and disappear in the confusion. There was no reason for him to stick around as "Jason" once all his relatives were dead.

Could he have faked the ghost of his father, using a photograph and some kind of video projector, as well as ventriloquism? Or had that been an authentic message from Cyrus to Mrs. Lawrence, to sell the house?

Her mind grew weary with the possibilities. Thinking about Patrick's schemes and plans did nothing to help her and Tommy gain their freedom. She needed to concentrate on that task, and put the rest out of her thoughts.

She yawned and the clock yet again. It was one o'clock now, and the others had probably seen the note she wrote, puzzled over her strange departure but dismissed her from their minds to go to bed with "Happy New Year" greetings echoing in the shadows as they turned off the lights and went to sleep.

Madeline thought back to her first night here, and how strange it had been to wake up suddenly and see that glowing apparition.

And then she'd met the live man, the next day, and he'd done something to her heart. She'd never be the same. And now she knew that Mrs. Lawrence was right when she said Luke was a good man.

All of the manipulations and lies by "Jason" had confused her, but now she knew that Luke could be trusted.

If only he'd realize somehow that she needed him, and come to her now! But Luke had told her that he tuned out other people's thoughts in order to preserve his own sanity.

He wouldn't magically read her mind, and rescue them.

She started to cry, overcome by discouragement, despair and fatigue. The gag hurt her mouth. Tears rolled down her cheeks and she had no way to blow her nose. Laughing a bit hysterically inside, she sternly pointed out to herself that, if only to be practical, she needed to get her emotions under control.

With a glance at Tommy, she was glad he was still sleeping, although he looked uncomfortable.

The rainstorm increased in tempo. It seemed of hurricane intensity, but she knew that California never got hurricanes. The ocean temperature wasn't warm enough for that type of storm system to develop.

Madeline reassured herself that she and her son would get out of this situation. She could not give up hope. Not yet.

She knew she was forgetting something important, but the combination of fatigue, physical discomfort and fear made her mind slow and dull.

To keep alert, she thought over the events of the past days, smiling to herself as she thought of Tommy's happiness when Mrs. Lawrence said he could keep the "Christmas" ball he enjoyed so much.

The crystal ball.

What was it Luke said about crystal balls? That they didn't have any actual power, but they helped the psychic focus their thoughts. That's what she needed to do: shove aside these stray, rambling thoughts of hers, and pinpoint her mind's power on contacting Luke.

Her glance fell on the needlework bag on the bed. If she could get over to it, the crystal ball was in the outer pocket.

It was worth a chance. She had nothing else to work with. She had hoped to use the scissors to cut her bonds, but her hands were tied behind her back and she couldn't reach into her pocket for the stork scissors.

But if she could get the crystal ball, and funnel her thoughts like a laser focus, thinking only the words "Luke, help us!" again and again... maybe he would detect her urgency.

She painfully scooted and wriggled her chair, inch by inch getting closer to the bed and the things Patrick had piled there so haphazardly.

Tommy woke up and mumbled something.

She looked at him, but his eyes drifted closed once again and he slumbered on. Trying not to make much noise, she steadily moved to the bed.

Once there, she was glad she'd left the bag near the edge because now she was able to use her chin to nudge at the bag. She managed to roll the crystal ball out of the bag just enough to have it in her sight, without risking its rolling off the bed.

With a quick prayer that she would be able to access the untapped psychic powers that both Luke and Frankie said everyone had – but which most people, including Madeline, had not developed – she focused on the crystal ball, while mentally pleading, "Luke, help us" over and over again, not allowing any stray thoughts the chance to sneak in.

Relentlessly, she repeated silently, "Luke, help us," firmly believing that if Luke was indeed emotionally connected to her, he would hear her... somehow, in some way. And he would come.

The smell of smoke woke her up.

She opened her eyes, confused that she couldn't move. Memory flooded back. She quickly looked at Tommy, tied to the chair nearby.

After scooting to the bed for the crystal ball, she was now behind her son rather than beside him. She hoped he had not awoken and thought she was gone. But he seemed to still be sleeping, and she didn't want to risk disturbing him by grunting or making noises to get his attention.

A quick glance at the clock told her she'd only been asleep for about an hour. She felt exhausted. Trying to stretch, she glanced around the room.

And saw Luke.

She pleaded with her eyes for him to notice her predicament. He seemed to be looking directly at her, but it was his astral body, as she now knew to call it.

There was the long silver cord, trailing from his head. She knew it kept his spirit connected to his physical body and without the cord, he'd be "dead."

His mouth moved, but she heard nothing. It was a similar experience to the one she'd had her first night here, but at least this time she knew who it was.

Excitedly, she wondered if she had called him with the crystal ball. She jerked her head in Tommy's direction, wanting to be sure that Luke saw the boy. She wriggled her shoulders and torso as best she could, trying to point out that she was tied up.

Not knowing how much he might be aware of during his out-of-body experience, she hoped to make a deep impression upon him that they needed to be helped, right away.

The smoke was getting stronger. She thought of Patrick's expertise with electrical systems, and wondered if he had arranged for a fire that would appear to have been caused by faulty wiring.

Wondering if Luke could hear her now, she looked at him intently, thinking, *Can you hear me? Nod if you can.*

The glowing apparition nodded slowly.

The house is on fire! Wake up, Luke. Come to the third floor. We are in the locked room three doors to the left of the stairs. Save us!

The silver cord grew taut. The apparition sped backwards, as it had done before, and zoomed out the locked door.

She gave a sob of mingled relief and despair, knowing her best hope had just gone out that door, but not knowing what the outcome would be. With him, she sent a heartfelt prayer that he would return soon in the form of a living, breathing man who would break the door down and get them to safety in time.

THIRTY

Madeline coughed. The small room was thick with smoke.

Tommy stirred, then apparently awoke and discovered he was bound and gagged. She could hear from his distressed moans that he didn't know where he was.

She scooted her chair closer and gave him a reassuring smile, not knowing what else to do.

"Maddie!" Luke's voice came from the hallway.

In here, she tried to call out, but the gag meant she was making only a muffled noise. She rocked her chair up and down the best she could.

"Where are you?" He called out, running past, his voice getting fainter. "Maddie!"

Desperate, she flung herself sideways, not caring about bruises. The resulting fall on the floor made a big clatter.

Moments later, Luke was rattling the knob and pounding at the door. "Are you in there?"

Tommy wriggled his chair, imitating what his mother had done, and the noise was enough.

"Okay!" Luke called in to them. "I hear you. Don't worry. I'll be right back."

Tears filled Madeline's eyes as she looked up from the floor at her son and they grinned at each other despite the bandannas tied around their mouths. She nodded at him, transmitting hope to allay his fears.

Shortly, they heard the door being pounded against from the other side, then the sharp edge of an axe poked through. Strong hands widened the hole and soon the door was open, minus its doorknob.

Smoke poured in, and in the midst of the swirling mist, Madeline thought she saw another apparition of Luke rushing toward her. *Oh no! Not another astral body – I need the real one!*

As if he knew what she was thinking, Luke said as he untied her gag, "Don't worry, honey. It's really me. Let's get you two out of here."

The moment the bandanna was off her face, Madeline wet her lips and gasped. "Thank God, it worked. Take care of Tommy first."

Luke kissed her hard.

She beamed at him, her eyes shining.

"Hold on, my darling," he said softly. "Let me get you both free. There's plenty of time for that other stuff later. Years and years. Right now, the house is on fire and there's no time to waste."

As soon as he got the rope off Tommy, the boy stretched, too confused to ask questions.

Madeline hurried to him the moment she was free and hugged him tight. "My brave boy."

Luke held a finger to his lips and pointed.

She looked into the hall and saw Patrick hurrying from the stairs, looking at something in his hand.

He hadn't yet noticed that the locked door was open and his prisoners had a hero.

She whispered to Luke, "He's Patrick. Be careful!"

Luke shot her a look, and then understanding followed. He nodded.

Patrick paused. He held a hypodermic in his hand and filled it from a small bottle. And then he looked toward the door.

Luke faced him. "What's that, Patrick? Were you planning to knock out Madeline and Tommy so you could untie them and unlock the door? Then when their bodies were found after the fire, no one would suspect foul play."

Patrick rushed toward him, his head lowered as if to ram into Luke.

"Look out!" Madeline pushed Tommy aside so he'd be safe. She hastily grabbed the video camera she'd seen earlier in the closet, thrust it into Tommy's backpack and scooped up their stuff. She left behind the long brass trumpet, video projector and other paraphernalia that she deduced Patrick had used to fake ghostly manifestations. "Come on, Tommy. Can you run?"

The little boy nodded.

She knew it would be foolish to go near Patrick, because he would take them hostage, so she waited with Tommy for the right chance to escape.

Luke sidestepped Patrick and slammed the back of the burly man's neck with a karate style chop.

Patrick staggered. He dropped the hypodermic and bottle.

Luke kept his advantage by punching at the other man's kidneys, weakening him.

Reeling, Patrick stumbled toward the door.

Patrick glared at Madeline and her son. "Shoulda gone when I told you to."

"I see," she said coolly, hiding her fear. "And when I didn't, you decided to kill us. What did I ever do to you that was so bad?"

"It was the perfect plan."

Luke picked up the cord Patrick had tied up Madeline with. He slipped up behind Patrick and flung the cord around his chest, pinning his arms to his sides, but as he was trying to tie the rope, Patrick broke free and ran into the hall.

The smoke was choking them now. They all coughed, trying to breathe.

As they ran out of the room, Madeline heard a cat meowing from behind one of the closed doors.

While Patrick and Luke continued to fight with their fists, ducking and jabbing, she grasped Tommy's hand and took him with her to investigate the apparent cat.

She realized it was near where she and Frankie had seen the calico cat ghost, and wondered if she was only hearing a ghostly echo and not a real cat.

"Where's the kitty?" Tommy asked, frowning.

"So you hear it, too?" Madeline tried the door and found it locked. She jiggled harder and opened it. A cat shot out past them. Inside the room, she saw signs that the cat had been kept prisoner here.

"Calli!" The little boy broke away from his mother to scamper after the cat.

"No, Tommy!" Madeline screamed.

As Tommy ran past, chasing the cat, Patrick reached out and snatched the boy. Tommy wriggled and kicked, but could not escape that iron grip.

"Let him go," Luke said, calmly.

"Or what? You're about as effective as my mother. All threats, but no action."

"And you? You're blind action. You rush headlong, with no thought of the damage you do to others." Luke seemed to sense that Madeline was next to him. He gestured a staying motion behind his back, as if hoping she would not try to do anything rash to get Tommy away from Patrick.

She stayed quiet, hating the inaction, but knowing Luke was right. It would be better to talk Patrick into letting Tommy go. Now that his plan had been discovered, he seemed less dangerous, but she remembered the knife he had held against Tommy earlier.

"Now that I know who you are," Madeline said to Patrick, "those ghostly voices make more sense. Your mother told me you won a prize for a talent contest… as a ventriloquist."

"And you were always doing things to the electricity," Luke said to the other man, "so I suppose the fire in the walls is something you've done. We all need to get outside now. So why don't we continue this conversation there? Aunt Agatha will be thrilled, of course, to have her long-lost son back."

"They'll lock me up again," Patrick said, in a low rumble, as if looking back in time to a dark place. He came to a decision, shaking his head.

Suddenly he set Tommy down and made a run for the final flight of stairs that went up to the roof.

"The belvedere!" Madeline cried, warning Luke. "It's dangerous!"

"You two run downstairs and get out of the house before the fire traps you!"

Madeline nodded. "Be careful! He has a knife."

Luke raced after Patrick and flung himself up the stairs.

She held Tommy safely in her arms. "Come on, honey. Can you carry your backpack? We need to get outside and make sure the cat is safely out, too." She set down her son and picked up The Calico Tapestry. "We'll get this cat to safety, too."

He happily went with her toward the stairs.

As they reached the front door and opened it, the welcome sound of fire engines screamed up the canyon road toward them.

The storm was over, for now.

Hurrying outside with her burden clutched in her arms, and Tommy at her heels hugging Calli, Madeline was relieved to see that Frankie was taking care of Mrs. Lawrence. All the others had gotten out safely, including Rosa the housekeeper.

"Frankie!" Madeline called out. "We have to help Luke!"

Madeline left all her things and Tommy with Rosa. "Please watch him."

"Who's this?" Mrs. Lawrence said, spotting the second cat. The other one was in her lap.

"It's the real Calli," Madeline said. "Tommy was right. There were two cats. The one in your lap must be an imposter that Patrick brought so the whole family wouldn't wonder why Calli hissed at him all the time. You might have guessed 'Jason's' true identity."

"You mean–?" Mrs. Lawrence looked at her in confusion.

"I'm sorry, Mrs. Lawrence," Madeline said softly, "but Jason is actually your son Patrick, and he's the one who caused the fire. I think he's sick, mentally ill from the war. I'll explain more later, but now I have to go help Luke."

She turned and ran off, grabbing Frankie's arm. "I need your powers."

"What's up?" Frankie asked, running with her toward the house.

"Luke chased Patrick up to that belvedere you and I were on."

"Patrick?"

Madeline knew the word would spread quickly from Mrs. Lawrence to the others, but Frankie needed to know now. "Jason is really Patrick. He wanted to kill everyone, including Tommy and me, so he could come back later as himself and inherit everything."

"Holy sh–" Frankie trailed off, stunned.

They reached the side of the house with a view of the upper roof area and the wrought iron belvedere.

"Look!" Madeline pointed.

Luke and Patrick were still punching each other, both growing tired, but each determined to win.

"Frankie, do you remember the other day up there with me?"

"Well, yeah. Of course. I wasn't totally out of it. Just kinda depressed."

"Remember that big, heavy weather vane I tripped on?"

They looked at each other, understanding the plan.

Frankie stared up at the belvedere and focused her energy.

Madeline watched eagerly, hoping to see something in the dark. The half moon shone through fleeting clouds. "There it is – Look, it's moving – You've got it! Keep it going."

The old weather vane shot up and hovered in the air, then swiftly moved toward Patrick's head.

Just then, the heavy-set man ducked and turned, evading a jab from Luke's fist. Patrick pulled his knife from a pocket.

"Wait, Frankie! You're aiming for Luke!"

"Damn! They need to hold still," Frankie muttered, concentrating hard. She kept control over the weather vane.

Then it appeared that Luke noticed it moving.

Madeline seemed to feel that he knew she was there on the ground, trying to help him.

She sensed the moment was exactly right.

"Now, Frankie!" she cried, and in that instant, Luke ducked, so the weather vane struck Patrick's head and knocked the man out.

Frankie laughed, breathless. "Wow…."

"You were fantastic! Awesome!" Madeline grabbed Frankie and hugged her tight.

Looking down from the belvedere, Luke called to them, "Nice teamwork, girls." He whipped the cord from his pocket and tied up Patrick, then called down, "Okay, I've got him trussed up, and he's not going to hurt anyone again."

Madeline blew a kiss up to him, her eyes shining with love.

Frankie chuckled to herself. "It's about time something I wished for came true."

THIRTY-ONE

Watching the firefighters salvage the house, Madeline and her son stood close to Luke.

"Since it started in the walls with the electric wires," Luke explained, "the fire got well-established before we realized it. That's why there was so much smoke."

"Looks like Patrick's plan was that we would all die of smoke inhalation or be trapped in the burning house. It's amazing the fire department got here."

"Someone driving by on Pacific Coast Highway saw the flames. That Good Samaritan called 9-1-1 and described the house."

"You can't even see the house from PCH, can you? Maybe it was my grandmother," Madeline said, "or your spirit guide Stephen. Intervening to prevent a tragedy."

"Maybe so," Luke said, smiling.

The fire captain had Patrick under guard until the police arrived.

"I feel bad for your aunt," she said to Luke, nodding toward the older woman. Mrs. Lawrence kept staring at Patrick, as if not believing that Jason Malone was actually her missing son. "But I sure am glad you found Tommy and me in time."

She smiled at him, marveling that she had been able to get a message to him with that "Christmas" ball of Tommy's, and let him know she needed help.

Luke grinned. He sang a parody of the Santa Claus song, "He knows what you've been thinking…."

"I'll have to be careful what I think from now on. But we may never find out the answers to all our questions," Madeline said. "I think Patrick was afraid of having an outsider around when the family was here. That's why he kept trying to scare me away. Hiding Tommy from me so I'd get spooked enough to leave. I guess the ghost walking on the stairs was him – he could project that sound of climbing footsteps somehow. And the trumpet, of course, and maybe the one of Cyrus, too? But what about my grandmother's ghost?"

"That green glow and the whisper to get out was probably Patrick, faking another warning to scare you. But I think the message you got when I was in a trance was valid," Luke said. "Your grandmother did give you a usable clue about the calico cat, along with the evidential about Tony Chestnut. But some of the other things, if not all of them, were manufactured by Patrick with video, ventriloquism and other tricks."

"I have the delightful feeling that my Tommy proved to be too much for him to handle on at least one occasion, because when I asked my son about mud on his shoes he talked about a tall man getting him to crawl in a tiny door to play with a cat."

"I've already figured out that Tommy has a vivid imagination. But picking out the details that make sense, what do you think happened?"

"My guess is that Patrick carried him outside, maybe planning to drive off with him somewhere so I couldn't find him on the premises. Maybe he had put him in his truck, and already had Calli in there, too. But if the cat ran off, Patrick might have needed him to crawl into some small space that seemed like a door to Tommy, to get the cat out of hiding."

"This old house has a lot of secret hiding places I loved as a boy. There was an old door under the veranda stairs that leads to a crawl space. Maybe the cat got away from Jason, I mean Patrick. You're right, we'll probably never know all the answers. He doesn't seem inclined to answer questions." Luke nodded toward Patrick, who sat sullenly, his mouth grimly shut, his head averted from his mother. "But at least it does look like the house will be repairable, so everything turned out okay."

"For everyone except that mouse 'Jason' sacrificed to try to scare me off."

Frankie came over with the cats and put them down. "Guess what? My parents got such a shock at the idea of losing me in the fire that they decided I can stay home and go to high school with my friends instead of going to that residence school."

"That's great news, Frankie!" Madeline hugged her.

"And my mom is going to try rehab again," Frankie added shyly. "I know she's got a drinking problem, and this time me and my dad are going to do what we need to do, to support her. No more pretending it's no big deal. The ads all say it's a disease, and I want her to get well."

Madeline and Luke smiled at her.

"Can we keep the cats?" Tommy asked.

"We'll have to see about that." Madeline ruffled his hair, grateful they were all safe.

Frankie picked up one of the cats. "Which one are you? Oh, kinked tail. You need a better name. So Tommy was right. It was Calli at first, and then it wasn't. Calli must have escaped and Patrick hid away the wrong one for a while and let the real Calli roam around the house."

"He saw me notice it one day when the cat hissed at him," Madeline explained. "So he had to switch the cats again. They really do look a lot alike, except for the tail."

"An imposter cat!" Luke shook his head, in amusement.

They discussed it further, realizing that the look-alike cat was friendly to Patrick, but this second cat had a kinked tail and so "Jason" had tried to keep anyone from noticing that by bribing the cat with catnip to follow him around.

"He had to keep people from petting it or picking it up," Luke said, "and discovering the difference. It must've made him nervous when Tommy pointed out the broken tail and got us all talking."

"He wasn't counting on a little boy's curiosity," Madeline said, patting Tommy's shoulder proudly.

"That's what Madeline's grandmother meant in her message about a calico cat," Frankie said. "Figure out the cat mystery and you realize that Jason is really Patrick." She left to join her grandmother and watch the firefighters.

Nancy, Frank and Brad had been so shocked that Jason was actually Patrick, that they huddled together, talking over all the possibilities of what their next plan of action should be.

Daphne had convinced one of the firefighters to bring out her suitcases filled with designer clothes and expensive jewelry. Now she was hanging around the fire engine, flirting with the men, clearly having given up on Luke completely.

"Won't last," Luke commented dryly, and winked at Madeline. "Firefighter's paycheck is too small for her taste."

Tommy tugged at Luke's jacket. "Are you going to be my new daddy or not?"

Madeline gasped, embarrassed.

"Looks that way," Luke said, nonchalantly. "If you'll both have me."

Tommy cried out, "Yes!"

She slanted a look at Luke, thinking: *Is that a proposal?*

He nodded solemnly.

"Please tell me you can't read my thoughts all the time," she said.

With a laugh, he put his arms around her. "You're easy to read, honey. It doesn't take any special power. All I have to do is look in your eyes."

"But I know the reason you found Tommy and me is that I gazed into Tommy's 'Christmas' ball and focused on calling you to me. And then you came, in that astral body like you did my first night here. A few minutes later, there you were, breaking down the door with an axe! So don't try to tell me it's all a coincidence."

"I must've been asleep," he said, puzzling it over. "So my astral body understands we're meant to be together. Soul mates." He grinned at her. "But there's actually a more prosaic reason I knew to rescue you."

"Really?" She felt a bit dismayed that she hadn't drawn him to her with newly developed powers.

"Frankie couldn't sleep. She went hunting for gum, thinking you might have left a pack behind when you left – my aunt had read your note to all of us – and when Frankie looked in your room, she discovered your boots."

"And she knew darned well I would not have marched out in the mud wearing those satin high-heeled sandals she loaned me from your aunt's closet. Good for Frankie. She's my hero instead of you, I guess." She laughed. "But I still think the crystal ball played a big part in this."

Reaching into his backpack, Tommy pulled out the crystal ball. "Can I see the future in here?"

"We make our own futures, Tommy," Madeline said. "But that will make a great paperweight for your desk when you're a student and then someday when you're a big success in whatever you decide to do."

Tommy's jaw dropped in awe. "You can see all that in there?"

"Hey, I see something, too," Luke said. "May I?" He took the ball from Tommy's hands and gazed into the depths of the crystal.

"Okay, what do you see?" Madeline asked, teasing.

"I see you," he said softly. "And Tommy. And me. The three of us, together. I even think I see a calico cat, there in the background. Is that all right with you?"

"The cat?" she asked.

"The family portrait."

"It's more than all right," Madeline said, knowing in her heart that she'd found her true love. "But there's just one thing."

"What's that?" Luke asked, worried. "You do love me, don't you? Because I fell in love with you the moment I saw you."

"You did?" She smiled, thinking *Me, too.*

"And I have to tell you that it will break my heart if you push me away. I know I'm moving fast, but after I give you some time to know me better, the minute I think the timing is right, I'm going to insist that we get married and set up housekeeping."

"That's the part I want to talk to you about." She looked at him gravely.

He frowned. "You don't want to get married and live together?"

"I just want to be sure that wherever we live, it's not a haunted house!"

Laughing, he enfolded her in his arms and kissed her.

The two calico cats padded over and sat at their feet.

"I don't understand why Patrick let the original Calli live," Madeline said. "I'm glad he did, of course, but wouldn't it have been simpler not to?"

"He was always superstitious about cats, and probably feared what would happen if he killed it. That ghost of the original Calico apparently was visiting the one in captivity when you saw it." He smiled at her. "Or at least that's what I'd like to believe.

Tommy squatted to play with the cats. "Let's keep both of them!"

Luke began nibbling Madeline's ear. His kisses left a hot trail down her throat and then he approached her mouth, whispering tender words of love as he held her close.

"Okay, Tommy, whatever you say," Madeline said, heedless, her thoughts totally engrossed in kissing Luke, something she planned to do as often as possible, for as long as possible, for the rest of her life.

"Hey, darling," Luke whispered mischievously, "that's what I plan, too."

The End

www.ingramcontent.com/pod-product-compliance
Lightning Source LLC
Chambersburg PA
CBHW060326260626
47160CB00007B/2688